# An arrow hissed through the door, clattering against the back wall of the control room

Ryan and J.B. dropped to their knees behind the last row of desks, the one-eyed man glancing to the rear to see that everyone else was in the chamber, standing, blasters ready.

Trader often said that life generally came down to two choices: a bad one and the other one. If he and J.B. turned and ran for it, jumping into the chamber and slamming the door, it would give the natives precious seconds to come after them and trap them before the jump mechanism operated.

So there was the other choice.

"Get on the floor," he yelled to his friends.

"Ready," Krysty called a few moments later.

"We stay," he said quietly to J.B.

Ryan rose onto hands and knees and powered himself forward to slam the armaglass door, triggering the jump mechanism. "Wait for us," he yelled. "Be along when we can."

A long arrow struck the door, so close it nicked Ryan's sleeve. He dropped to the floor, crawling back to join the Armorer.

Behind him he knew that the metal disks in the floor and ceiling of the chamber would be glowing, and fine tendrils of mist would be gathering near the top of the six-sided room. In less than a minute his companions would be somewhere else.

He and J.B., oldest and best of friends, hunkered in their limited shelter, blasters ready for the inevitable attack.

**Also available in the Deathlands saga:**

# JAMES AXLER

# DEATH LANDS®

## Emerald Fire

A GOLD EAGLE BOOK FROM
# WORLDWIDE®

TORONTO • NEW YORK • LONDON
AMSTERDAM • PARIS • SYDNEY • HAMBURG
STOCKHOLM • ATHENS • TOKYO • MILAN
MADRID • WARSAW • BUDAPEST • AUCKLAND

Ruby sparks from a piñon fire, soaring into the black
velvet of an Albuquerque sky. The best of memories.
This is for Carla and Jim Wright, with much love and
great affection. The best of friends.

First edition October 1995

ISBN 0-373-62528-6

EMERALD FIRE

Printed in U.S.A.

The art of the Incas, the Aztecs and the Mayas is amongst the most beautiful in the history of mankind. Sadly those civilizations also produced some of the most barbarous and inhuman cruelties the world has ever known.

—From *The Sun, the Pyramid and the Knife*, by Jedediah Alnwick, published by The Free Press of Corrales, NM

# Chapter One

The sick darkness was passing.

Ryan Cawdor steadied his breathing, conscious that the jump had been one of the easiest that he could remember. There had been none of the hideous gibbering dreams that sometimes swam out of the black horror of a bad jump.

He felt slightly sick, there was a throbbing pressure behind his eye and his stomach felt as though it had gone ten rounds with a rabid mule.

"Fireblast," he whispered to himself, still not risking opening his eye.

Ryan was conscious that his hand was still being gripped by Krysty Wroth. That in itself was a sign that the mat-trans unit had functioned well.

All he needed to know now was whether everyone was all right and where the jump had taken them.

He breathed in slowly, aware that the air felt very hot and moist. And green.

Ryan opened his eye.

# Chapter Two

When civilization was blown apart in the massive nuclear holocaust of 2001, the world had been geared for all kinds of military action, most of it supposed to be top secret at the highest level. But many people had heard about the Totality Concept, the cover-all policy that ranged from time travel to self-supporting space stations packed with laser-guided hardware.

One of the subsections of the Concept was called Overproject Whisper, and one small part of that was Operation Chronos, which was concentrating on the largely doomed research into time traveling, or "trawling," as it had become known. The idea of pulling targets from the past or pushing them into the future was interesting. But in practice there were less than a handful of successes.

One of them, Dr. Theophilus Tanner, was recovering in the mat-trans chamber across from Ryan Cawdor.

The matter transmitter had been developed in a laboratory complex in Maryland and was one of the limited successes of the Totality Concept. The mat-trans units were often an integral part of the secret military complexes—known as redoubts—hastily and secretly built all across the United States, with a few elsewhere in the world. These "gateways," as they were called, were developed in those shadowed, paranoid days that closed the twentieth century, and made it possible for people to be sent instantly from one location to another.

"How're you feeling, Doc?" Ryan's voice sounded flat and hollow in the hexagonal chamber. The color of the armaglass walls varied from place to place. This time they were an odd shade of pallid green.

The old man ran a hand across his face, smiling and showing his oddly perfect set of gleaming teeth. His light blue eyes twinkled at Ryan.

"Upon my soul, dear friend! Relative to a rare good day, then this is still some way less than adequacy. However, compared to an average mat-trans jump, I feel as frolicsome as a dog with two tails. Or a monkey with six paws. Or an elephant with three trunks. Or a—"

"I get the picture, Doc. Not a bad jump, was it?"

The silver-haired old man fumbled in one of the capacious pockets of his frock coat, so ancient that the black material had a strange greenish patina that Doc swore stoutly wasn't mold. He pulled out a blue swallow's-eye kerchief and mopped his brow.

"By the Three Kennedys! The jump was passing fair, but the heat here puts me much in mind of the botanical gardens in London, at Kew. There was some verse, but I confess that its remembrance seems to have dodged away from my poor corroded old brain."

Doc had been a leading academic back in Omaha, Nebraska, in November of 1896, living a happy and contented life with his beautiful young wife, Emily, and his two beloved children, Rachel, who had been three years old, and Jolyon, barely past his first birthday.

The white-coated scientists, whom he had come to detest with a bitter loathing, had plucked him from the past and drawn him forward to 1998, as part of Operation Chronos. It was then discovered that their success with Doc had been a freakish event, with virtually all of their other experiments failing horribly.

Doc himself was such a stubborn and recalcitrant time traveler that the scientists, in December of 2000, propelled him many years into the future—into the postholocaust United States, which had become known as Deathlands. Most of the time his mind functioned reasonably well, but stress sometimes sent him spinning off onto some alternative thought beam that was all his own.

He reached out to retrieve his lion's-head ebony cane, which concealed a gleaming rapier of Toledo steel, stretching his long, skinny legs in their cracked knee boots. Then his hand automatically went for the unusual handblaster that was holstered at his hip.

It was an ornate Le Mat, a weapon that dated back to the early days of the Civil War. The blaster was engraved and decorated with twenty-four-carat gold as a commemorative tribute to the immortal memory of James Ewell Brown Stuart—Jeb Stuart, the greatest cavalryman of his country. The massive cannon, weighing over three and a half pounds, had two barrels and an adjustable hammer. It fired a single .63-caliber round, like a shotgun. As well, a revolver chamber held nine .44-caliber rounds.

At any range around twenty feet it was devastatingly lethal. At much over fifty feet it was fairly innocuous in the old man's hands.

The Armorer was also sitting next to Doc, feeling for his neatly folded spectacles in a pocket of his worn leather jacket, finally perching them on the bridge of his narrow nose. Five feet eight inches tall, and just about reaching one-forty when soaking wet, John Barrymore Dix was Ryan's oldest friend. They had both joined the legendary Trader and his armored war wags when they were young men, filled with sand and gall. And they had learned many things from Trader, mostly about surviving, about mistakes not made.

J. B. Dix was undeniably the greatest authority on weaponry in all of Deathlands.

His own armament consisted of a 20-round 9 mm Uzi automatic machine pistol, and an unusual scattergun. The Smith & Wesson M-4000 didn't fire ordinary rounds. It held eight Remington 12-gauge cartridges, each with twenty fléchettes, tiny, murderous inch-long darts.

J.B. grinned at Ryan and picked up his beloved fedora with his left hand, blowing dust from the crown and placing it carefully on his head.

"That's one of the best jumps I ever had," he said. "But it's hot and wet, isn't it? Where in the black dust have we jumped to this time?"

He turned to look at the stocky black woman who sat next to him, reaching out to hold her hand as she jerked back into consciousness.

Mildred Winonia Wyeth was in her middle thirties, the daughter of a Baptist minister who had been burned to death by Klans in a firebombing back in 1965.

A leading expert in her field of cryogenics and cryosurgery, she was also a brilliant shot with a pistol and had won the free-shooting silver medal in the last Olympic Games of all time, in Atlanta in 1996. The event four years later had been canceled due to the terminal deterioration in world politics.

Three days before the end of the year 2000, Mildred had been admitted to hospital for a minor operation. Unpredictably the anesthetic produced a near-fatal reaction. In a desperate bid to save Mildred's life, her doctor had, ironically, frozen her, putting the woman into suspended animation in a nuke-powered hospital, hoping to revive her at some future time from the coma that had claimed her. There she had stayed in an endless, dreamless sleep, until Ryan and the others, ragged Prince Charmings, had come along and awakened her from both the coma and her suspended state.

The tiny beads in Mildred's plaited hair rattled as she moved her head.

"Guess I don't feel too bad," she stated.

Mildred was wearing a quilt-lined denim jacket, and reinforced military jeans tucked into black calf-length boots. On her hip was a Czech-made target revolver, the ZKR 551, from the Zbrojovka works in Brno. It was a 6-shot blaster, chambered to take a Smith & Wesson .38-caliber round, with a solid frame-side rod ejector and a short-fall thumb-cocking hammer. Mildred used to claim she could take out a gnat's eye at forty paces with the weapon.

She wasn't joking.

Next to her, still sleeping, was eleven-year-old Dean Cawdor. He had his father's dark complexion and shock of black, curly hair. It was only in the last year or so that Ryan had ever known that he had a son, the result of a single sexual encounter with a woman named Sharona. The boy and his mother had roamed Deathlands until she had died, rad sick, handing over responsibility for Dean to a friend who had eventually met Ryan and the companions in a chance encounter in Newyork.

"Gaia!" The voice belonged to the flame-haired woman sitting next to Ryan. "Wonders never cease. I actually don't feel sick, lover. It's hot in here."

Krysty Wroth was Ryan's partner, lover and friend. Her long red hair was strangely sentient and reacted to a threat of danger. Now her tresses were curled tightly and defensively at her nape. The woman herself had a mutie quality, being able to sense the presence of other life forms and identify them as a possible menace, though she wasn't a full-fledged doomie, able to pinpoint what was going to happen.

She yawned and stretched, catlike and graceful, looking around at the others and seeing that Dean was the only one not yet back with them. "Air feels triple moist, like being in a Hopi sweat bath," she said.

"Must be somewhere south," Ryan replied. "Down the keys or the bayous."

The seventh and last of the group of traveling friends uncoiled himself from the corner of the chamber, next around in the circle from J.B.

Jak Lauren was sixteen years old, standing a bare five feet four and tipping the scales at a little over one-ten. He had the lean body of a trained acrobat, and wore a ragged collection of cotton and leather clothing. His obvious weapon was a satin-finish .357 Magnum Colt Python, holstered on his hip, but Jak wasn't keen on blasters and preferred to rely on his hidden arsenal of leaf-bladed throwing knives.

But the first thing that everyone noticed about Jak was his mane of hair, as white as a magnesium night flare, then his eyes glittering like molten rubies. The young man was a true albino.

Jak had traveled with Ryan and company on two separate occasions. They'd first encountered one another in the swamps of Louisiana, when they'd helped him against the vicious Baron Tourment, murderer of his father. Some time later Jak had met and married Christina Ballinger and they'd had a daughter, Jenny, sharing a brief happiness on their New Mexico spread.

Happiness in Deathlands was something you grabbed at as it rode by. And it didn't often last long.

It wasn't all that many weeks since Jak had buried his wife and child.

And now he was back with Ryan and the other companions.

Dean was finally coming around from the effects of the mat-trans jump, blinking open his dark brown eyes and looking immediately for his father. "All right, Dad?"

"Yeah. All right. Seems to have been a good jump. How do you feel?"

Dean sniffed and raised a hand to his face, coming away with a smear of blood on his fingers. "Nose," he explained. "Think I must've banged it on my knee or something. Apart from that I feel like a real hot pipe."

Ryan nodded, though he still made no effort to get up. His brain felt the feathery, tumbling sickness that always came from a jump, but the discomfort was nothing compared to the usual bone-deep nausea.

"Everyone take it easy for a few minutes," he warned. "Don't get fooled into thinking that we're all aces on the lines, just because we haven't thrown up or stuff."

While he sat resting in the locked gateway chamber, Ryan checked out his own array of weapons.

The eighteen-inch panga was sheathed on his hip, its tip like a needle, its double edge honed to a whispering sharpness. On his other hip was the powerful SIG-Sauer P-226. It had a four-and-a-half-inch barrel and held fifteen rounds of full-metal-jacket 9 mm bullets. The built-in baffle silencer was no longer as efficient as it had once been, but it still muffled the sharp explosive crack when the trigger was squeezed. His Steyr SSG-70 bolt-action rifle fired ten lethal 7.62 mm rounds. It also had a laser image enhancer and a Starlite night scope.

As Ryan looked over his weapons, he noticed out of the corner of his eye that the Armorer was doing the same with his own blasters.

Once he was satisfied, Ryan glanced around the six-sided chamber. "We all ready to move on?"

There was a nodding of heads and a muttering of agreement from everyone.

"Double red," Ryan said. "Here we go."

# Chapter Three

The pale green armaglass door clicked open.

"Phew!" Dean exclaimed. "Even hotter. Think the place is on fire, Dad?"

Ryan shook his head. "No." But his forehead wrinkled in puzzlement. "Never known it quite as hot and humid as this. Not even in the bayous."

"We are aware how the long-term effects of the nuclear wipeout have included major changes in climate," Doc said in his best lecturing voice. "Not counting the volcanic action and the nationwide earthquakes. Perhaps we are in a region that has become tropical."

Doc was right about the changes between the old United States and Deathlands.

Though there weren't the scientists of the laboratories to verify it, there were rumors that the planet had actually been tipped a few degrees on its axis by the war that truly did end all wars.

The weather changed radically and became more extreme. First had come the long winters, which completed the 99.9-percent recurring megacull of human life that had commenced in the missile-hungry days of skydark.

Though the mighty San Andreas Fault was one of the first to let go, the world was seamed with tectonic activity. California virtually disappeared into the Pacific, and volcanoes erupted from Seattle to Mount Washington. Acid rain fell, strong enough in the first years to strip the flesh from a man's bones in a matter of minutes. There were ferocious chem storms with brilliant purple-pink lightning and endless thunder. High-rad detritus constantly tumbled from the skies, the useless relics of the world powers' attempts to use space for military purposes.

Nearly a hundred years had passed since the nuke-caust had been triggered and civilization had died, but the repercussions were still everywhere in Death-lands. Not just in the weather and the landscape. There had been horrific genetic damage among the few survivors, resulting in amazing mutations of every sort among every level of life: birds, fishes, reptiles, insects.

And human beings.

Particularly in human beings.

"Smells like swamps on hottest day ever," said Jak, standing behind Ryan with his blaster drawn.

The usual procedure in mat-trans units was to find the gateway opening into a small anteroom, generally stripped bare during the evacuation at the time of skydark.

This time was much like the others—a room eight feet square, with two rows of empty shelves and a backless chair. Nothing else.

Through the next doorway they could all see the main control room to the unit, containing rows of desks, comp screens and keyboards, endless banks of dancing colored lights and flickering crystal displays.

And beyond it was the familiar sight of the closed vanadium-steel sec doors that sealed the gateway off from the rest of the military redoubt.

"If the doors are clamped tight, then how come the air feels so hot and damp?" J.B. looked around. "And how come there's no mold or nothing like that?"

"Anything," Mildred corrected.

"What?"

"You should say that there's no mold or *anything* like that, love," she repeated.

Ryan grinned back at the Armorer. "Nice to see someone else getting their knuckles rapped for a change for not speaking proper."

"Properly," Krysty corrected.

"Fireblast!" He pulled a face at her. "Anyway, I reckon that the basic air conditioner's folded. But the stuff they pump through to chill germs has kept the place clean."

Doc nodded, reaching out and rubbing his hand down the wall of the anteroom. "It is most fearfully moist. But no trace of any sort of sphagnum growing here."

"Wonder what the redoubt'll be like?" Krysty said. "Could do with some decent washing facilities. And if there happened to be some canned food..."

"Noticed that the control room is smaller than usual?" J.B. asked.

Ryan nodded. "Right. Mebbe it's a smaller redoubt, as well. No reason they should all be the same."

"Can I open the door, Dad?"

Dean stood by the lever at the side of the hugely strong sec door, one hand resting on it. From previous experience, they all knew that the green lever, pointing downward, would open the door when it was lifted.

"As usual, son," he said. "I'll get on the floor and look out underneath as it rises. Rest of us fall back in a loose skirmish line. Stop it rising when it's about six inches up to let me check the corridor outside. Drop it like goose shit off a shovel if I shout to you. And don't take it up any higher until I tell you."

"I know all that, Dad, don't I?"

Ryan smiled grimly at his son. "I hope you do. No point in waiting until there's been serious grief for all of us to find out you'd forgotten something important."

"Sure, Dad. Sorry."

"Never apologize," J.B. began, starting to quote one of the Trader's favorite sayings.

"It's a sign of weakness," everyone else chorused, including Dean himself.

"There appears to be something written on the wall, just here," Doc observed.

"Graffiti?"

"I think so, my dear Krysty. But it is carved small and my sight is not, frankly, quite as good as once it was."

The woman moved across to look at the spidering scratches in the cream-painted concrete. Everyone else waited, Dean with his hand already gripping the lever.

"'*Un lobo no muerte a otro,*'" Krysty read slowly. "Is that some sort of Mex?"

"Read it again," Doc said. "I believe that it might be Spanish."

"*Un lobo*... That's a wolf, isn't it? *No muerte a otro. Muerte* is death."

Doc put his head on one side as he considered the graffiti. "A wolf will not kill one of... will not kill another wolf," he said finally.

"Funny seeing a foreign saying." Mildred looked around at the others. "Any of you ever seen anything like that before in any other redoubt?"

Ryan answered for all of them. "Not like that. I guess it means that you don't turn on your own kind. Man doesn't chill his own brother."

"Yeah." Krysty stared at it. "Must've been done in the last days before skydark."

"Last hours," the Armorer suggested.

"Least no sign of Japanese killers."

Ryan looked at Jak. "True. Won't have to watch out for an ambush with sword or arrow from those... What was the name you said they had, Doc?"

"Samurai. Professional warriors with a strong code of honor. I remember their names. Takei Yashimoto had his bow broken by Dr. Wyeth here. And I think I wounded him in the face with the Le Mat. The one that trusty Ryan slew was called Tokimasha Yashimoto, brother to the first named."

"This might be a part of Deathlands that they haven't reached," Ryan said, "though we've been hearing rumors of these Oriental bandit gangs all over the store."

It was only on their recent jump to Washington Hole that they had seen clear proof that the rumors were true. The companions also had an overwhelming suspicion that the murderous samurai were also using the gateway network.

The graffiti was forgotten.

"Ready, Dad?"

Ryan crouched, holding the cocked SIG-Sauer in his right hand.

"Take it away," he said.

The lever moved upward. "Quite stiff," Dean hissed. "Doesn't seem to... Yeah, it's going."

They all heard the familiar sound of gears beginning to operate, perhaps for the first time in nearly a century, working in their sealed unit, using hydraulics to lift the enormous weight of the sec door.

"It's so massive," Mildred whispered as the first tiny crack of daylight appeared.

"Take a low-yield, high-penetration nuke missile to blow it open," the Armorer replied. "Nothing less than that would have any effect on it."

"Stop," Ryan ordered. "Hold it there, Dean." The movement ceased immediately, leaving a gap of about six inches between the bottom of the sec door and the concrete floor.

"What do you see, lover?" called Krysty, crouched behind one of the rows of control consoles.

"I see... green."

"Green?"

"Yeah. Just like that was the very first thing I noticed when I came around from the jump. That smell in the air was warm, wet and . . . green."

"You mean green paint? Or green plants and stuff?" J.B. called.

"Plants and stuff. But . . ." Ryan flattened his face against the gritty floor, pressing his good right eye to the gap. "I don't see any corridor out there. No sign at all of any walls or even a ceiling."

"Must be covered with lichen," Mildred suggested.

Now, even through the narrow crack at the bottom of the door, they could all taste the strong flavor of humidity and green vegetation.

"It is damnably reminiscent of the tropical hothouse," Doc said, breathing deeply. "Perhaps we have found ourselves in a redoubt that had its own green conservatory. It is not beyond the bounds of possibility."

"I guess not," Ryan agreed, still lying on the floor, trying to puzzle out what he was seeing. "But there's what I'd swear was filtered sunlight. No sort of roof up there, unless it's made of glass."

"That'd fit in with Doc's theory." Mildred smiled innocently at the old man. "It would be *so* wonderful if one of Doc's theories actually came true."

Doc took off an imaginary hat and dropped the woman a deep bow. "May the bird of paradise fly up your nose, dear lady."

"Hold the noise," Ryan called. "I don't know about this. Looks like the outdoors. Dean?"

"Yeah, Dad."

"Just take it up another six inches, will you? Then stop it. And keep on triple red to drop it at my signal."

"Sure. Here goes."

The hidden gears hissed and the door trembled for a moment, then moved up smoothly another six inches. Ryan still held the SIG-Sauer at the ready.

There were several seconds of silence.

"Well?" Krysty queried. "Come on, lover. The suspense is chilling us."

Ryan moved to a kneeling position and dusted of his hands. "I don't know."

"But what do you see?" J.B. asked. "Is that indoors or out of doors?"

"Out. Definitely out."

"Should I take it all the way up, Dad?"

Ryan stood. "I guess so. Just wait a moment, though."

He turned to the rest of the companions in the main control room of the mat-trans unit. "There's so much lush vegetation out there that you can't see very far. It's not like anything I ever saw before. Don't recognize half of the plants. So I don't know where in the dark night we've jumped to."

"Time jump?" Jak asked.

Ryan looked at the albino. "I don't... Hadn't thought about that, Jak, but I guess it's not out of the question. Fact is, nothing's out of the question so we'd best all stay on triple red until we know a bit more. Okay, Dean, take her up, but keep on the edge of dropping it again."

The boy nodded, lifting the green handle and gripping it in both hands.

The sec door slid inexorably upward, settling into place at the top of its rise.

"By the Three Kennedys!" Doc was the only one to break the silence as all of them finally saw the amazing sight outside the entrance.

Directly in front of the door, there seemed to have been some effort made to clear away the rich bank of vegetation, but on either side the wall of greenness soared a hundred feet high. The smell was overwhelming, the moist emerald scent overlaid with the sweetness of flowers. Great trees could be seen, their massive, moss-covered trunks wound with lianas and flowering vines.

They could hear the cheeping of insects and the sounds of other distant creatures, howling, barking and snarling in the undergrowth.

Mildred giggled. "Sorry," she said. "Can't help it. I just thought that we should be real careful. It's a jungle out there."

# Chapter Four

"I don't believe we're in Deathlands," J.B. said quietly. "I don't even recognize those trees or the bushes. Could be we're in those islands out in the Cific."

"Hawaii?" Krysty stared out at the alien landscape. "Suppose that would make some sense."

"Perhaps the most practical move would be for John Barrymore to use that quaint little sextant of his and try to locate our actual position," Doc suggested.

Ryan shook his head. "Not for a minute, Doc. Like Mildred said, it looks more like a jungle out there. Could be all sorts of dangers we aren't ready for. Gotta take this one a single careful step at a time."

Everyone stood and waited, stupefied by the abundant array just outside the open sec door. Gradually, as their eyes became accustomed to the richness, it became possible to note some of the details.

The green canopy was dotted with color.

To the right was a shrub that bore brilliant tiny red flowers, like points of living fire. One of the vines that clawed its way around the trunk of the tallest tree, whose crown was out of sight among the other vegetation, had cuplike flowers of ivory pink, attracting hordes of small turquoise insects.

The ground was covered with mosses, so dazzling a green that it almost hurt to look at them.

"Definitely someone been here recently," J.B. said, pointing. "See the hacked ends of some of the bushes where they've kept open that narrow path."

"Place like this'll close up in couple days," Jak said. "Reminds me of home."

Doc stood next to the teenager and patted him on the shoulder. "It puts me in mind of an old verse, dear boy, about an old road through the woods. But wind and rain have undone it again, and now you would never know that there was ever a road through the woods. Something like that. I disremember the exact wording."

"Look at the butterflies." Dean had left the control level locked in the open position and had joined the others, his Browning Hi-Power cocked in his right hand. "Dozens of them. They're beautiful. Know what kind they are?"

Doc peered out through the doorway. "Well, they are certainly tropical. The brown ones with the eyes are owl butterflies. Brassolidae family. The pale one with the black freckles around the wings is a green morpho."

"Wow! What about that one—black and green and splashes of red and white? The big one?"

"I believe that's called a southern cattle heart, Dean. You know, there's something very odd here. None of them are indigenous to the United States. They all come from either Central or South America."

"Look at this one." Mildred pointed at a butterfly, larger and more beautiful than any of the others, that had come hovering inside the control room. "What's it called, Doc?"

It had an overall width of at least eighteen inches across, and its wings had elongated, feathery tips that added another six inches to their length. The leading edge of each wing was brilliant vermilion, shading into dark crimson. Then came a strip of golden white that darkened into the trailing tips, which were a rich purple color.

Doc shook his head as the butterfly danced around them, circling, rising, falling, flying closer to Dean, who watched it with a hypnotized fascination.

"Don't know. Some kind of a swallowtail. But I never saw one with that coloring, and I am certain-sure that I have never in my life seen a butterfly of that extraordinary size. Positively giganticus."

"Seems to like you, Dean," Mildred said, watching the butterfly hovering nearer and nearer to the boy.

Dean was smiling up at the delightful mutie creature, holding out his hand for it to perch. But the whirligig of serendipity color seemed to be flirting with him, swooping lower, brushing his curly hair with its wings, then rising high toward the ceiling of the control room.

"So beautiful," Krysty whispered, as though she were frightened of scaring the butterfly away.

One moment it was over in the far corner of the room, hanging in the air like a living splash of painted colors, next moment it had come diving in toward

Dean, fastening itself onto the side of his throat, just below and behind the left ear.

At the last moment the boy cried out, waving his hand at it, ducking away, meaning that the attack missed the carotid artery by less than an inch.

Ryan reacted fastest.

There had been something unearthly about the staggering beauty of the large butterfly, something that had brought a prickling to the short hairs at his nape, a sure sign that his combat instinct was giving him a warning. A warning that all wasn't well, a warning of possible danger.

The moment the butterfly folded its beautiful wings and dived at Dean, Ryan was already moving, his mouth open to start a shout of alarm.

The SIG-Sauer was switched to his left hand in a flicker of movement, and his right hand reached toward the butterfly, where it clung to Dean's neck like a bizarre piece of living jewelry in stunning colors.

As he grabbed at it, Ryan was surprised by the fluttering power of the long wings beating against his fingers. But he closed his hand, wrenching the creature from the pale skin, seeing the blotch of brilliant crimson that it left smeared behind it, as though a part of its magical coloring remained behind on the boy's throat.

"Kill it, Dad," the boy cried, his voice high and thin and ragged with shock.

Ryan crushed the mutie creature and flung it to the floor, lifting his foot to stamp on its dying struggles.

"No!" Krysty called. "Let me look at it."

Dean had turned and clung for a few moments to his father, arms locked around Ryan's waist, his whole body trembling. "Thanks a lot, Dad.... That fucker..."

"You all right?" Ryan rubbed his finger at the trickle of blood, seeing how close the bite was to the artery. He carefully examined the small wound, seeing what looked like the injection mark of a hypodermic syringe.

"Might be poisoned," Jak warned.

Krysty was crouched over the butterfly, opening up the bruised, shattered wings with the short barrel of her blaster, peering cautiously at it. "Gaia."

"What?" Mildred asked.

"Bastard's got a stinger about six inches long, just like a needle. Hard, like steel. Looks more like something to poke in and suck blood rather than anything for pumping out poison," she said, pulling a disgusted face.

"Best not take a chance." Ryan lowered his head toward the circular bleeding wound.

"Watch him, Dean," Doc warned. "Ryan has probably been a vampire all along, just waiting for his moment to suck your blood and turn you into one of the undead. Listen to the creatures of the night!"

"You haven't got any sores in your mouth, have you?" Mildred asked, ignoring the old man's teasing. "Doctor friend of mine tried this on a woman who got bitten by a moccasin snake down on the Brazos. Forgot he'd got a little ulcer in his lip. Woman lived and he died."

Ryan hesitated a moment. "No."

He placed his lips against the warm flesh, sucking gently, tasting blood and spitting it out on the concrete floor. He repeated the procedure, harder. This time he was sure there was a strange, metallic taste in with the salt blood, and he spit out more quickly. He sucked and spit a third time.

"You all right, Dean?" he asked.

"Reckon so. Thanks again, Dad."

Ryan squeezed the boy's arm. "Done good."

Mildred looked anxiously at Ryan. "Sure you got no problems from that?"

"No, not really. Thought there was an odd taste and my tongue and lips are a bit numb."

"Bad?"

"No. Wearing off already."

"Loc an," said J.B., who'd been looking at the butterfly over Krysty's shoulder. "Paralyze its victims."

"Yeah. Guess so."

Krysty straightened. "Evil-looking thing. So pretty, so deadly. If that had struck an artery, it could easily have done some serious harm."

She lifted her booted right foot and slammed it down on the feebly fluttering butterfly, crushing it into the floor.

"There," she said.

Ryan looked outside. "Shows us the hidden dangers. Still don't know where we are, but it's a strange and hostile place. Let's keep it on triple red, friends."

As they readied themselves to leave the gateway, Mildred glanced back, seeing the dull smudge on the gray stone. "It always amazed me that creatures could manufacture something like a local anesthetic in their bodies. Ah, the way of nature! Still, it's a pity. It was so pretty," she said.

RYAN WENT FIRST, the others following him in a close skirmish line, J.B. bringing up the rear. Everyone had blasters cocked in readiness, all of them aware of the dangerous strangeness of the place.

A narrow path between the trees showed the same signs of having been recently cut from the lush wilderness with machetes.

The sun was bright, occasionally visible, filtered in golden shafts through the overwhelming green of the forest's twining branches. The heat was oppressive, and all of them were quickly soaked in sweat.

"Can you use your sextant, J.B.?" Ryan asked. "Doesn't make that much difference, but it'd be good to know where we are. I swear I've never been here before. Wherever 'here' is."

"I can try it." The Armorer reached for the miniature scientific instrument, one of the rarest examples of surviving predark navigational gear. He squinted through it at the sun, having made all the necessary calculations and settings, then looked at the dial and shook his head.

"Well?"

"Nothing, Ryan. It's either malfunctioned or we aren't in Deathlands anymore."

"Well, we ended up in Moscow that one time," Ryan said. "Can you change the settings to give us an idea?"

"Sure. But I can't give any real kind of accuracy at all. Even if I try and reset all the base parameters on it. Let's see . . . If we . . ."

They stood still, waiting. A skinny monkey swung past overhead, its pelt a leprous yellow. It paused and stared down at them from red-veined, protruding eyes.

J.B. sniffed. "Well, near as I can figure it, we're someplace like the middle of the Amazon jungle. But there's one lateral reading that doesn't seem to register properly. I guess we could be on the narrow bit between Deathlands and South America. Could be."

"The isthmus of Panama," Doc suggested. "Home of the great canal and every kind of disease-bearing insect known to humanity. The white man's grave."

"Farther south is more likely." J.B. put away the minisextant. "Best bet is that we've jumped to some kind of secret base that got built in the jungles of Brazil or a place like that." He took off his glasses to clean away a blur of perspiration. "Have to admit that my geography's not too hot once you get south of the Grandee. And we're way south of that."

Ryan glanced behind them. They'd all checked out the exterior of the building that housed the mat-trans unit. The one thing that seemed certain was that it wasn't a normal redoubt. It was too small for that, though it was built of the same nuke-resistant materials.

Some scratches and deeper gouges marred the reinforced walls at the side of the open door. Instead of the usual lever to close the door, there was the kind of protected number-and-letter digital-display pad that was normally on the outside doors of big redoubts.

Taking a chance, based on previous experience of exits from sealed redoubts, Ryan had keyed in the numerals 2 and 5 and 3.

It had worked, and the massive sec door had slid closed. There were more shallow scratches and minor dents on its outside, as if attempts had been made to break in—but totally ineffectual attempts.

"Like the one in Russia," J.B. had observed. "Just the mat-trans unit hidden away without a major redoubt to guard and protect it."

"There goes my hopes of a hot shower," Krysty moaned. "With this soaking heat I need it even more."

"Me, too," Mildred agreed. "Maybe we'll find a nice limpid crystal pool somewhere close by."

"Probably will," Jak said. "Filled piranhas."

THE PATH RAN for about a hundred yards.

Doc called for a halt. "Might I ask a short and simple question?"

"Sure," Ryan replied. "Shoot, Doc."

"Since the gateway was sealed and had obviously not been opened since the days of skydark, what is the point of this path? It appears to lead through an otherwise impenetrable region of dense forest to a locked door."

"Good question."

They all stood and pondered it. Apart from the narrow path, there was no other sign of the existence of human life, though the undergrowth was so thick that there could have been a sixteen-lane highway just a hundred yards away and they wouldn't have known it.

"Mebbe part hunting trail," Jak suggested. "Plenty game around."

"Could be." Ryan wiped sweat from his face, pulling away the patch from his missing left eye and mopping the puckered socket dry.

"What are we looking for, Dad?"

"Don't know until we find it. Somewhere to get some food. Just move on a ways until we come across some sort of ville."

Less than thirty seconds later they encountered the locals.

# Chapter Five

Ryan had just started moving again when the path came to an abrupt end. The wall of forest opened into a wide clearing, hacked clear and kept cropped. Immediately opposite was a wider track, winding toward the west.

But what immediately caught Ryan's eye was the trio of men standing by a large circular block of stones at the center of the clearing.

They were dark skinned, with short hair that was covered in some kind of oil or grease. Two of the stocky men wore cotton shirts and pants, the third a beaded loincloth that barely covered his genitals. All of them had necklaces, and dangling rings through their ears. Bows were slung across their shoulders, as were quivers of feathered arrows. Two of them also had blasters. One was carrying what seemed to be an ancient Mauser rifle. The other had a pistol tucked into the waist of his pants. It wasn't a model that Ryan recognized at all.

They were arranging the body of what looked like a small antelope on top of the block of stone, but they stopped at Ryan's sudden appearance from the surrounding greenery. None of them made any effort to draw a weapon.

The one-eyed man had already hissed a warning to his companions, but the natives didn't seem to present any major threat. He had the SIG-Sauer drawn, but didn't open fire. The men were about fifty feet away from him, close enough for him to have felt confident in taking out all three.

Ryan led the way as the friends filed into the clearing, all with blasters drawn. The trio of locals watched, muttering at the sight of the red hair. Mildred's dark coloring also seemed to fascinate them.

But total amazement was reserved for the last but one of the party.

Jak Lauren.

When the albino, with his shock of pure white hair, walked into view, the men were galvanized. They dropped the bloodied corpse of the animal in the grass and actually staggered backward, clutching at one another.

"Watch it!" Ryan warned, wondering what kind of danger the reaction might mean.

But the natives didn't seem to have any thought of attacking the seven strangers. They stood there, slack jawed, repeating a word that sounded to Ryan like *blanco*. He knew enough Mex talk to know that the word meant white, and he assumed it had to be some sort of reference to the teenager.

Though you didn't call it body language in Deathlands, it was an important part of survival to be able to read the way a man stood and acted.

It was obvious to Ryan that the trio of locals were torn between fear and aggression and something else that he couldn't identify, something like an unusual kind of respect mingled with understandable suspicion against outlanders who had suddenly appeared in their hunting grounds.

"We don't intend trouble," he called, holding up his empty left hand in the universal sign of peace, while making sure that the 9 mm automatic kept the trio covered.

The three men exchanged glances, whispering intently to one another.

Then, without a breath of warning, they turned tail and ran toward the wide track.

"Don't shoot," Ryan snapped. "Let them be."

In eight beats of the heart, the olive-skinned natives had vanished into the jungle that lined the trail.

"Well, they didn't seem too impressed with meeting the bold explorers," Doc said. "From the appearance of them I would have said that John Barrymore was roughly correct. They had the physiognomy of natives from Central or South America. Perhaps from the basin of the Amazon, or the Mato Grosso."

"Blasters were interesting," J.B. said, looking at Ryan. "You recognize them?"

"Rifle looked like a Mauser. Didn't know what the handblaster was. You pick them?"

The Armorer nodded. "That's what's interesting. Spanish and Portuguese used to be active in these parts, didn't they? Doc, you know about—"

Mildred interrupted him, coughing to attract attention. "I know Doc is the source of all information from aardvarks to memorable zeugmas, but could I just mention that I'm the one in the party who minored in American Indian sociological groupings. You could try asking me, John."

"Sorry." He patted her arm. "Was I right about the influence of the Spanish and the Portuguese?"

She smiled at him. "Course you were, love. Incidentally, did anyone else notice that the guy without the shirt or pants was tattooed?"

"Me," Jak said. "In thick ridges, like snakes."

"Right. Coils and also hundreds of dots around his thighs. Made him look like he was wearing Lycra cycling shorts. Not that any of you would know what Lycra cycling shorts are. Where was I?"

"Conquistadores," Doc prompted.

"Right. Most of the continent was overrun by European explorers. Most came from Spain or Portugal. Had a very strong influence right up to skydark."

J.B. nodded. "Unusual weapons. Only seen either of them in armaments books from predark. Good guess on the Mauser. Bolt-action rifle, 6.5 caliber. Mauser-Vergueiro. The M-1904 model. Odd gun. Like to have a look at one. The bolt handle is set in front of the receiver bridge."

"More like a Mannlicher?" Ryan asked.

"Yeah. Handblaster was also Portuguese. It's a Savage M-915. Antique. Got some interesting details from what I remember about them."

"What?" Jak asked.

"Shouldn't we be moving out of here?" Mildred asked. "Sorry to interrupt all this male-bonding talk about guns, but those three might come back with a bunch of friends."

Ryan nodded. "In a minute, Mildred. They can't get back with help just yet."

He turned to J.B. "Go on." It was always profoundly interesting tapping the Armorer's unparalleled knowledge of weaponry.

"Delayed blow-back action. Bit like the Model 12 Steyr. Way it's built, the actual barrel rotates. Slows the action down just a little. But it all starts to operate the moment you initiate the firing sequence. Spur cocking lever. Set where you'd find the hammer. A spring-loaded striker on the old Savage gets itself released by the sear."

Ryan was fascinated by this arcane piece of blaster lore. "So the cocking lever doesn't hit on the firing pin, like the hammer does on most handblasters?"

"Right. So you're careful not to have a round in the chamber when you let the cocking lever down."

"Real old blasters," Jak said.

"Yeah," the Armorer agreed. "Real old."

"How come natives with bows and arrows also have blasters like that?" Krysty asked.

"Find it a lot all the way across Deathlands. Dirt-poor squatters, in a stinking frontier pesthole so low the pigs eat better than people, can end up with a top-quality Python or Magnum." J.B. shook his head. "Those blasters could be well over the hundred-year mark."

Mildred was looking around her. "I've never been down this far south," she said. "Spent a little time in Mexico. College days. Checking out some Toltec and Olmec ruins. All part of the great Aztec empire."

"I read about the Aztecs," Doc said. "Fascinating, the strengths and weaknesses of their way of life. Staggering beauty and appalling violence. I read an excellent book on them once. So long ago. Also covered something of the Mayas and the Incas, farther south."

"They tribes, Doc?" Dean asked.

"Civilizations, son. The Lakota and the Chiricahua could be called tribes, I guess. But when you start thinking about the old ones, like the Anasazi, then you are talking about an entire civilization."

"What's the antelope for?" Dean asked, walking forward. "And what's this triple-weird stone for?"

Mildred glanced at Doc before answering. "My best guess is that the animal is a sacrifice and the stone is likely some kind of altar."

Doc nodded, joining the boy. "Flattened top and a channel to carry the blood over one side. Maybe to be caught in a vessel of some kind. And there's a crude sculpture of a man with a snake issuing from his mouth. Serpent god. For once Dr. Wyeth and I find ourselves on the same side of the fence."

"Altar?" Ryan repeated. "They come all the way out here to leave a sacrifice to their gods? The gods of the jungle?" A thought struck him. "Wait a minute. That hacked-out trail runs from here all the way to the gateway entrance. Almost like they're sacrificing to that."

THEY MOVED CAUTIOUSLY along the fifteen-foot-wide track, heading roughly westward, though it curved and twisted in on itself like a poisoned rattler.

The jungle pressed in closely on both sides, with impenetrable walls of brush, some of the shrubs with murderous spines six inches long. And everywhere was the overpowering scent of flowers and the humming of insects.

Krysty was at Ryan's heels. "Be a great ace-on-the-line sort of place for an ambush, lover," she said quietly.

"You feel anything?"

"No. Sort of seething life, but all of it seems to be away in the background. No immediate threat."

"Could be a hundred armed men within fifty feet of us, and we wouldn't know." Ryan looked behind, checking that everyone was keeping a proper spacing.

"Thought Trader didn't approve of taking chances like this. What would he think?"

Ryan smiled. "He'd have thought there was no choice. Then chances don't come into it."

"Where's that crystal pool you were talking about?" Mildred called from farther behind. "We're all dehydrating at the rate of a pint an hour. Maybe more. We go on too far, Ryan, and we'll all get ill. And after that we'll all get dead."

THEY TOOK A BREAK about ten minutes later, resting in another clearing, all of them flopping to the ground, close to exhaustion.

"Never known anything like this humidity and heat for sapping strength," Ryan said.

"Doc's not handling it well." Mildred had walked over to join Ryan and Krysty.

The old man was sitting fanning himself with J.B.'s fedora, his lips moving as he muttered to himself. In the stillness it was just possible to hear what he was saying.

"Catch the blood in the vessel with the pestle. Not the flagon with the dragon. Which has the true brew? Truth has the witch's brew." He smiled to himself as he mopped his brow with his blue kerchief. "Chalice from the palace? Or is that the one that holds the poisoned pellet? Caught at the court of King Arthur. If you have a boil, you must lance it a lot."

"Off his head," Krysty said. "Babbling total nonsense, poor old bastard."

"Can I recce, Dad?"

Ryan nodded. "My orders are very simple. To go on a recce and find us some good fresh water, within less than a hundred yards from here. And if you sort out some food, then you get a double-plus point."

"On my way."

"And Dean . . ."

"Yeah?"

"Careful."

"Sure."

Ryan lay back on the lush grass and closed his eye, thinking about the location of this latest jump somewhere to the south of Mexico. His knowledge of the geography of Deathlands was second to nobody. But that knowledge extended only a few dozen miles south of the big Grandee.

He dozed, his last sentient thought involved with wondering whether this might be the Shangri-la that he and Krysty were endlessly searching for. Their Paradise. Their Promised Land. The Golden City.

In Ryan's mind there was water and pasture and maybe mountains. A small homestead, secure and solid. And himself there with Krysty and with Dean. It was a place of safety, where a man could finally stop all the running and the feuding and the fighting and the chilling.

And maybe there would be more children. That part of the picture always seemed to be a little blurred.

Someone was shaking him.

For a fraction of a broken moment, Ryan's hand fell to the butt of the SIG-Sauer, his fighting instinct taking over.

"Dad."

The hand moved from the blaster.

"Dad!"

"What is it, Dean?" Ryan sat up and opened his right eye, feeling the beginnings of a headache lurking somewhere behind the ruins of his left eye.

"Found it."

"What?"

"Water. Just around the next corner. And there's loads of fruit there."

Ryan blinked, aware that his son's excited face was streaked with sticky threads of yellow juice. "Sure it's good to eat?" he asked.

"Course. Delicious. Peaches and nectarines and some other stuff I don't know the names of."

Everyone else had sat up as the boy came running excitedly into the clearing. Even Doc seemed to have snapped back into the real world.

"What kind of water, boy?" Mildred called.

"Hey, little water boy, set your water bucket down," Doc sang tunefully. "And bring me a long cool drink, there's a sweet Ganymede."

Dean turned to the old man. "Doc, that's not my name. Are you feeling . . . ?"

"Feeling double fine and looking triple good, thank you, Dean Cawdor. Though I confess that I was fatigued for a moment or two due to the lack of access to the best produce of Adam's brewery. But now you bring us the finest news. Ganymede. Cupbearer to the gods. It is drinkable, is it, lad?"

"Sure."

"Tried it?" Jak asked, standing up. The teenager seemed to suffer from the damp heat less than the others, though Ryan knew that a hot bright sun was bad news for his deathly white skin.

"Sure."

"No piranhas?" Mildred asked.

The boy's smile vanished and his eagerness evaporated. "Don't think there's . . . Never looked."

"Hell," Ryan said, "let's go see."

# Chapter Six

There were no piranhas.

Dean led them along, scampering like Puck, beckoning for them to follow him around the curving track, past a bank of fragile violet orchids.

"Right here!" he shouted, his bright voice muffled by the surrounding walls of dark vegetation. Behind him, a small furry animal skittered across the path and disappeared, but Dean never even saw it.

Everyone was infected by the boy's enthusiasm, running behind him, though Ryan, J.B. and Jak still had their blasters drawn and cocked.

And suddenly there it was.

"By...by all the stars that shine in the bright diadem," Doc breathed, leaning on the silver lion's-head hilt of his ebony cane.

It was possibly the most beautiful place that Ryan had ever seen.

The pool was about one hundred feet across, surrounded by banks of emerald grass. Beyond that came a circle of flowering bushes, dripping delicious scents into the still air. And surrounding the shrubs were the mighty trees, great giants of the tropical rain forest, soaring two and three hundred feet into the cloudless blue sky.

The water in the pool was clear and limpid. Waxen lilies were scattered across the surface, filling the day with their deep, sensuous smell.

"Like a picture in a kids' book of the Garden of Eden," Mildred said, awed.

"Gaia! I can't believe that a place like this exists in Deathlands." Krysty shook her head. "Stupe! Course. Forgot for a moment we aren't in Deathlands."

"Can I swim, Dad?"

"Hold off a minute. Don't just go jumping in blind, son. Let's take a long, careful look at this. See the way the sun's reflecting off the surface?"

"Sure. So what?"

Ryan sighed. "Times I don't think you'll ever learn anything properly, Dean. Sun means you can't see much of anything. Can't see what's living in the pool. Could be gators, snakes, any kind of dangerous mutie creature."

"But it looks so lovely, Dad."

"Prairie rattler's one of the most beautiful of God's creatures," J.B. said. "Doesn't stop him from putting you in the boneyard, Dean."

"I guess so. But..."

Ryan walked on the lush grass, shading his eye against the dappled sunlight that lanced through the gently waving branches above him. The pool seemed to have a bottom of clean stone and looked to be roughly ten feet deep. But the water was so crystalline that it was very difficult to judge the true depth. As far as he could see, there was no menacing life lurking in the pool, just a large number of slow-moving, tiny fish, brilliantly patterned in the brightest of colors.

"Don't know," he said finally. "Those pretty little fish might be the kind to strip an ox to its bones in thirty seconds. Then again, they might not be."

Mildred had knelt and cupped water in her hands, sipping at it, rolling it around her mouth before swallowing it.

"Good?" Jak asked, licking his dry lips. "Good, clean water?"

"Well, if it's been poisoned, then they used something midway between ambrosia and nectar," the woman replied. "Because that is as sweet and pure as anything I ever tasted. If you could've bottled this back in the predark times, you could have knocked all the other designer waters down the drain."

The others didn't need any invitation. Dean, Doc and Krysty threw themselves down flat at the side of the small lake, drinking in great gulps, letting the water run through their hair and over faces and necks.

"It is quite wonderful," Doc gasped. "Washes away all the horrid, beastly stickiness of the humid forest. Cleanses in a magical moment."

Ryan, J.B. and Jak were, instinctively, much more cautious. All of them peered around the clearing, looking and listening for any threat of danger.

"Seems quiet," the Armorer commented. "Want me to cover while you all drink?"

Ryan nodded. "Sure. Do the same for you in a couple of minutes."

Jak knelt, head turning as he lowered his face toward the mirrored surface of the water. His dazzling white hair drooped down, becoming wet, the fine strands clinging together.

Ryan laid the Steyr in the grass, kneeling and cupping his hands to drink. The others had been right. It was cool, fresh and utterly wonderful.

Even as he sipped at the delicious water, Ryan looked around the clearing. Trader used to say that as long as you always expected trouble, you'd never be disappointed and you'd never be taken by surprise.

J.B. had his turn, then straightened, wiping his mouth on his sleeve. He reslung the scattergun across his shoulders, holding the Uzi at the ready.

Krysty finished next, followed by Jak.

"How about risking a bath?" Mildred asked as she knelt by the side of the pool. "Something that tastes this good has just got to be safe."

"A typically female piece of logical thinking," Doc commented, dabbing at his mouth with his blue kerchief. "Or should I rather say *illogical* thinking?"

Mildred looked ready to rise to his baiting, then she changed her mind. "Doc, it's just too hot to bother with your teasing. And unless anyone has some serious objections, I'm going to peel off some layers and have a swim."

"I'm still kind of worried by those natives we saw," Ryan said. "And this sacrifice stuff. There's a mess of things here that we don't begin to understand."

"How about a swim?" Mildred repeated. "If I smell like the rest of you, then my armpits sure aren't charmpits. Being funky's all very well, but..." She allowed the sentence to trail away into the green stillness.

"All right." Ryan looked around. "But we do this careful and safe."

"I don't mind if we do this swinging from a flying trapeze, Ryan, just as long as I can get cleaned up."

"I'll vote for that," Krysty added, lowering her voice as she stood close by Ryan. "Got my monthly, lover. A good wash'd be the best ace on the line."

"Right. Ladies go first, with Dean and Jak. Doc and J.B. and me'll stand watch. Then we change over."

"Sounds good," Mildred whooped, dropping her denim jacket in the grass and sitting down to unlace her boots.

Krysty was already out of her Western boots and was unholstering her blaster. Off came the pants and the white shirt, which left her in only her bra and panties, standing poised at the side of the lake like a carved goddess.

"Diana refreshing herself after a day's hunting in the forest," Doc said softly.

"Watch the woods," Ryan warned.

He turned his back on the pool to look around the open space, checking the flower-covered trees.

"A pleasure," the old man replied. "Truly this is a *vista encantadora*. A most enchanted place."

As Ryan surveyed the area, he saw the four swimmers, and he became doubly conscious of how sweat crusted and sticky he felt, literally itching for the chance to get in the cool clear water himself.

Mildred floated on her face, wearing bra and panties like Krysty, her muscular shoulders exposed to the sunlight. Dean was ducking and diving with a sinuous ease, his dark body vanishing into the depths of the pool, then propelling himself upward, shaking his head amid a crown of scattered diamonds, laughing in sheer delight for the pleasure of it.

Krysty swam very slowly, her fiery hair burning on the surface of the pool. She waved to the watching Ryan with a negligent hand.

Ryan was looking at Jak, the youth's white body burning like a column of ice, his red eyes glowing like fire at the center of the mane of tumbling hair, when he heard J.B.'s quiet whisper. "Company. Two. Nine o'clock from where you're looking."

Since the Armorer hadn't opened fire with his Uzi, Ryan figured there was no immediate danger. He turned slowly, ninety degrees to his left, looking casually where J.B. had indicated

He saw them immediately.

Though the first glimpse had been very quick, Ryan thought he recognized the two as the natives they'd seen a little earlier. Only their faces were visible, but they didn't look threatening, more like curious.

At first Ryan guessed that they were probably fascinated by the seminaked bodies of the two women, but he noticed straightaway that their dark eyes were fixed on the languid body of Jak Lauren, who was floating on his back, spitting up a stream of water like a broaching dolphin.

"Want me to take them both out?" J.B. asked in a calm, conversational voice, as though he were asking Ryan whether he thought the meat needed a touch more salt.

"No. Not unless we have no choice about chilling them. Best to arrive someplace else and not start butchering the locals. Just watch them double careful.''

"Watch who?" Doc boomed. "Whom should we be watching, Ryan, my dear fellow?''

"Nothing, Doc. Keep a watch on the far side of the pool and tell us, *quietly,* if you see anyone over there. But don't do nothing hasty."

The two pair of eyes were still watching Jak as he swam slowly around the edge of the pool.

It had to have been obvious to the natives that their presence had been spotted by both J.B. and Ryan, but they still made no attempt to move back into deeper cover.

They whispered to each other, revealing that their teeth had been filed to points. Ryan glimpsed tiny flecks of blue-green stone embedded in their central incisors that he guessed were chips of turquoise.

Jak had stripped to his shorts for the swim, and was now picking his way out of the pool, his pale body gleaming in the sunlight. His hair fell across his shoulders like a shawl of snow.

He looked across toward Ryan and the Armorer, suddenly spotting the two faces peeking out at him. He gave a yell of warning and pointed a finger, as white as wind-washed bone, at the pair of intruders.

"Look out!" he yelled.

The natives vanished as quickly as if they'd been grabbed from behind. There was a brief flurry of rustling from the undergrowth, and then silence again.

"Same ones?" Jak called, standing still, the water barely reaching his knees.

"Reckon so," Ryan replied. "Or someone very much like them. Didn't seem to mean us any harm."

"What do they want?" Krysty asked, walking from the pool, the water streaming over her breasts and stomach and thighs. "Just curious?"

Ryan nodded, holstering the SIG-Sauer. "Reckon so. You people had long enough to swim and freshen up. Our turn now. Get the blasters as soon as you're dressed and keep a lookout. But don't start shooting unless there's a good reason. Place like this, wild jungle, probably isn't a good place to upset the locals with a firefight."

THE WATER FELT EVERY BIT as good as it had looked and tasted.

Ryan peeled off his clothes, leaving them in a neat pile, but carried his blaster to the edge of the pool and placed it on the rich grass.

The small lake wasn't big enough to extend himself and swim properly, but Ryan luxuriated in moving up and down its length, mouth open to draw in great drafts of the fresh water. Like the albino teenager, he had stripped down to his shorts, relishing the movement of the cool liquid against his skin.

J.B. wasn't a great swimmer and he moved nervously from side to side, taking care not to ever get himself too much beyond his depth.

Doc had pulled off his cracked knee boots and stained frock coat, hesitating before divesting himself of his ancient breeches. He peeled off the white shirt to reveal a tattered undershirt that buttoned high up to his neck and undershorts that covered him all the way down to his skinny knees.

"By all the saints, Doc!" exclaimed Mildred, who was in the middle of getting herself dressed. "That is one of the damnedest things I ever did see."

"Well, your body, ma'am, hardly seemed to me to present a perfect picture of God's gift to mankind."

"Hey, watch your mouth, Doc," J.B. snapped angrily. "Mildred didn't—"

But the woman quieted him with a raised hand. "All right, my dear. I can fight my own battles, particularly against a shrunk-shanked old goat like Doc here."

"I don't think I shall be taking the waters after all," Doc muttered.

Mildred realized that the old man was genuinely hurt and embarrassed. "Hey, Doc, I'm sorry. Me and my big mouth. Wasn't very funny, was it?"

"No, I confess I was less than amused by your comments, Dr. Wyeth."

"Come on, Doc. Time's passing," Ryan called, paddling on his back, staring up into the deep green of the overhead branches, blinking at the occasional shafts of bright sun.

Doc stalked toward the inviting pool, looking like a somewhat disheveled heron, clutching to him the ragged underclothes and his ragged dignity.

THEY ALL LAY in the grass, letting hair dry, resting from the swim, enjoying the cool shade. A light wind had risen, taking away the top layer of the stifling humidity.

Three tiny piglike animals that Doc said were peccaries came and drank from the pool, ignoring the presence of the seven humans. Dean had hissed to his father that they should butcher them for meat, but Ryan had refused.

"Don't need it yet. Forest seems to be brimming with food. We've all eaten our fills of those fruits you found. Ones that taste like peaches."

"And those cherries," Krysty added. "Best ones I ever had, even back in Harmony ville."

Ryan stretched and stood. "But now I reckon it's time to be moving on."

# Chapter Seven

They followed the continuation of the trail. It ran roughly west, picking up on the far side of the pool where the two natives had been hiding.

Ryan led the skirmish line, spaced out at about five yard intervals, with J.B., as usual, bringing up the rear of the small column.

The overwhelming humidity had mercifully eased, helped by the freshening easterly breeze that rustled the topmost branches of the mighty trees. Though they saw little of it, Ryan was aware of the profusion of wildlife that moved unseen through the forest around them.

A couple of times he spotted monkeys swinging noisily among the dangling fronds of liana, and once a deer crashed out across the trail, pausing to stare haughtily in the direction of the human invaders. It would have been absurdly simple to put the handsome animal down with a single bullet, and Ryan made the first instinctive move to shoot.

But he held back, partly to avoid the sound of a shot ringing through the trees. Partly because, as he'd said to Dean, there seemed to be more than enough fruit around to hold off starvation forever and a day.

The trail was well trodden, wide enough for a wag in most places, running over mainly level ground. Every now and again it was crossed by narrower side tracks that he guessed were probably for hunters.

"Trees thinning out some," said Krysty, immediately on his heels.

"Yeah. Seem to be moving steadily downhill. Could be heading toward a river."

He held up a hand, stopping and looking around him. Krysty was right. The giant forest of a couple of miles back had diminished, and they had just passed through several clearings.

"Look at that bird, Dad," Dean called, pointing up into a circle of blue sky.

Ryan squinted into the brightness. "Eagle of some kind."

"I believe that the bird in question is most likely to be a giant condor," Doc offered. "It was always a splendid bird, but that specimen seems unusually large."

Ryan's guess put the wingspan at thirty feet. The bird was circling lazily, riding a thermal, its keen eyes scanning the green carpet below for some sign of edible life. It had noticed the seven two-legs, attracted initially by the blaze of white that was Jak Lauren, but had rejected them from experience, knowing they would fight back too hard.

"What's that?" J.B. asked, pointing with the muzzle of the Uzi along a transverse trail that cut in from the right. "Some kind of statue?"

They all walked the hundred yards or so to examine it.

It was obviously extremely old, dating back to well before skydark. The stone of the double columns was deeply carved, but time had worn away the sharp, clean edges, blurring the design.

"Dragons?" Mildred suggested.

Doc peered closely at them, shaking his head. "No. I think not. I believe that they are the famous plumed serpents that typify the culture of the old Aztecs. See that they stand ten feet tall and have their jaws gaping open?"

"Oh, yeah." Jak sniffed. "What got in mouths?"

"Skulls, I believe," Doc replied. "Representations of human skulls. But moss has grown over them, and it's a little difficult to make out."

Mildred was on tiptoe, staring at them. "My guess is that they aren't carved skulls, Doc."

"But the eye sockets and the teeth that… Oh, by the Three Kennedys! I take your meaning, Dr. Wyeth. They aren't carved skulls at all. They are real human skulls."

Ryan was more interested in what lay scattered around the base of the two pillars of stone.

There were bunches of flowers, already faded and dull, a large earthenware dish of fruits, mostly rotted, gnawed by predators, and the ragged carcass of what had probably been a large pig.

"Sacrifices?" he asked.

"The Aztecs were very fond of all manner of sacrifices," Doc pronounced, gripping the lapels of his frock coat as though he were about to deliver a lecture. "Their religion was totally dependent on them. In fact, it was not just fruit or animals that their blood-eyed gods demanded as visible tokens of their devotion and love. They were a deal more famous for their barbaric—"

"Hold it, Doc," Ryan said, lifting a warning hand. "Think we might be close to company."

His attention had first been drawn by the cessation of the background noises of the jungle, the cheeping of insects and the fluid songs of the brilliantly hued birds. The forest had become unaccountably quiet, and even the fluorescent clouds of butterflies had vanished.

Then his acute hearing had detected other noises, faint and distant but coming closer: a sound like the cracking of a whip, someone crying out in pain or anger, laughter, coarse and brutish, and a strange metallic tinkling.

"Take cover," he said.

"Here or on the main trail?" the Armorer asked. "Be good to see what's coming. Wouldn't see nothing from back here."

"Wouldn't see *anything*," Mildred corrected, but J.B. took no notice.

"Yeah. Undergrowth's thick enough to keep us well hidden." Ryan glanced around. "Everyone stay still."

He ran back onto the main trail, pausing to check that nobody was in sight. But the trail curved in the direction of the noises, making it impossible to see more than about eighty yards ahead. Ryan eased himself quickly into the bushes, picking one that was covered in bright orange trumpet-shaped flowers that had a bittersweet perfume.

The others rapidly followed his lead, hiding on both sides of the trodden path, vanishing instantly into the banks of green vegetation.

The only sound was a muffled oath from Doc as he found himself uncomfortably close to a colony of red ants. He moved sideways a few yards, rustling the bushes until he found somewhere more amendable.

Now it was easier to identify the approaching sounds.

It was undoubtedly a whip—several whips—snapping against naked flesh. And the voices reflected pain, not anger. The bursts of laughter were brutish, and the metallic tinkling was almost certainly the noise of steel chains.

All of which combined to point in only one direction.

"Slavers," Ryan breathed.

THERE WERE A DOZEN or so of them, sallow faced, with a look that was partly Mex and partly something else.

They were a ragged bunch, dressed mainly in cotton shirts and pants, stained with sweat. All had either rifles slung over shoulders or handblasters tucked into belts. The common factor in their faces was coarseness. Most had drooping mustaches, and a few had straggling beards. Their eyes were hard and dark, puffed around the rims like those of habitual drinkers.

The leader rode astride a lame burro, smoking a thin cigar. He wore a battered panama hat with a ribbon of red and yellow knotted around it.

By the time he had ridden slowly past Ryan, it was possible to make out the victims—the slaves, for Ryan's guess was obviously correct.

They looked identical to the natives that Ryan and the others had already seen. He counted twenty-four— nine men, eleven women and four children. All of the children were female, looking to be prepubescent.

The entire group was completely naked, and all of them showed bleeding welts from the short, viciously plaited whips of their captors.

Ryan noticed that most of the prisoners had long arms and broad feet. None of the men had any facial hair at all, though their torn and bleeding ears showed where the ornamental rings had been torn out.

The other thing that caught Ryan's eye was the amount of tattooing that was visible on the natives, mostly on the men, clusters of raised blue-and-purple patterns across legs and body and face.

The chains were fastened around the left ankle of each prisoner, meaning that they were forced to shuffle in a clumsy march to avoid tripping one another.

They looked to be thoroughly cowed and resigned to their fate, heads lowered, occasionally crying out at a particularly vicious cut from one of the whips.

Ryan peeked through the fringe of dark green leaves, looking back down the trail. At the tail end of the column, to his disquiet, he spotted a pair of the slavers walking together, with four dogs on leashes. The animals were slavering brutes with underslung jaws and the red eyes of killers.

They were tugging ahead, snarling at the heels of the last of the line of slaves.

Ryan tried to ease himself back into the undergrowth, praying that the overwhelming scent of the colorful flowers covered his own smell and hid it from the hounds. In his right hand, the SIG-Sauer was already cocked, his index finger resting lightly inside the trigger guard.

Now most of the sorry column had trudged by. Not one of the natives had lifted his or her head to look at the surrounding brush, and none of the guards seemed to be bothering with checking against a possible ambush.

Slavery was endemic in some parts of Deathlands, generally where there was some sort of crude manufacturing or processing plant set up, or where old mines were being reopened and reworked. In all those cases, the work involved was bitter and arduous, and it simply wasn't possible to attract paid workers.

So the barons and owners used slaves.

Over the years Ryan had encountered slavery on several occasions. Trader's rule in life was not to interfere unless there was some good reason—generally commercial—to justify it. For the miserable victims, condemned to dwell at the very bottom of the poverty heap, slavery was a way of life. If you tried to combat it and free a few poor wretches, then others would be taken and the circle would remain unbroken.

The only way of stopping it was to totally wipe out the slavers themselves, and there wasn't often much profit in trying to do that.

One of the young girls stumbled and fell, dragging down the next two in line.

For a moment there was chaos, with screaming and yelling and dogs barking. Whips raised and fell, cracking into defenseless flesh. The fattest of the slavers grabbed the girl and heaved her to her feet, slapping her hard across the face to teach her a lesson to be more careful.

"Don't spoil the merchandise," called the man on the burro's back.

"Stupe bitch went down on purpose," the angry man replied. "I'll show her to be trouble, tonight."

"No, you won't, Manuel. Not unless I say so."

There was a clear note of warning in the voice, and Manuel let the girl go, snatching a chance to brush the flat of his hand over her budding breasts, making her wince more than the slap had. "Sure, boss," he called out.

Ryan frowned, wondering about the accent. They spoke reasonable American, but there was a heavy guttural accent to it that he couldn't place.

Now the prisoners were almost past him.

Ryan felt movement and looked down, seeing that a tiny lizard, vermilion in color, was industriously climbing over the toe of one of his combat boots.

He noticed that it had a triple row of needle-sharp teeth, and it was trying to gnaw its way through the toughened leather. Moving with infinite slowness, Ryan hefted the two pounds of cold metal that was the SIG-Sauer P-226 and brought it down firmly on the back of the reptile's skull, cracking its head open in a puddle of gray-pink brains, sending it toppling lifelessly into the leaf mold that lay all around.

The dogs were level with him when he risked a glance through the fringe of leaves, and one of them, a brindled brute with scarred flanks, was heaving on the leash, as though it had managed to scent him.

But the guard took no notice, cursing at it and tugging savagely at the spiked choke collar.

"Come on, Diablo, you piece of shit! Walk on, will you."

He kicked at the dog, which turned and snarled at him, showing its teeth.

Ryan crouched lower, part of his attention fixed on the death throes of the little lizard, which was on its back, legs jerking convulsively, a thin trickle of green blood seeping from between the pointed teeth.

The column of slavers and their victims had almost gone, moving safely along toward the east, passing unsuspectingly by Ryan and the others.

Ryan relaxed his grip on the blaster, ready to ease down the hammer, when Dean leapt from the undergrowth immediately opposite him, yelling at the top of his voice.

# Chapter Eight

Ironically it was only the total chaos that prevented a bloody firefight.

Dean's totally unexpected appearance took everyone by surprise, including Ryan and the other companions.

The slavers swung around, and blasters were drawn and leveled. But the dogs had gone crazy, pulling the guard off his feet, knocking over his companion. Also, at least half of the natives fell down in screaming panic, pulling one another to the ground, making it impossible for anyone to hope for a clear shot at anyone else.

It was a hair-trigger moment.

Ryan took a chance and stood, holding his automatic in his outstretched hand, pointing it toward the tops of the trees, shouting as loudly as he could.

"Don't shoot! Nobody start shooting or there'll be a load of dying."

To his relief, J.B., Krysty and the others all stayed hidden and silent in the undergrowth, meaning that they didn't tip his hand, didn't show that they were outnumbered almost two to one by the slavers.

Dean was rolling on the track, beating at his body with flailing hands. From where he stood, Ryan could see the problem, the same problem that Doc had so narrowly avoided.

Ants.

Dean had inadvertently chosen a nest of fiery red ants for his hiding place, staying still and quiet for as long as he could, stoically enduring the repeated bites until they became unendurable.

"Sorry, Dad, sorry," he kept repeating, weeping bitter tears with the acidic agony of dozens of bites, all over the most tender parts of his body.

Ryan ignored his son, focusing his attention on the slavers, particularly on the man in the panama at the head of the raggedy procession, who had slipped agilely from the saddle of the burro, dropping to a kneeling position behind the skittish animal. He held a battered Armalite that looked the identical twin to the blaster that the Trader always carried.

"Who the fuck're you, mister?" he shouted. "Best you tell me pretty quick."

"Name's Ryan Cawdor. No call for anyone to get slippery-fingered and start shooting. No need!"

"I am Rodrigo Bivar. I like to hear you say this. How many blasters you got, amigo?"

"Enough."

The man threw his head back and laughed, showing that he had more precious metal in his teeth than the lost Dutchman Mine. "Enough. That's a big joke, friend. You better tell me or mebbe we start to do some shooting."

"First man squeezes a trigger means you get your head blown away."

"You got people with blasters."

"I promise you we have."

"Promises!" The slaver roared with laughter.

Ryan looked at the gang, seeing the edginess and tension, knowing that one wrong step and there'd be a lot of blood spilled on the bright green turf.

"See that white flower," he said, "halfway up that tree there, in among the creepers?"

Heads turned and Bivar nodded. "Sure I see it. What about it, Cawdor?"

"Look at it." He turned to the bushes. "Mildred?"

"Yeah?"

"Hey, you got ladies there, friend? They pretty ladies? We sure like pretty ladies, amigo."

"Our pretty ladies got stings. Mildred. That flower. Take it out for me."

"Sure."

There was a short pause, then the familiar light crack of the ZKR 551 revolver. And the flower, fully thirty yards off, disappeared in a pulp of watery spray.

The slavers chattered among themselves until Bivar barked something at them in a language that Ryan didn't recognize. The slaver chief stood and removed his stained panama. "Hey, lady, I take my hat off to you. That real pretty shooting you done there."

He turned to Ryan. "How many's enough, friend?"

"Enough."

The man cautiously emerged from behind his burro. "I get it now. You in the same business as us?"

Ryan didn't hesitate. "Could be. Same sort of line. You got a good crop there."

The slavers were still nervous, though some of the tension had seeped out of the atmosphere. Bivar slung his Armalite ostentatiously across his shoulder, though Ryan would have bet his life that the man had at least one other concealed blaster.

"You don't want to trade for them?"

"No. Take our own," Ryan said.

"That's plenty good, friend. Just so's you don't try to steal the ones we got. Men like us, we don't fall out over a few slaves. I figure that'd be blasphemy, mebbe."

Ryan smiled. "Guess that's an ace on the line."

Bivar looked puzzled. "Ace on line. What the fuck's that mean? That outland talk? Where you say you come from, amigo?"

Ryan pointed vaguely toward the north.

"And where you goin'?"

This time Ryan pointed in the opposite direction.

Bivar roared with laughter again. Behind him, some of his men had gotten the slaves back on their feet, using the whips to restore a cowed order. The guard with the dogs had also kicked them into a whining submission.

"You know this place good, friend?"

Ryan shook his head. "Not that good. Heard there was a big village not too far off in that direction," he guessed, pointing back along the trail where the slavers had come from.

"You heard good. But you best be real careful for a day or two. Like a nest of bees when the honey's been robbed. You know what I mean?"

"Yeah, I know."

"Help us, *señor!*" called one of the natives, holding out his hands helplessly toward Ryan.

The nearest guard clubbed him down with the butt of a remade percussion-cap pistol, knocking him senseless.

Bivar found it all profoundly amusing. "If God had not wanted them sheared, then he would never have created them as sheep, would he, amigo? Is that not so?"

"That's so."

"And he calls to you for help. Like a baby in the jaws of the lion who cries to the wolf to save him." The sally was greeted with raucous laughter from all of his listening men.

It crossed Ryan's mind to give the word to open fire and massacre the slavers, but he and Dean were out in the open, vulnerable.

Things could easily go wrong—a few lucky shots— and the trade wasn't worth it.

"Hey, outlander?"

"What is it?"

"You seen any of my friends around here?"

"No. Just a couple of natives who ran away before we could get to them."

"Is strange. Got more of my men scouting. Should've met up with them by now. You see them, tell them we head for camp. Keep these sheep awhile and teach them all good manners. You tell my friends that?"

"Sure."

"*Gracias.*"

Ryan nodded. "I see them, I'll tell them. How many of them, so I recognize them?"

"You not have that problem. There's—" he looked down at his fingers, lips moving "—I don't number so well, friend. Not so many as us. But, like you say...enough."

"I'll tell them."

"Now we go. Listen, I leave one or two of my men a way behind, just in case of any little misunderstanding about you following us. I do that."

Ryan held out his hands. "I'm going the other way, Bivar. No worries."

"Watch for them angry bees, then. Adios."

He waved his panama hat and clambered aboard the sway-backed burro again.

His men slowly holstered their blasters and began to shepherd their reluctant flock along the trail.

Bivar turned in the saddle and gave a great flourish with his hat as he vanished around the bend. A minute or so later and they'd all gone, the noise of their passing fading away into the distance.

Ryan waited, managing a reassuring smile to his son.

"Dad, I'm real—"

"Never apologize, Dean. Sign of weakness. Like Trader always used to say. I understand."

"The ants were—"

"Next time, look down a bit more carefully before you pick a hiding place."

"All right for us to come out?" J.B. called.

"Sure. Everyone out."

Krysty was first back onto the trail, brushing faded petals from her clothes. "That was a son-of-a-bitching encounter, lover," she said, her face set like cold Sierra granite. "Should have done something."

"What?" Ryan looked at her. "Way you stay alive in Deathlands is by listening to your head and ignoring your heart. Think I didn't feel any pity for those poor, sorry wretches? Sure I did. But a wrong move, and me and Dean could easy have bought the farm. They all had blasters and looked like they knew how to use them. A good dozen of them."

Krysty wasn't going to be that easily satisfied. "All that bullshit! Head and heart! It doesn't mean a bastard thing, Ryan. We could've saved them and cleansed the earth a little by chilling those cold-eyed slavers." She bit her lip. "Could've done it. Should've done it."

Ryan suddenly felt the familiar swelling of anger, the red mist that often came in a killing field. The seaming scar that ran from his right eye to the corner of his mouth began to throb.

He took a step toward Krysty. "Fireblast! I read in old predark books about what they called bleeding-heart liberals. Folks want to do the right thing, without stopping to think about what the fuck the right thing might be. Sure, we could almost certainly have taken the slavers out. Let all the natives go. Free to run around the forest. Killing's a craft, just like any other. Get good at it and you stay alive. I figured the risk wasn't worth the taking."

Now they were face-to-face, toe-to-toe, glaring at each other. When Krysty spoke, her spittle dashed against his cheek. "There's times you don't put yourself first. Gaia! There's things you can't just ride around.''

"And getting me and Dean chilled is one of those things, is it? Well, is it?''

"No. Of course not.''

Ryan took a long slow breath and turned away, wiping at his face with his sleeve. "If there'd been any way of doing it without risking our lives, don't you think I'd have thought of it? There wasn't.''

"We could still go after them.''

"They'll be ready. Not like taking candy from a blind baby, Krysty. Slavers aren't specially trusting sort of men. They'll be watching real careful. Could even be they might try a counterstrike first. Get their retaliation in before we move against them. No. Not worth it.''

There was a silence that extended to twenty heart-beats, which was broken by Doc.

"I fear that I must ally myself with Master Cawdor, my dear Krysty. History is full of vain sacrifices against hopeless odds. One remembers occasions like the Pass of Thermopylae and the Alamo and Sir Richard Grenville against the Spanish navy. Even Custer's last stand. But all resulted in terrible mortality for the side of right. There is truly a time for the head to rule the heart. I would not wish to be saying prayers over the burials of Ryan and Dean here.''

There was a stillness after Doc's words, and the only sound they could hear, by an acoustical freak, was the faint tinkling of the steel chains, far off and small, like the noise of a rat's feet across broken glass in a dry cellar.

Krysty turned away, tears glistening in her emerald eyes. "You might be right, Doc. So might you, Ryan. But being right doesn't make it right, does it?"

He reached out and touched her hand, feeling his own anger diminishing and shrinking to nothing. "You're right from your side, lover, and I reckon that I'm right on mine."

THEY CONTINUED along the track, on into the late afternoon, seeing the scuffed turf and broken branches where the slavers had driven their prisoners.

"Not quite the paradise it looked," Ryan commented. He and Krysty were walking side by side, rebuilding the bridges between them.

"Never is. Got to have a serpent in the garden, or it's not a real garden."

"Wonder where the rest of them are. The leader, Rodrigo Bivar, said to watch out for another group of them."

"If we find them, we could mebbe do something about it," she said.

"I'd go with that," Ryan replied. "Yeah, I'd carry that one to the wire."

RYAN'S WRIST CHRON SHOWED a time of five o'clock in the afternoon. But he had no idea at all of what local time might be.

"Be dark in a couple of hours," he said.

"Reckon it'll be a good idea to find somewhere to camp for the night." J.B. looked around them. "Forest like this could harbor all kinds of predators."

"Trail still winds downhill." Ryan rubbed at his chin where an insect had stung him several minutes earlier. "Could be we might find water soon."

Jak had squatted, checking the trail. "Still backtracking slavers," he said. "Reckon we—"

He was interrupted by the noise of sporadic gunfire, sounding like it came from nearby.

# Chapter Nine

They moved fast along the track, closing up, J.B. right behind Ryan.

"Smell the black-powder smoke," he said. "Sound like muskets. And could be those Portuguese Mauser-Vergueiro rifles. Might be the second party of slavers."

Ryan nodded. They were jogging fast, raising the sweat so that it trickled down faces and necks, across chests and stomachs, down legs.

The sun was well sunk toward the western horizon, and the shadows grew longer.

The trail was climbing steeply. It was obvious from the noise of the firefight that it lay in a dip beyond the next rise, less than fifty paces ahead of them.

Ryan held up a hand, slowing to a walk, not wanting to burst over the crest of the small hill and find himself smack in the middle of the shooting.

He moved to the left side of the wide track, slipping the last few yards through low bushes covered with tiny yellow berries that burst as he brushed against them, filling the air with the scent of apples.

The scene unfolded in front of him as though he were looking down on a stage. But the players weren't actors and the spilled blood, crimson against the vivid green of the grass, was real.

It was obvious what had happened.

A group of six natives cowered behind a huge fallen tree near a small lake. They had been caught out in the open by the slaver's sneak attack, and three bodies lay stretched on the lush turf.

The natives had two rifles between them and one handblaster, but it was clear that they were running short of ammo. The shots were coming slower.

The slavers were directly below Ryan, their backs to him. There were eight of them, well concealed from the natives by a stack of felled timber. Most had single-shot muskets, though one was using an M-16, keeping up a steady fire against the natives.

"Just matter time," said Jak, at Ryan's side. "Nowhere to run."

Krysty touched Ryan's arm. "What do you think this time, lover?"

The one-eyed man reached and slid the Steyr SSG-70 off his back, bringing the polished walnut stock to his shoulder. He peered through the Starlite scope, using the powerful laser image enhancer, working the bolt action and levering a 7.62 mm round into the oiled breech.

"I think it's time to take a hand," he said.

The others drew their blasters, J.B. moving a few steps to the left of the others to give himself a clear field of fire with the Uzi.

Mildred held the Czech target pistol in her right hand, down at her side. "I'll take the pair on the extreme right," she said. "Leave the rest to y'all."

The slavers were fish in a barrel.

At less than forty yards' range, even Doc had a reasonable hope of doing damage with the ponderous Le Mat.

The execution lasted barely five seconds.

Mildred took her first man through the base of the skull, the second one just behind the left ear as he started to turn. Both were instant kills.

Ryan took out the man on the left with the first shot from the rifle, the big full-metal-jacket round smashing into his back, a little below the left shoulder. He levered in a second round and killed the skinniest of the slavers, who'd been quickest to react to the ambush, starting to run in a crouch to the right toward the thick cover of the forest. It wasn't a good idea to leave any survivors running free. The 7.62 mm slug hit him in the side of the throat, leaving a blood-spurting exit hole the other side of his neck the size of a fist, almost ripping his head off his shoulders.

The other four perished where they lay, their bodies twisting and jerking, fountaining scarlet blood under the impact of the lethal hail.

Ryan didn't need to call out for everyone to hold their fire. The stillness of death made it obvious enough.

The stink of the shooting faded as the wind carried it away, and the clearing below was quiet.

Ryan took a chance and stood, empty-handed. "We're friends. Anyone speak American?"

There was no answer from the cowering natives.

"The men who were shooting at you are all dead," Ryan called. "Danger's gone."

"You friends them?"

The voice was harsh and guttural, the accent difficult to understand. But it was definitely a kind of American.

"No. We chilled them to save you. Can we come down and talk to you?"

One of the natives stood, holding a bullet wound in his left forearm. "Come down kill?"

Ryan shook his head. "Course not, you stupe," he muttered under his breath, then he raised his voice. "No. We have killed your enemies. We will not kill you or hurt you."

"Come," the man said, beckoning to Ryan with his good hand. The other natives also stood, a woman running clumsily across the clearing and throwing herself onto one of the bodies of her people, weeping loudly.

"Let's go, friends," Ryan said.


THE NATIVE INDIANS WERE, understandably, still on the ragged edge of panic, all of them trembling and almost all of them gray with shock.

They were obviously the same tribe as the others that the companions had seen earlier, with the same oiled hair, tattoos and heavy golden earrings.

Mildred tore a strip off the sleeve of one of the dead slavers and offered to bandage the arm of the wounded native. But he backed away, shaking his head.

"I mean to help you," she said briskly. "Now just stand still and I'll bandage it. Clean wound. Looks like it was a musket ball, and it's gone clean on through."

Jak had paused on the hillside to reload his Python and was the last of the group to walk into the clearing, picking his way past the puddles of blood.

His appearance had a startling effect.

The leader of the group, who'd been hurriedly backing away from Mildred, dropped to his knees, mouth open, then fell facedown in the grass.

Each of the others, as they saw the teenager, followed suit and prostrated themselves.

"What fuck they do?" Jak said crossly. "Stupes!"

The Indians were chanting, repeating a single word over and over again, but it was in a foreign tongue and made no sense at all to Ryan. He turned to J.B., who'd just finished reloading the 20-round Uzi. "How do we stop them? I don't want to stay here for long, just in case Bivar and his men heard the firefight and come running to see what's happened."

"Try," Jak said, stepping forward and stamping his foot, gaining the attention of the natives. He gestured to them with his hand. "Get up. Now."

They all stared at him, hesitating.

"Try again," Krysty suggested.

"Get up," the teenager repeated, lifting a hand to flick a few strands of the snow-white hair from over his red eyes. "Come on. Get up, now."

Slowly, not looking at Ryan or the others, the natives rose to their feet.

"What is this?" Ryan asked. "You all understand me, and you can speak American. What is it about Jak?" He pointed to the young man. "Why's he special?"

The wounded man, blood still trickling from his fingers, muttered something, repeating it at Ryan's insistence. "He is like a god in old stories. Back in oldest times, before time of black skies and air that choked."

"A god!" Dean exclaimed, gurgling with laughter. "That's a hot pipe, Jak. Can you make miracles like gods do? Turn water into whiskey?"

"Shut up," Ryan snapped. "You might think it's funny, son, but these people don't."

"I suspect that it must be the color of our young friend's hair," Doc offered.

Mildred nodded. "If these people have roots back to the Aztecs or Mayas or Incas, then there could easily be some myth of a stranger with hair like dazzling snow and eyes like rubies, come to lead them to a better world. That kind of thing. It's a common thread in legends of many civilizations."

"Cargo cults of the Pacific," Doc said runically. "There are peoples on obscure islands who once, in wartime, had airplanes bring supplies and the specious trappings of civilization. Then wars ended and the planes went away. These poor superstitious natives built model planes of branches to try to lure the real thing back and give them prosperity once more."

"Why is Jak special?" Ryan asked, tapping the teenager on the shoulder.

For a crazed moment he thought that the stocky native was going to take a swing at him, but the man checked his movement. "Can't tell. Tell breaks circle. But he is the waited one. Can't tell you more."

Mildred stepped forward again, still holding the strip of torn cotton. "Jak?"

"Yeah?"

"Make him stand still while I bandage that bullet wound. Stop the bleeding."

The albino teenager nodded. "Sure."

He turned to the native. "Stand still and she puts on bandage on arm. Make better."

The man shrank from the advancing woman, but his nerve held and he finally stood still for the bandaging, wincing as though Mildred were applying a poultice of pure acid.

"Ask him where his village is, Jak. Tell him we'd like to visit and mebbe stay a night or two. Get some food." Ryan glanced at the sky. "Soon be dusk."

"You ask. Speaks all right."

Krysty smiled. "You even sound like they do, Jak. Way you talk, sort of clipped and... What's the word, Doc?"

"Elliptical. Meaning that certain words are missing from the dear boy's sentences."

Ryan sighed. "Fireblast! Can we get this done? Dark's not far off. If they'll house us for a while, we need to know. Just ask them, Jak."

The teenager looked at the natives. "Need shelter and food. Can we come back your village?"

"All of them?" The man with the bandaged arm didn't seem enthusiastic at the idea of bringing seven strangers to his village. "Just you."

Jak shook his head. "No. We are all friends."

"They are friends of you?" He sounded disbelieving. "You do not have friends. Only those who..." He struggled for a word. "Who kneel to you."

Jak shook his head, making his hair froth out like a blizzard. "No! Fucking listen me. These my friends. You take us your village. Find houses for us. Food."

"Just you," the man repeated stubbornly.

"No, for... If you think I'm powerful, then best do what I say."

The native turned to his companions, drawing them close, speaking to them quickly and quietly in the strange foreign language.

"If they decide against us, then I reckon we might do well to go back to the gateway," Ryan said. "Take a chance on running into Rodrigo Bivar and his gang."

But the native preempted him. Facing Jak, he bowed his head. "You and friends welcome us village."

# Chapter Ten

The village was about three miles away, along the winding track, and it was close to full dark by the time that they reached it.

Only one thing of any interest happened during the trek along the trail.

As they skirted another pool, they all heard moaning coming from some tall bushes with spiked stems.

"One of the natives, wounded by the slavers and left to die," Ryan said, drawing the SIG-Sauer and leading the way into the undergrowth.

But the man lying there, knees huddled to his chest, was an Anglo, with the same swarthy complexion as the slavers. He was doubled over, blood soaking through his clothes from a deep stab wound in the stomach.

The natives gathered around, staring blank-eyed at the moaning man. The lone woman stepped close and spit in his face, mouthing a curse.

Ryan holstered his blaster and drew his long panga, not wanting to waste a bullet on the man when cold steel would do as well.

As he leaned forward, the leader of the natives stopped him. "He is taker of us. Chainer of women and girls. Stealer of men for the holes and tunnels where the silver lives. Turner of women into sluts."

"So he's better dead."

"No. He will speak to gods for us. We take him to Teotihuacán where he will meet Coatlicue, and where he will help bring winning to us."

"You want him as a prisoner?" Ryan asked. "Well, I sure don't want him for anything. Yeah..." He waved his hand. "Take the son of a bitch and welcome."

The man had stopped weeping, his eyes staring wide at the gleaming polished blade of Ryan's panga. As soon as he realized that he wasn't going to be chilled on the spot, his first reaction was one of grinning relief. Then, as he was jerked to his feet by the natives, his wrists bound behind him with strips of whipcord, he began to cry again.

"You're white," he said, his voice cracking. "Don't let them take me. You don't know what they'll do."

Krysty pointed a finger at him. "I've seen what your brutish gangs do. Anything that happens to you from these people's going to be triple deserved."

He tried to scream at them, but the native woman stooped and picked up a clump of dirt and grass and rammed it hard into his open mouth, tying it tightly into place with two more of the rawhide strips, silencing him. Fresh, brighter blood showed against the dark patch where he'd been stabbed, the wound that had obviously resulted in his being left behind by Bivar.

"Our home," said the stocky native, pointing ahead of them with his good arm.

"Where we will bury our dead ones," the woman added. "We could not carry them now. But in morning bring them to homes."

Ryan had wondered about that, surprised that they hadn't made any effort to bury their own dead. The corpses of the slavers had all been dragged together while the male natives urinated on them, then they had been lifted by wrists and ankles and thrown into the pool.

"Look over there," J.B. said. The muzzle of the Uzi indicated an amazing structure about a quarter mile off, to the right.

It was a kind of pyramid, more than a hundred feet in height, with steps scaling its four sides. The top was flattened and seemed to have some kind of altar on it. The structure lay to the east of the fenced village, which stood on the edge of a large lake.

There looked to be about seventy huts, nearly all of them thatched with wide palm leaves. The light was mostly gone, and the cooking fires looked as bright as diamonds. Ryan sniffed, starting to salivate, scenting the delicious odor of what he guessed was probably roasting pork.

"Food smells good," he said, smiling at the native with the wounded arm, but the man looked back at him with no change of emotion.

"Meal for dead. Those taken by slavers are dead to us and to the gods. It is hard for those left behind to walk tear-blinded on path between night and day."

"Yeah, guess it is."

One of the other men with them had run ahead, calling out in the language that was a strange mixture of harsh gutturals and liquid syllables. It didn't take an expert translator to know that he was warning the village about the arrival of strangers, of the battle and of the dead—and of the slim youth whose eyes glowed like smoldering coals in a fire of ash and whose hair was whiter than the eternal crest of snow on the high peaks.

Drums began to beat in a fast staccato rhythm, totally unlike the slower meter of the drums of the Native Americans on the high plains.

And there was the strident sound of a brass trumpet, ripping apart the quiet of the evening.

"Giving us a welcome," Dean said, walking closer to his father.

"Yeah. We got nothing to fear, son. All we've done them, so far, is a big favor."

"Long as they don't reckon us for slavers," J.B. said softly.

Ryan had already considered that one, and he'd been glad to see that native go racing ahead, babbling out the tale of what had happened that afternoon. The village would already be stricken by the loss of so many of their number at the hands of Bivar and his men, and any pale-complexioned outlanders were likely to risk a hostile reception.

"By the Three . . . !" Doc was wiping perspiration from his forehead, but he hastily put away his swallow's-eye kerchief as he saw the reception party coming toward them through the high, spiked gates. "It's either the Akond of Swat or the great panjandrum, or perhaps it's Atahuallpa himself, long-dead monarch of the Inca people.''

Ryan had been met by some bizarre-looking men and women in his time, but he'd never seen anything to match the arrival at this obscure, isolated village, somewhere in Central or South America.

There were eight of them making a stately progress toward the strangers—all males, judging by their height and build.

But it was impossible to be sure, as all eight wore amazing, intricate masks. They were built on a thin wooden frame, covered in huge nodding feathers of turquoise, green and coppery blue. The faces were stylized, with eyes of white shell, teeth of jade and cheeks made from a black stone that Ryan guessed was probably obsidian.

The effect was impressive and, to be honest, Ryan thought, more than a little frightening.

The men wore long cloaks down to their bare feet, fringed with the same gorgeous feathers. The cloaks looked to be woven from linen and were a range of colors. Black predominated, with red, yellow and green.

Only one man wore an emerald cloak and he was the tallest, walking at the center of the half circle. His mask was even more ornate than the others, and he carried a long sword at his hip, made from the same black stone.

Mildred's brow was furrowed, as though she were struggling to remember something from the past. "Green means royalty, I think," she said. "And yellow is connected with food. Black was either priests or nobles. I can't recall which. Red might be warriors. The color of blood, you know."

The drums continued to beat from the village until the man in green held up his hand, flourishing the black sword. The crowd of nearly two hundred natives at his back fell silent, along with the drums.

He called out in his own tongue, and the native with the wounded arm replied at length, gesturing toward Ryan and the others, miming them opening fire and then acting out the deaths of the slavers.

Finally he pointed at Jak, though he didn't look at the young man. He touched his clenched fist to his chest, then to his forehead, and finally to his lips in what was undoubtedly some kind of religious ritual.

"Play this cool, Jak," Ryan whispered out of the corner of his mouth.

"Sure."

The sword dipped and every man and woman and child dropped to their knees, temples touching the dirt.

"The man who would be king," Doc said, thoughtfully. "I'm certain our guesses are correct. They regard the lad as some kind of long-lost god or monarch. Or, perchance, a combination of both."

Only the green-clad man remained standing, his face invisible behind the feathered mask.

"You are come to us," he said in a ringing voice. "The wait has been long. If you had come a day sooner, then the men with whips and chains would have been scattered and we would not be in mourning."

"We scattered some for you this afternoon," Ryan said, not wanting the moment to slip away.

"We heard this. And we thank you. Thanks to the servants of the awaited one."

"Friends, not servants," Krysty pointed out, but nobody seemed to hear her.

"My name is Itzcoatl. In your way of speaking it means the Serpent of the Black Stone. The brother who you helped is called Chimalpopoca. Smoking Crest. We are the people. Called, in our tongue, Macehualli."

"Aztec names," Mildred breathed. "Mother of God, but these are lost descendants of the ancient Aztecs."

"How do you come to speak our own language?" Ryan asked. "Are there other Americans near here?"

"Americans." Itzcoatl savored the word in his mouth as though it were a suspicious new herb and he wasn't altogether sure whether he liked the flavor or not.

"Are there any?"

"No. We have not seen Americans for..." He hesitated. "More moons than there are fingers on the hands of many warriors. Not in the memory of any person of the tribe."

"But there were Americans here?"

Itzcoatl considered the question, his face invisible. The smoke from the many fires billowed around him, making him look like a creature from ancient myths, rather than a human being. "There is a... temple. Right word? Temple some miles from here with a door that is never opened."

"The gateway," Krysty whispered to Ryan, who nodded his agreement.

"That is part of many places where Americans built in the years before the crops failed. Our fathers' fathers' fathers worked for them. Helped them in their preparation for war. When they departed it was a sad day for all of the people. The dead they left we buried in honor. Some took their own lives. None stayed alive. We learned their way of speaking, and because we thought that they would return, we have kept up learning of their speech. I think I speak it more good than other man. But it becomes harder with each child. One day it will be lost."

"What is the other language you speak?" Mildred asked. "I don't know it."

The feathered head turned toward the woman, the white shells gazing blankly past her. "We call it Nahuatl. The old tongue we know from the far-off old days."

She nodded, then said to the others, "I'm sure that's a word from the Aztecs."

One of the men dressed in a black robe leaned toward the leader of the tribe and said something. Itzcoatl nodded. "Quauhtlatoa, who is called Speaking Eagle, reminds me that we are poor... What is the word? Someone who receives strangers."

"Hosts?" Krysty suggested.

The man nodded. "Yes. You bring us the waited one and save the lives of our brothers and sister. And we remain beyond the walls, breathing out empty air and words. You will all stay and eat with us now?"

"Thanks," Ryan said. "Just a couple days, perhaps, then we'll have to be on our way."

There was something in his remarks that upset the Macehualli people. The plumed masks gathered close, and all the body language showed tension and anxiety. Ryan could hear the fluting exchanges between the leaders of the tribe, but it was Itzcoatl who quelled it, snapping out an order and holding up his left hand. His right hand dropped to the jewel-studded hilt of the polished black-stone sword on his hip, producing silence.

The voice from beneath the mask sounded strained. "We fear you leaving soon. We cannot repay the debt if you leave quickly. So stay as long as you want."

"Thanks again. Be glad to stay awhile."

This was obviously a reassuring remark as the tautness eased from the listeners.

"Good, good." Itzcoatl muttered something over his shoulder. Two men moved forward and took the arms of the prisoner, with surprising gentleness, and led him away.

"You'll chill him?" Ryan asked, not caring much one way or the other. As Krysty had said, being a member of the slavers' gang carried its own risks.

"He will be used," the chief replied. An odd choice of words, Ryan thought.

Throughout all the exchange, it had been glaringly obvious that the real subject of interest was Jak Lauren. Since they had all scrambled upright, every eye in the crowd was glued to him, following his every movement. When he brushed a hand through his magnesium hair, a fascinated ripple ran through the natives.

"You will be shown to your huts. Will two be enough for your needs?"

Ryan nodded. "Sure. Be fine."

"The meal being cooked now is not good enough for—" the white eyes in the mask moved toward Jak "—not good enough for any of you. Go to your huts and rest, and women will bring water for washing. Then, later, we can feast."

He turned and walked back in a stately manner, followed by what seemed to be his inner council, through the tall gates, the crowd of natives parting like the Red Sea. They all moved back even farther as Ryan led his friends into the village.

The drums resumed their slow, ponderous beating, and the trumpet blared once more.

As Jak strolled through the gates, the entire gathering fell again to its knees in salute.

"Never been god before," the albino whispered. "Could get used to it."

The air was filled with the smell of oiled bodies and smoke and cooking meat.

Ryan felt very hungry.

# Chapter Eleven

Ryan called everyone together in the hut that he had picked for himself, Krysty and Dean. It stood next door to the building offered to the others.

The structure was made from thick logs and sealed with clay. The roof was layered palm leaves, the floor packed earth. There was no door, just a curtain of wooden beads. The fifteen-foot-square room was divided into what appeared to be cooking and living-sleeping quarters. A small fire burned in the center of the cooking area, most of the smoke finding its way to the roof, out through a hole in the thatch.

Silent women had brought in pots of cold, clean water and bowls for washing, keeping their dark eyes averted from the group of outlanders.

"Take care about drinking too much of it," Mildred warned. "Not sure about their hygiene here, or the way they dispose of their waste products."

"They seem healthy," J.B. commented.

"Sure they do, John. They've had fifty generations to get used to whatever toxins might be present in it."

"All right, listen up," Ryan said. "This is a new situation on me."

"On all." Jak pulled a face.

"Sure. Way I see it, we're safer than safe here at the moment. Our stock's higher than a snake in an eagle's beak with these natives. Partly for the help we gave and even more for the fact that they seem to think that Jak here is just a short step away from Christ himself."

"Man who would be king," Doc muttered. "Oh, I believe that I might already have picked out that literary reference. Have I? Did I? Or was it the one-eyed man becoming king in the country of the blind? I disremember which. Could be the one or it could be the other. Oh, my burning brain of fire."

Ryan waited until the ramblings had faded away, then he carried on. "Only thing is, these aren't like any people we've ever met in Deathlands. No way of knowing how they'll react to any given set of events. Don't let the blasters out of your sight. Don't go anywhere on your own. That applies to you, Jak, even more than the rest of us. All right?"

"Why me?"

"Because nobody here knows how gods get treated."

"Very well," Dean said, grinning. "Mebbe I can sort of be the god's best friend."

Mildred patted the boy on the back. "I'll let you be in my dream, Dean, just as long as I can be in your dream."

THE MEAL WAS HELD out-of-doors, in front of the main building of the village, which was a longhouse where the official business of the place was enacted.

Itzcoatl, deprived of his mask, had told them that. He was revealed to be one of the tallest men in the village, with gold rings through his ears so heavy that they had pulled down the lobes, almost to his broad shoulders. Across his chest, he had a tattoo of twin serpents, entwined, openmouthed. Each held a human skull in its gaping jaws.

He still wore a green robe decorated with the same beautiful feathers as the masks.

When Ryan and the others came out of their huts, summoned to the meal, the chief was standing at one end of the table, beckoning for Jak to take the seat at the very head.

"The place of most honor," he said, seating the others on either side, staggering them with the senior men of the village, including Chimalpopoca and Quauhtlatoa.

The food reminded Ryan of meals that he'd had close to the Grandee, in the south of old Texas and in the very northern regions of old Mexico.

There were plates of corn tortillas and bowls of red beans and chili to go with a large caldron of fish stew. Maize bread was piled all along the table for everyone to help themselves.

The drink was an herbal-flavored liquor that Ryan's neighbor told him was called *octli*. Vaguely reminiscent of pulque, it seemed bland enough as you sipped and swallowed, but once it was halfway down the gullet it began to burn with a ferocious fire that belatedly warned you of its high-alcohol potency.

After the fish stew came platters of assorted meats, roasted, with charred skin on the outside, pink and with seeping blood on the inside.

Ryan recognized duck, turkey, venison and what he guessed was some variant on the small pigs that they'd seen running free and wild in the forest. It was delicious and he ate freely, using his hands, dipping into other dishes of mushed vegetables spiced with chili.

Itzcoatl clapped his hands and beckoned to one of the row of young women who knelt submissively between the long table and the bank of cooking fires. "Bring the very best food for our special visitor."

"For Jak?" Ryan asked.

"Yes. Must we call him by that name of the earth? We have a word that means burning snow and it would be better for him. What do you think?"

"I think name's Jak," Jak said.

The woman was approaching, carrying a platter of wood with something at its center, concealed by a cover.

"She is called, in your language, Rain Flower. We call her Quiauh-xochitl." The chief smiled. "Give it to Jak." He smiled proudly at being allowed to use the given name of the visiting god. "Enjoy," he said to the teenager.

The cover was whisked away, revealing the dish.

"Gaia!" Krysty breathed.

"That's disgusting," Dean said, his jaw sagging, a piece of venison dropping from his greasy fingers.

It was the head of a large mutie rat, with the top of the skull hacked off. There had been no cutlery visible on the table for the preceding courses, but there was a metal spoon with a long handle sticking out of the gruel of brains and blood that brimmed from the cranial cavity.

"The food of the gods," Itzcoatl announced. "You take all the cunning of the rat into your being by devouring its brains. Eat it, Jak."

The albino opened his eyes wider, reflecting the bright orange flames of the fire in their ruby depths. "Pass on this. Thanks, but no thanks."

The native didn't seem at all worried at the refusal and beckoned for the woman, Rain Flower, to take the dish away again. "Unless you, Ryan, or any of your other buddies might wish to eat and become cunning?"

The companions declined the offer, shaking their heads.

"For dessert we have *atolli*."

"What's that?" Mildred asked. "Eye of newt and toe of frog, I guess."

"Or perchance the wool of a bat and the tongue of a dog," Doc added. "As the immortal bard of Avon has it."

The *atolli* was a sticky mixture that looked extremely unattractive.

"Eat," the chief said, waving his hands to encourage his guests.

Doc took the first plunge, inserting two fingers from his right hand into the mess and cautiously licking them. He screwed up his face for a moment, then tried another gobbet, sucking his fingers clean. "Interesting," he said.

"What's 'interesting' mean?" Mildred snapped. "You mean like it's buffalo shit, but it's real interesting buffalo shit?"

"Try it for yourself, my dear Dr. Wyeth. You above all should not be the one to eschew experimentation. It's fascinating. You have, I am certain, sampled Chinese dishes that are sweet and sour?"

"Sure."

"Well, this combines both sweetness and fieriness. There must be both honey and finely chopped chilies in this, unless I miss my guess. Am I correct, Chief Serpent of the Black Stone?"

Itzcoatl smiled broadly. "You are right, wise one. Chilies and wild honey mixed with maize. You like it?"

Now everyone was dipping in.

"Good," Krysty said. "Real good."

Dean scooped up a handful and lapped it like a dog. His eyes watered at the heat of the peppers, but he grinned through the discomfort at the delicious sweetness. "Ace on the line," he mumbled through his third mouthful.

"My lips feel like they've been double bee stung," J.B. called. "Need something cool to drink to salve them."

"Too much *octli* and man sees Citlaltépetl," Speaking Eagle said with a lopsided smile.

"What's that?" the Armorer asked.

But the native's grasp of American wasn't good enough to explain what he meant. His chief took over the task.

"He say that you get drunk as skunk and see the Mountain of the Star. This is like a—" he fumbled for the word he wanted "—Mountain of the Star is a vision. Yes. We have a drug called *yauhtli* that is for dreaming, as well."

"Is there any more of that rather splendid maize and honey and chili concoction?" Doc asked. "If pressed, I do believe that I could force down a tiny portion more of it."

Mildred laughed. "Follow it up with a wafer-thin chocolate mint, Doc?"

"If such a delicacy were available, then I would welcome it. But until then, I shall remain content with *atolli*. If that is the correct name for it?"

The chief nodded. "Yes, there is more. But, Jak, you have eaten little. Is that the way of gods?"

"No, it's not. I don't know. Just that dish of rat's brain took away appetite."

Ryan sighed, breathing out, relishing the feeling of fullness. It wasn't often during his travels that he'd enjoyed having eaten and drunk so well.

Itzcoatl was looking at him across the table. "I ask you a question?"

"Sure. Go ahead."

"You have good firearms. Better than we have."

"I guess so."

"Better than men with whips and chains?"

"The slavers? From what we've seen I reckon we could give them a run in a firefight."

"We have trouble with them."

"Since when?"

The short question threw the native for a while, until he puzzled it out. "Since when not long time. Four moons. Maybe five moons."

"Where do they come from?"

"From north. Across rivers and mountains. They have taken our people three times. Bad. Very bad. We have angered the gods to make this happen."

He looked at Ryan as though it had been a question rather than a statement.

"Mebbe you have. More likely you're just sort of unlucky. There's slavers all over Deathlands."

"Lands of death?"

"Deathlands. Name of where we come from."

The native was on his feet, spilling his beaker of *octli*. His hand went to a small ornament on a cord around his neck. "You are from the land of death?"

He turned to his comrades around the table, his voice carrying to the people of the entire village, who were sitting quiet and patient in the shadows beyond the fires. He called out to them in their tongue.

From their reaction it was obvious he was telling them that the strangers in their midst were some kind of gods of death, bringers of death. Living dead?

Everyone cried out and Ryan could see the shuffling movement, hear their fear. The row of serving women also broke and edged away. One of the men at the table, wearing black, made a stabbing gesture at Ryan and Jak with his fingers, obviously trying to avert their evil eyes.

Ryan jumped to his feet, clapping his hands, causing a few more seconds of panic. He shouted to the villagers. "We are not dead men. We are not gods. We come from the land of living men, this side of the grave.''

He looked at the chief. ''Tell them, damn it! Stop this stupe terror.''

Licking his lips nervously, Itzcoatl stammered out a version of that Ryan had said, calming the natives.

''Tell them that if we can help while we are here, then we'll do what we can.''

After he'd translated that, the chief sat down again, beckoning urgently for more liquor. ''There is not just the men with whips and chains.''

''No?''

''There is another village,'' he said, pointing across the lake, ''a half day from here. They have been at war with us for all the years in the world.''

''Why? I mean, why has the war been going on so long? How come one side or the other hasn't won?''

The Indian shook his head sorrowfully. ''Our numbers are always about the same as their village. And the gods are pleased with the blood spilled in the wars, with the gifts that we make to them. So we keep fighting. Now, the slavers have taken many from this village. Not from our enemies. We are becoming weak and may lose all.''

''You'd like us to stand the fight on your side against them? Is that it?''

''They are the Jaguar people. That is the nearest in our tongue to what you understand. The ferocious animal, holy to us. Like a cougar.''

''Sure, I know what a jaguar is, Itzcoatl.''

"It has been our plan, when the gods will permit it, to throw the bones and risk all and go against them. But the odds are very long."

"And life is very short," Doc added.

"Truth. Life is short. But to give it in battle means the gods will smile."

Smoking Crest said something to the chief in their tongue. Itzcoatl looked around, considering the sky.

Ryan guessed what was going on. "Time is passing," he said. "And we have journeyed long and fought hard." He found himself slipping into the old-fashioned, stilted manner of speech of the chief of the tribe.

"You wish to go to the beds?"

"I think so. Was a good meal, Chief. Thanks for it. Talk again in the morning."

Sitting cross-legged on the floor had been a strain, and Ryan winced as he stood, feeling any number of old wounds tugging at muscles, cartilage and tendons. He managed to steady himself without making it too obvious.

Everyone else rose, with varying degrees of ease and difficulty, Jak at one end of the scale and, not surprisingly, Doc at the other.

"You are content with the huts?" The chief looked worried at the thought that the visitors might not be happy with their accommodation.

"Good," Jak replied, receiving a relieved beam of delight from Itzcoatl.

The firelight was playing across the chest tattoo of the entwined snakes, making them come alive, writhing. Ryan yawned, aware of how filled the day had been. He was ready for bed.

There was a distant crackle of thunder, snatching the attention of all the gods. "Rain is needed," Speaking Eagle said. "Comes from smiles of gods. Buy smiles with blood of enemies. We need many enemies for blood for smiles."

"Guess you would," J.B. agreed.

Ryan nodded. "Then we'll say good-night and go off to the huts you've let us have."

He led the way through the crowd, which folded away from him as though the natives feared that his skin might contaminate them in some way.

Itzcoatl called after him.

"We will send women for you and the men."

# Chapter Twelve

"What?" Krysty's response would have shattered a plate-glass window at fifty paces.

"It is our way."

J.B. winked at Ryan. "Sounds like a good way to me. What do the rest of you reckon?"

"Dean's too young," Ryan said straight-faced. "Much too young."

"And Doc's likely too old," the Armorer added. "Be wasted on him."

"Oh, no it would not, John Barrymore Dix! There may be snow upon the roof, but there is a positive inferno still capable of blazing in the hearth."

"How about me?" Jak said. "I'm the god, so I get first picking."

"I don't believe this." Mildred stamped her foot. "How can you guys possibly...?" Then she caught the smirk that passed between Ryan and J.B. "Oh, I get it. You bastards!"

The chief had watched the byplay, looking puzzled, trying to work out what it was that the Anglos were saying. He finally sensed that some kind of a joke or a trick was being played, and he started to laugh.

"You men say you want our women, but your women say not," he spluttered. "But you not want them." The broad smile vanished as quickly as it had been born. "Why it is that you not want our women?"

"No reason. Just that where we come from—"

"The dark land of death?"

"No." Ryan hesitated. "Well, yeah. Back there we pick our own women."


DEAN FELL ASLEEP QUICKLY on the grass-filled mattress in the far corner of the kitchen. He'd dragged it there without anything being said. Though there wasn't even a curtain between the two parts of the house, he gave Krysty and his father a semblance of privacy and modesty.

They lay together, Ryan having done no more than take off his heavy combat boots. He had suggested to the rest of the friends that they take care sleeping, not post a watch, but not get undressed, in case something roused them fast in the middle of the night. And they were to keep their blasters close to hand.

He reached out and put his arm around Krysty, feeling for the warm swell of her breast. But she eased away from him. "Told you, lover. Wrong time of month."

"Tomorrow?"

"Likely."

"Be nice."

He could almost feel her grinning in the smoky darkness. "Sure it would. If you want it real bad, lover, then I'd be happy to slide down and give you—"

"No. Not tonight. Too one-sided. Like it to be two-sided."

She sat up and patted him on the cheek. "Hey, not bad. Not bad for you, lover."

Outside, the village was falling into sleep.

Itzcoatl had told them that the warriors always kept a watch, though they didn't expect the slavers to run at them again for at least another month. That had become the pattern of their savage raids. But there was always the threat from the Jaguar people, out there in the blackness of the forest.

The dogs of the settlement had quieted, and the only sound was a baby crying in a nearby hut, a noise that quickly faded away into stillness.

Then there was only the jungle.

RYAN AWAKENED ONCE in the night. He could hear the regular sound of Krysty's breathing at his side and Dean carrying on a mumbled conversation with himself, still locked deep in sleep.

The fire had crumbled into itself, leaving only a pile of white ash, speckled with tiny glowing embers. Through the beaded curtain that was the front door to the hut, Ryan could see that it was a brilliant, moonlit night, throwing sharp shadows across the dirt floor.

Outside, there were the ceaseless night sounds of the tropical forest, insects chittering and hunting birds crying out, the occasional barking snarl of some larger predator.

Ryan wondered what had awakened him. There was slight pressure on his bladder from the *octli* that he'd drunk. The surprisingly potent liquor had also given him a sick headache, with pressure behind his good eye.

He decided to go and take a leak.

It didn't seem a good idea to wander off and risk being shot by one of the guards. Ryan had noticed that some of the natives carried small leather pouches with rawhide thongs attached—stone-throwing slings. As well as the archaic blasters, they had bows with long arrows, and a few had blowpipes slung across their shoulders. Any of them could strike him down from the darkness unless he stepped carefully.

He walked to the rear of the hut, looking out past two more buildings, seeing the surrounding fence through the gap. There was no sign of any of the sentries.

Ryan felt the short hairs begin to prickle at his nape, and he padded back to the sleeping room and picked up both the SIG-Sauer and the panga, holstering one and carefully sheathing the other.

He stepped down into the open space, his head turning from side to side, suddenly realizing what had disturbed him. The background of noise from the trees beyond the fence had ceased and the night was unnervingly still.

It crossed his mind to go back and wake Krysty, to stir the others from sleep and go out to see if there was anything wrong.

But there was always that moment of serious doubt that everything was fine, and he would have roused J.B. and the others for no good reason.

And he was already outside, breathing in the rich night air.

Ryan moved with infinite caution, picking his way between the houses toward the fence. His shadow preceded him, etched on the cropped grass of the compound.

When he reached the perimeter he stopped for a moment, puzzled that he hadn't yet seen any of the sentries or been seen by one of them.

His hand had been hovering over the butt of the blaster, but now he relaxed a little. He unbuttoned himself and started to piss against the high fence, playing the amber jet back and forth, watching as it trickled down the smooth-barked logs, soaking into the turf.

He buttoned up his pants again and started to turn away from the fence, when two things happened.

His eye caught a glimpse of a pair of naked feet sticking out from the deep shadow of the nearest building. Someone was either sleeping there, or something had gone very seriously wrong in the village.

Before his mind had taken a vital second or so to try to rationalize what he'd seen, Ryan was dealt a crunching blow across the throat.

He hadn't seen it coming until the last fraction of a moment and didn't have time to parry it successfully. He managed to get up his right hand to slightly deflect and dull the force of the hit, and if he hadn't, then he would certainly have been killed.

Ryan staggered two steps away and slumped to his knees, all of his fighting instinct rallying to stop him going down into the darkness.

The man who'd attacked him was an etched silhouette, holding a long club shaped like a baseball bat. He was certainly a native, but wore a necklace of teeth and claws from some kind of forest predator.

A jaguar, Ryan thought as the club started to whistle down toward him for a second, killing blow.

He ducked and rolled, trying to yell out a warning to the village, but his vocal cords had been damaged by the attack and all that came out was a strangled whisper.

The club hit the turf, inches from his skull.

There wasn't time to stand and try to draw either the panga or the SIG-Sauer. Any attempt would have opened him up to a terminal blow from the native.

If you couldn't get safe away, then try to get in close. Trader's advice for intimate combat situations was always valid, and Ryan followed it instinctively.

Even though he was still hovering on the right side of consciousness, he powered himself up from hands and knees and ducked inside the third swing of the club, taking a glancing blow into the ribs that made him gasp.

He grappled with the man, his fingers slipping on the oiled skin, immediately aware that his opponent was nearly as tall as he was, and felt, at first contact, at least as strong.

The native grunted something, dropping his useless club, trying to knee Ryan in the groin. A half turn parried it with his thigh, but there was a jar of pain.

Ryan tried to grab at his enemy's genitals, but the man was quicker, moving sideways and drawing him off-balance, his own hands reaching up for a stranglehold.

To negate that attack, Ryan pressed himself closer, pushing his face against the native's neck, sliding upward and managing to get his arms around the barrel chest. Both men were soaked in sweat, panting hard with the desperate effort of trying to kill without being killed.

Ryan could hardly breathe through his damaged throat, was unable to cry out. He tried to bite the man's muscular neck, but the heavy coating of grease defeated him.

The bitten nails on his adversary's stubby fingers were digging into his own neck, clamping off what remained of his breath. The man dipped, trying to lift Ryan off his feet, but the Anglo's slightly greater height defeated him.

The necklace of claws and teeth was digging into Ryan's cheek, and he could feel blood trickling down his face.

It occurred to him, like a shock of Sierra meltwater, that this nameless native from a stinking little village in the middle of nowhere was going to chill him.

They struggled face-to-face, Ryan not daring to relax his grip on the man's body.

The moonlight was stark enough to show the flat features in sharpest detail, the patterned tattoo across the forehead and the streaks of black paint smeared over each cheek, and the eyes. The dark slits showed no emotion, no hatred or anger, and stared incuriously back at Ryan.

Acting on a primitive, atavistic impulse, Ryan opened his mouth, pressed his lips against the bony cavern of the socket and sucked as hard as he could.

For a moment he thought that there couldn't possibly be enough suction.

But there was.

He felt the eye move, quivering with uncertain life, and the grip on his throat relaxed for a moment.

Ryan sucked harder, pushing his face in closer, the muscles in his neck and shoulders like cords, his jaw aching with the unbelievable pressure.

Once more he felt the slippery orb move, feeling moisture flood between his lips, the eye sliding from the socket like a boiled egg, entering his mouth.

The hands fell away from Ryan's throat, and he drew in a shuddering gasp of air, pushing the native away and spitting out the eye, where it dangled on the native's cheek.

The man opened his mouth and began to scream in mind-blanking horror at what had been done to him. His vision was shot. One eye showed the moonlit fence and the powerful figure of the Anglo, the other a swinging, confused picture of the grass and his own staggering feet.

Ryan gave a sickened groan, spitting to try to clear the bitter taste from his mouth. But while he took a couple of stumbling steps away, he reached for the cold butt of the 9 mm blaster, leveled it and squeezed the trigger.

The old baffle silencer had been through some hard times, and it didn't do much to muffle the sharp crack of the explosion. Ryan felt the jolt run up his arm, past the elbow to the shoulder, the muzzle of the SIG-Sauer jerking upward.

But the bullet had already done its job, hitting the screaming native through the center of the chest, blowing his lungs apart, exiting and taking the splintered shards of four spinal vertebrae with it.

The agonized cry of horror was choked off and the dying man tottered backward, hitting the fence and sliding down, leaving a slick, snaillike trail of blood, sable black in the unforgiving moonlight.

As he fell, the extruded eye dangled on the painted cheek, swinging back and forth like a young child's toy, connected to the skull by a narrow strand of nerves and muscle.

Ryan looked down, holding the smoking automatic. His left hand reached up and unconsciously touched the patch over his own missing left eye.

"You get used to it," he said softly.

THE SCREAM AND THE SHOT roused the entire village.

Within a handful of seconds, Ryan had Jak, J.B. and Krysty at his side, all carrying drawn blasters.

"Attack?" the Armorer asked. "Saw dead man under the hut there as I came to... Dark night!" He'd spotted the monocular corpse lying crumpled by the tall fence. The eye was still swinging gently from side to side. The necklace of claws and teeth glinted white.

Krysty touched Ryan by the arm. "You're shaking, lover." She lifted her face to kiss him on the lips, her eyes showing hurt when he pulled away from her.

"Tell you later," he said.

The warriors of the village poured from their huts, carrying a rich variety of weapons, muttering to one another when they saw what the tall outlander had done to one of their most bitter enemies, the manner of the Jaguar man's passing.

ITZCOATL arrived at the hut, where Ryan was sitting with the others, telling them what had happened.

"There were four of them," the chief said. "Come from the lakeside on logs that... What is word?"

"Drifted?" Doc suggested.

"Yes. Drifting logs. We think one guard slept. But his wife's sister's youngest son was taken by the Jaguar people two moons ago. Perhaps he was leaned on to help."

"You catch them all?"

The chief shook his head, the necklace of small feathers around his neck rustling softly. "You wasted one. We took two alive, but wounded. One escaped into the woods. Perhaps they will learn we have a god and his friends now fighting with us and not come again." He didn't sound convinced. "Perhaps."

"How many dead you got?" J.B. asked. "Saw the one under the hut."

Itzcoatl brightened. "This is good news of good news and bad news. Two of my people have gone to help the rains fall and the winds blow and the wheat rise and become gold. They lost more than we lost."

Ryan nodded. "Right glad to hear it. Yeah, triple happy for you. Now I'd like to get back to sleep."

The native nodded and walked out of the hut. J.B., Doc, Mildred and Jak stood and followed him, leaving Ryan alone with Krysty and Dean.

"What?"

"How did you pull that stupe's eye out?"

"Go to sleep, son," Ryan said. "Just go to sleep."

# Chapter Thirteen

There was one further disturbing footnote to the night's battle.

As they all went blinking into the early-morning sunlight, Smoking Crest, the elder of the council, began to explain to them about the funeral arrangements they were making for the two dead warriors.

"It is always our way that we go back into earth in place of homes."

"You mean that it is your practice to inter your fallen comrades inside the village?" Doc asked.

"Yes. No."

"Which?" Ryan asked.

"In village, but more. In house where living. One you saw, you sleep in his hut. Moved out for you. Now must be buried there. Under floor."

"Under the floor of the hut we're sleeping in?" Dean asked with a mix of disgust and fascination. "He'll rot and stink us all out!"

The native shook his head, smiling at the boy, showing his filed teeth, the inlaid jade glittering in the sun. "No stink. No way stink. You see. We have way of doing this. Be done this morning after eating."

"Not sure I feel all that hungry," Mildred said. "Glad it's not my hut."

One of the village's drums began to pound, and the shrill blast of the trumpet sliced through the air. Ryan had already realized that the instruments, including the delicate fluting of sets of panpipes, were used as a way of measuring out the day, marking time to eat or time to wake or sleep.

They all sat together, cross-legged on the floor, in the open space at the heart of the settlement.

There was an air of tension and excitement among the natives after the events of the previous night. Now some of the adoration for Jak had transferred to Ryan. Many of the warriors—particularly the younger ones—kept nudging one another, whispering, often touching their eyes as if they were talking about the horrific way that their visitor had mutilated the jaguar man.

The food was more of the *atolli,* the maize-based gruel, flavored with both chili and honey, as well as smoked ham and a mess of scrambled eggs that was scorched and liberally speckled with bits of shell. Mildred was delighted to see large wooden platters of fresh fruit, hardly any of which she recognized.

"That's a mango and a kind of kiwi fruit. These are nectarines, only a lot juicier. Pineapples. But I don't know what that one is. Or those gold-speckled berries. Or that one."

Itzcoatl was subdued, concentrating on his food, hardly speaking at all.

Finally Ryan leaned across and asked him what was wrong. "We won last night. They'll think twice before they risk a midnight raid like that."

The native nodded. "You are the straight arrow, Ryan. And you hit a good lick for us. But I think you will move on soon. Then there will be no joy in Mudville. Take Jak with the snow hair and we will be left very alone. Caught between . . . between rock and strong place."

"Hard place," Krysty corrected. "You say caught between a rock and a hard place, Chief."

He nodded solemnly. "I thank you. The slavers and the people of the Jaguar. We between them."

"Could get in firstest with the mostest," J.B. suggested. "Reckon we could easy set the death bell chiming with the Jaguars. Probably bloody the noses of the slavers, as well."

Ryan looked across at his old friend. "We haven't talked about this," he said, not bothering to conceal his anger. "Don't go making offers we might not be able to follow up on."

The Armorer stared calmly back at him, the sunlight reflecting off the polished lenses of his spectacles, making it impossible to see his eyes. "We don't argue in public, Ryan."

"Stick to our rules, J.B., and we won't have anything to argue about."

"I only said that we *could* lend a hand. Didn't say that we would."

Itzcoatl looked from man to man, understanding that there was a bitterness in the argument. But both men were speaking quickly and quietly, so it was difficult for him to follow what was being said.

"Cool it out, guys," Mildred said. "Not saying either of you is right. But carry on like this, and you both finish up being wrong. Save it."

Ryan bit his lip, busying himself with slicing a layer of hair-specked fat off the ham, nodding. "Right, Mildred. Sorry, J.B., but we—"

The Armorer interrupted him. "I'm sorry, too. Let my tongue do my talking instead of my brain. You're right."

"But there might be something we can do here," Ryan said. "Have to see."

AFTER BREAKFAST CAME the ceremonial burial of the men killed in the night attack.

Ryan and his companions waited in the hut where Doc and the others had slept while teams of natives worked in the other building, excavating a square hole for the interment of the slain warrior.

It was dug out beneath the fireplace and was roughly four feet deep.

Itzcoatl joined them, already wearing his full ceremonial robes of green linen. He carried the large feathered mask in his right hand, the obsidian sword at his hip.

"Will you honor us?" he asked, speaking to Ryan, whom he had come to recognize as the undisputed leader of the group. But his eyes strayed to Jak.

"Surely. The grave—the burial hole—is smaller than our people would use."

The native smiled at him. "We told of the long holes of your people, Ryan. But it is not necessary. You lie down to meet your gods. We sit ready."

A priest appeared, masked, in a black robe, beckoning to Itzcoatl and the others to follow him into the hut.

There was already a crowd in there, with the man's widow standing to one side, arms around her two young children. Her long hair was unbraided, streaked with ash, and raw, weeping furrows down each cheek showed where she had tried to mutilate herself with her nails. Her eyes stared blankly ahead, and she seemed to be in another world.

Mildred noticed it and whispered to Ryan that she thought the woman had been drugged.

The corpse rested on a low platform. It was naked, placed in a squatting position with cords around the legs, arms and upper body to keep it steady. There was a long wound down the belly, crudely stitched, and a strangely bitter, herbal smell filled the hut. The eyes had been removed from their sockets and replaced with the same white shells that decorated the masks.

"Like the Egyptians," Doc observed. "They've opened him and taken out all the main organs. Used oils and stuff to embalm him. Stops him swelling and bursting and also cuts down on the maleficent odors."

"His brain has also been removed," Itzcoatl said. "It is in the sealed earthenware pot and will be buried with him."

"How do they do that?" Krysty asked. "I can't see any scars or marks on the skull."

"Long hooked wires," Doc replied.

"Fine, thanks. That's all I need to know, Doc. Enough."

"They insert them into the nostrils and draw the brain out that way," the old man insisted, ignoring her protests. "Again, like the ancient Egyptians."

"What's happened to his dick, Dad?"

Dean's voice broke into a sudden stillness in the hut, and everyone turned to stare at the boy.

"What?"

"Look at his dick. They tortured him or something?"

Ryan peered through the gloom, seeing that the dead warrior's penis was visible between the bound legs, wincing as he saw what his son had spotted. The end was frayed and sliced into narrow strips or tassels, so that it resembled the petals of a flower.

"Fireblast."

Itzcoatl now wore his ceremonial mask, and the white shell eyes turned incuriously toward the outlanders. "Sleeping Wolf did this himself."

"Why?"

"To win favors of the gods. They love those who give pain to themselves in their honor. Many of us have done this. Or things like this. Also, the tattoos are for the gods."

The priest coughed nervously, muttering something to the chief, who nodded in return.

"You ready to start?" J.B. asked.

Itzcoatl's mask fluttered back and forth, but he didn't speak.

The ceremony was relatively short. The gutted corpse was lowered into the square hole, where it rested, the head slumped forward on the muscular neck. Then his wife was given the pot containing his brain, but she nearly dropped it, seeming totally confused about what she was supposed to do. One of the priests took it from her and put it in the grave, between the dead man's bare feet.

Other small earthenware containers were added.

Ryan turned to meet Mildred's eyes, and he mouthed a question to her.

She read him correctly. "Food and drink. Corn for him to sow a crop when he reaches the other side of the dark river. Maybe some beads in case he needs trade goods."

Last of all came a short-bladed dagger of the familiar black obsidian stone.

The priest in charge made a brief speech in their own tongue, scattering a handful of dirt into the dark hole, where it lay on top of the greased hair. Then the wife was given earth to drop in, but her fingers didn't hold it properly and it spilled out onto the hut's floor.

At a muttered word from Itzcoatl, a couple of older women took the widow and her children out of the hut. She walked between them, unprotesting.

"She has been given the *yauhtli* powder," the chief whispered.

"What?"

"A drug. It removes some pain. It is given as a mercy to those who we send to meet the gods."

Mildred had been listening. "What used to be called Indian hemp, I think," she said.

The ritual was coming to an end. One by one the men present were stooping to pluck up a handful of the loose dirt that had been excavated from the grave, letting it fall on the body. At a sign from the officiating priest, Ryan led his six companions to play their own small part in the burying.

Once that was done they went outside, leaving a half dozen of the dead man's closest relatives and friends to fill in the hole and stamp the dirt hard and flat again.

"YOU SAID THAT THERE WAS an American base not far from here," Ryan said. "How far away? Is it still there? Mind if we go take a look at it?"

Itzcoatl had taken off his mask, but still retained his ceremonial cloak. Pitchers of *octli* were being passed around as the village feasted in celebration of the dead. The chief's speech had become slurred, and his dark eyes narrowed until they were almost invisible.

"Three questions," he said, giggling, holding up four fingers, squinting at them owlishly. "Or was it four questions?"

"Three questions," Ryan agreed. "First, how far away is the base?"

Itzcoatl considered that. "As far as tomorrow and as near as yesterday," he mumbled.

"Terrific. How long would it take us to get there?"

Another giggle. "As long as your past and as short as summer rain."

"Just tell him we're going," Krysty said.

"Got a better idea." Ryan turned and looked at Jak. "You ask him the questions. He won't dare to fuck around with a god."

"Don't want to. When we going from here?"

"Why? You got a problem, Jak?"

"Sure. Don't like way they treat me. Don't like heat and damp. Don't like food. Don't much like danger. My vote to leave and make another jump."

Ryan nodded. "Fair comment. Day or so and we'll leave. But we haven't talked much about what we're going to do while we're here. Will we help them against this neighboring tribe or not? Will we go after those slavin' sons of bitches?"

The teenager looked down and sighed. "Mebbe right, Ryan. Mebbe just me. Sure, I'll ask him." He tapped Itzcoatl on the shoulder, making him jump.

"What do you want, Jak? Women? Drink?"

"Just answer Ryan's questions. Where is old American base? How long to get there? Does still exist? We're going take a look."

Itzcoatl shook his head muzzily. "Haunted ruins, Jak," he mumbled.

"Haunted by what?" Ryan asked. "Ghosts of the old Americans who used to live around here?"

The native laid a finger along the side of his nose and winked at Ryan. Or tried to wink. He succeeded only in closing both eyes at once, which made him lose his balance and nearly fall over.

"Dark night!" The Armorer pointed at Jak. "Just ask him which way. We'll go find it ourselves."

"I will get Rain Flower to show you. You have seen her before. She will go with you, Jak, and will follow your orders. Sure will."


IT WAS A HEAVEN of a morning.

The young woman had listened to the drunken chief, nodding her submissive understanding. She wore a blouse of plain cotton over an ankle-length skirt that had been handprinted with large, bright orange flowers. Her hair was loose over her shoulders, and she had a Savage automatic tucked into a crude holster on a broad leather belt around her slender waist.

Ryan and his group carried all of their weapons, including the Steyr rifle and the Smith & Wesson M-4000 scattergun. It wasn't a time or a place to take any risks.

Rain Flower walked quickly, barefooted, through the gates, turning to follow the side of the lake for about a quarter mile. Then she cut off to the left along a clear track that took them close to the huge pyramid.

After another two hundred yards, they were all swallowed up by the jungle.

# Chapter Fourteen

Faint and far off, Ryan heard the shrill noise of the trumpet from the village. His guess put them at least two miles away, with the lake lying directly behind them. The track was growing narrower, and they were passing fewer and fewer side trails.

"How long before we get to the old base?" Ryan asked. The young woman hadn't spoken a single word since they'd left the village, and he was beginning to wonder whether she spoke American. Or whether she might possibly be mute.

"It is about as far as the distance that we have already come," she replied after a long pause.

"Easy walk?"

She nodded, half turning to glance over her shoulder at the one-eyed man. "Easy for me. I am used to walking. Not so easy for all of you." It seemed as if her eyes searched out Doc when she said that.

He smiled at her, showing his wonderful teeth. "My dear child, you do me wrong. It is perfectly true that there are certain segments of my body that function less well than once they did. But that doesn't apply to all the parts. I am still capable of keeping up on a gentle stroll through the forest." He plucked out his swallow's-eye kerchief and wiped sweat from his brow.

"Just as long as we pause now and then for the briefest of rests."

The young woman looked puzzled. Jak touched her on the arm, making her jump like a startled deer. "Doc says he can walk all right," he said.

"Yes. Oh, yes."

RAIN FLOWER TOOK DOC at his word, setting an even more brisk pace, deeper and deeper into the jungle. The trail grew more narrow, and she turned to ask Ryan to use his panga to hack away some overgrown strands of liana.

"Looks like this track isn't used all that much," he commented, wiping the sticky green ichor from the polished steel blade and resheathing it.

"We afraid spirits of past. Nobody comes this way for long years."

Krysty moved alongside Ryan. "Why are we going to look at this ghost-haunted place, lover?"

"Never know what you might find. Itzcoatl said something about there being a fight there in predark times. If the natives are scared of it, then you never know what might be there waiting, untouched."

"And whatever walks there walks alone," added Doc, who'd joined them in time to hear the end of their conversation. "As the wonderful Shirley Jackson once said."

J.B. was at their heels. "If it was an army base and it was sealed like the redoubts, then there's a good chance of picking up some ammo or some unknown weaponry."

"Soon there," Rain Flower said. "Water there."

"Could do with a drink," Mildred stated. "Amazing how quickly you can get dehydrated in such damp weather."

"IT'S AN M-551," J.B. said, surveying a rusted heap of scrap metal that lay almost buried in the undergrowth just off the trail.

"Tank?" Ryan asked, doubtfully. He could see the tracks, fallen into ribbons of orange decay, and what might have been the barrel of a heavy cannon.

"Light tank," the Armorer amended. "It had a four-man crew. Carried a missile launcher, as well as a range of machine guns. Used to be called the Sheridan. It was employed a lot out in Nam."

"Has it been here ever since the nukecaust of 2001?" Mildred asked. "I can't believe that there's anything left of it."

"No strong winds. No frost to break it up." J.B. reached out and touched a piece of the side paneling, crumbling it between his fingers like red sand. "Just rotting quietly away here in the jungle."

"What happened to its crew?" Mildred asked.

"I'll look," Dean chirped, eagerly vaulting up onto the front of the ancient vehicle.

Rain Flower rubbed her knuckle on her forehead, turning away, looking frightened.

"Don't worry," said Ryan reassuringly. "Any ghosts are long, long dead."

The hatch above the commander's control position was open, hanging on by a few threads of rusting steel. Dean knelt and started to lean in.

"Look for snakes," the young woman called, stopping him dead. "Big snakes here."

The boy hesitated. He banged his fist a few times, generating a hollow, dull ringing sound. Nothing happened, except for a flight of vivid yellow parakeets rising, screeching, into the upper branches of the trees.

He slowly lowered his head inside the turret of the old tank, staying motionless for a few moments. "Nothing," he called, his voice muffled and echoing. "Stripped bare."

"Come on back," Ryan said. "Best stay on the trail. What's left of it. Could be mined."

J.B. nodded. "Probably antipersonnel rather than magnetic. Wouldn't expect any big military move against the base. More likely paratroops. Light-armed skirmish unit. And any mines laid way back before the long winters must mostly have deteriorated by now." He took off his fedora and mopped his forehead. "They'd have antidisturbance devices fitted, as well."

"The trail's about vanished." Ryan stood still. "I can hear water falling close by."

The native woman smiled at him, recovering something of her nerve. "Yes. Close now."


THE BASE DIDN'T COMPARE to some of the massive redoubts that the friends had encountered over the past months. It wasn't built into a mountainside or hidden deep underground.

At first glance it looked like an average long-abandoned air base back in Deathlands: a few weather-stained administration buildings and Quonset huts surrounded by tumbled towers and fragmented coils of rusted razor wire.

But it seemed as if a camouflage expert had been at work, disguising the complex.

Most of the roofs had fallen in, the windows broken, and moss and vines were draped all over the ruins so that they almost vanished into the background of the forest.

Everyone stopped and stared at the lost relic from before the brief and bloody war that ended civilization as the world had known it.

"Kind of spooky," Mildred said quietly.

"I doubt we will find any human remains here," Doc said. "Not after nearly a hundred years of tropical weather."

"But there could be some hardware hidden away," J.B. stated hopefully.

"I not go in," the young woman said, seating herself comfortably on a fallen baobab tree. "Wait here you coming back. Much time."

"Frightened of ghosts?" Jak asked, sitting by her.

"Yeah. Am."

"But you have god with you. Nothing to be feared with god at your side."

"What kind of god is Jak?" Ryan asked. "What's the story about this?"

IN THE END, the process of discovery was protracted by the young woman's poor grasp of the American tongue, but they learned something of the background to Jak's godship.

As they stood there, close to a small, stagnant pool, a swarm of midges pestered them, forcing a move closer to the ruined base. They walked past the crumpled remains of the red-and-white pole that had once been the first step in the security of the place, now lying broken and neglected, overgrown with weeds.

They stopped by the old guardhouse, with its warning notice board almost illegible from age, showing warnings in American, Portuguese, Spanish and in what they guessed had to be the language of the local natives. There was absolutely nothing inside the building, except for a scattered carpet of splintered glass.

There Rain Flower finally unraveled a complicated tale of legend and myth.

It seemed that back in the long-lost times of first man and first woman, when the gods walked the earth in their various guises, there was a very beautiful girl, barely past puberty.

Her name was Tlazolteotl and she was beloved by many of the gods, who all desired to lie with her and father her firstborn child. Because of her rare beauty, they all knew that her son—it had to be a son—would be one of the most marvelous humans ever known.

But the maiden had no wish to be either the bride or mistress of any of the gods, for she truly loved a young warrior of her own tribe.

One night she fell into a deep sleep and dreamed a most mysterious dream.

She was swimming in the bottom of a deep and beautiful lake when a dolphin came to her.

Finding out from Rain Flower what kind of a creature it was took several minutes until Doc used the ferrule of his swordstick to scratch a sketch of a dolphin in the soft dirt in front of the old guardhouse.

The dolphin was a nameless god who was sympathetic to the weeping of Tlazolteotl, and he took her to a grotto filled with mountains of precious stones, glittering and dancing like living fire.

He touched a round piece of rare white jade, valued above price, no larger than a half-ripe pea, telling the young woman that she would be preserved from the lusts and unwelcome attention of the other gods if she would swallow the jade.

On waking, she walked in the forest.

It had rained, and some loose dirt had washed from a steep bank outside her village. And there, among the mud, lay a tiny berry of pure white jade.

She swallowed it and immediately became pregnant.

When the child was delivered nine months later, he was a boy, with eyes like rubies and hair as white as the driven snow upon the Mountain of the Star itself. Citlaltépetl.

He grew magically and was a full-grown man of twenty by the end of the first year of his life.

During that mysterious year the crops grew well and the rains came, and every battle was a victory.

But the young man vanished on his first birthday and had never been seen or heard of since.

But the legends told of him, told of what could come to pass one day.

KRYSTY HAD NODDED. "This young man will return and all will be well? Is that it?"

Rain Flower nodded shyly. "Yes. Old ones say this. Now he has come."

Jak had listened closely to the tale, finally shaking his head in disgust. "Old story's shit," he said. "Come from the swamps. Know my mother and father. Not god."

But the young woman wasn't to be persuaded of that. During the telling of the myth, her eyes kept turning toward the albino teenager, showing unquestioning worship of him.

"You sure you won't come farther with us?" Ryan asked. "Mebbe better than staying on your own."

She shook her head, covering her eyes. "No. You look for spirits of dead. Not me." She touched the holster with the 10-round Savage. "Be safe from whip men or Jaguar people."

"Right. We'll be back in not more than an hour or so. Come on, people."


THE CONCRETE ROAD into the base was barely visible beneath a carpet of moss. To the right Ryan spotted another of the small tanks, settled on its tracks, covered in a shrub with brilliant orange flowers.

The first building, still in sight of the guardhouse, was in a terrible state, with only one wall standing.

J.B. went closer to examine it, running his hand over the surface of the reinforced concrete. "Bullet holes and grenade fragments and burn marks," he said. "The natives were right. There was some sort of a battle here."

His foot disturbed something in the undergrowth and he bent down, picking up a bunch of twigs and clinging vines. It wasn't until he peeled them away that the others could see that he was holding a blaster, a long rifle.

"I recognize that," Ryan said, "from our run-ins with Gregori Zimyanin. It's a Dragunov sniper's rifle, 7.62 caliber, isn't it?"

The Armorer nodded. "Right. The old reworked Kalashnikov. Just like we saw the Russkies using."

Mildred shook her head. "You mean Russians landed down here? Wherever 'here' is."

Ryan nodded. "We heard stories of them dropping paratroopers in parts of Deathlands in the last hours of skydark. In the far northwest. Alaska and northern Canada. But nobody I know ever found any real proof of that. Least there's proof that it happened down here in the jungle."

"This place must've had a tactical importance." Ryan looked around. "Hard to imagine now."

"Might have been a comp comm center," Krysty said. "Radar and satellite links to all that hardware circling around up in deep space."

J.B. nodded. "Makes sense. They might have put them in from Russkie fleet exercises down in the Caribbean. Just drop a handful of specialized troops off a carrier. Surely been a firefight here."

Doc had sat on the grass, wiping his forehead. "By the Three Kennedys! This is one of the least welcoming environments I have ever encountered. I would appreciate returning to the village and that cool lake as soon as possible."

"Want to go back and keep Rain Flower company, Doc?" Ryan asked. "We won't be that long."

The old man stood, looking weary. "No. I think that I prefer to stay with you. I sympathize with the little mite. This is undeniably a little on the spooky side."

"There's a wrecked chopper over there," Jak said, pointing with a long white finger toward the edge of the forest.

"CH-47," J.B. said, dropping the rusted relic of the Dragunov back in the grass. "The big Chinook."

All of them turned toward the entrance of the base as they heard Rain Flower screaming at the top of her lungs.

# Chapter Fifteen

It was a gigantic mutie python.

The creature had obviously tasted the air and sensed the young woman, who was sitting alone by the entrance to the camp. It crept from the cool shadows, moving with a silent, sinuous power.

Before Rain Flower even guessed at the danger, the snake had wrapped itself around her ankles, crushing them together, making it impossible to escape.

She had screamed, warning the others, and managed to draw her rusted blaster from its holster and pressed it against the huge coils, a yard or so below the blunt shovel-shaped head.

She pulled the trigger. There was a puff of smoke from the muzzle of the Savage and a feeble popping sound.

"Misfire," Jak shouted, already sprinting back toward the guardhouse.

Ryan was at his heels, J.B. and Krysty sharing third place in the deadly race.

As they drew closer, they could appreciate the gigantic size of the serpent. Part of it was still hidden by the undergrowth, but what was revealed was fully thirty feet long, the central coils almost the size of a barrel. The skin was glossy, mottled in dazzling shades of olive, brown and gold.

"I'll use the scattergun on it!" J.B. yelled.

By now the young native woman had vanished into the swathing loops of the reptile, only one arm emerging from the side. Her hand was waving frantically, her fingers opening and closing spasmodically.

Mildred called out from a few yards behind the others, breathless. "Don't just shoot it, John. The reflex'll tighten and crush her."

"Shit!" The Armorer slowed, looking over his shoulder at her. "Sure?"

"Sure enough not to want to take the risk. Have to get it brain-dead straight off."

The great head was reared in the air, fully eight feet off the ground. Jak was way out in front, sprinting for the life of Rain Flower. He had heard Mildred shout the warning and had holstered his .357 Colt, hardly breaking stride.

Ryan had shrugged off the heavy Steyr rifle, knowing that this was going to be a close-in chilling. But Mildred's warning had also slowed him.

They all heard a muffled scream for help from somewhere within the serpentine coils of the python, but the voice was weak and fading.

"Let me!" Mildred yelled, stopping thirty or forty yards from the snake, panting for breath, drawing the ZKR 551 and leveling it, trying to steady herself.

But Jak was blindly oblivious to what was going on behind him. He was still running, arms pumping, white hair trailing like a flare of burning ice. His right hand held one of his concealed armory of throwing knives.

Ryan slowed, realizing that the drama was going to be played out one way or the other before he got close enough to take an active part.

It was going to be Jak.

Or nothing.

The python watched the darting figure, its flat eyes staring down. Waves of muscle ran along the hugely muscular body, slowly beginning to crush the frail woman, ready to pulp the meal to a more accessible size so that it would slip between the dislocated jaws and down into the squeezing labyrinth of its intestines.

The head was weaving slowly from side to side, like a rattler trying to hypnotize a rabbit.

Jak took no notice, every shred of his attention focusing on his target.

"He'll never..." Dean began.

Jak was the most amazing acrobat that Ryan had ever seen through all the long survival years in Deathlands. His lithe body was more agile than seemed humanly possible.

He took off from a flat-out run, as though from a springboard, performing a neat tucked somersault in the air, dodging the lightning lunge from the broad, patterned head and gaping jaws. He landed astride the upthrust body, hanging there like a monkey gripping a telephone pole.

The python hissed like a leaking steam boiler, its jaw snapping empty air as it tried to bite the irritating creature that clung to its immeasurably powerful body.

"Mildred?" Ryan called, not looking back.

"Moving too much. I'm too out of breath. Triple-big risk, Ryan."

"Wait," he said quietly. He had his own blaster, the SIG-Sauer P-226, cocked and leveled, but the chance of hitting a vital spot in the weaving head and body of the giant snake was remote. Better to let the teenager take his chance.

Rain Flower's arm hung limply, sandwiched between two of the thickest coils. The fingers were no longer moving.

Jak wriggled a little, gripping the python as if he were riding a starfishing bronco, giving himself leverage with his left arm. The short-bladed knife was in his right hand.

"The eyes!" Ryan shouted.

But the boy didn't need to be told.

The little blade pecked the sight from the right eye of the snake, darting instantly at the other side of the flat skull, pricking out the left eye.

Jak pressed the point home as hard as he could, clear liquid, tinted pink, running over his hand and down his arm.

The mutie serpent reared, fifteen, twenty feet from the floor of the forest, its head shaking to and fro with a dreadful violence, trying to dislodge the thing that had brought bright pain and a cloaking darkness.

"Let go and jump, kid!" the Armorer called.

But Jak wasn't finished.

Merely blinding the reptile wasn't going to be good enough. He wanted it dead.

Jak worked the sharp point deeper and deeper into the ruined eye, until he was wrist deep in the armored socket, driving the knife back through the optic nerve into the primitive brain of the great snake.

"Get ready to try and snatch the girl if it lets her go," Ryan yelled.

The lines were going down, the snake losing control of its own enormous fifty-foot-long body. Its tail thrashed from side to side uprooting a sturdy live oak as though it were matchwood.

"Loosening, I do believe," shouted Doc, who'd bravely moved closer to the part of the serpent that was holding the unconscious young native woman.

"Gaia!" Krysty screamed to Jak. "Let go of it and save yourself!"

The snake's death throes were stupendous, making the floor of the forest tremble. Its tail lashed out, demolishing the remnants of the guardhouse, snapping the red-and-white pole into shards of rusted metal.

As it fought against the coming of endless night, the python's coils relaxed, leaving the unconscious body of Rain Flower to tumble to the dirt. She lay limp and still, blood trickling from nose, mouth and ears. Doc was fastest, stooping beneath the thrashing scaled loops, whipping the native girl up into his arms and scampering with surprising speed away from the scene of death, toward the others.

"Well done," Ryan yelled. "Carry her well out the way. God knows how long it's going to take for this mutie bastard to buy the farm."

The writhing creature twice reared up to a phenomenal height, way above the lower branches of the taller trees. But still Jak clung, both arms and legs wrapped around the part of the body just below the blinded head.

Rain Flower blinked open her eyes, staring around in bewilderment. She whispered something in her own tongue, eyes widening, seeing the white-haired teenager riding the sky lanes with the dying monster.

"No!" she screamed, and passed out again.

The end came with a startling abruptness. Jak's knife finally probed through to the forepart of the mutie snake's brain and killed it.

One moment it had been reared up high, hissing, jaws working, frothing green spittle seeping over its bright scales. Then it fell like a tumbling redwood, shaking the earth again, flinging the albino from his hold, sending him rolling over and over into a stand of white lilies.

Doc stayed with Rain Flower, while the others ran toward Jak.

The teenager was standing up, examining a deep bruise on his right elbow, rubbing at it.

"You all right?" asked Ryan, the first one to reach him.

Jak half smiled back at him, blinking. "Eyes don't work too good. Shaken around. Big son of a double bitch, wasn't it? How's girl?"

"Fine. Passed out when she saw you riding the back of the beast," Mildred said. "You sure you're all right, Jak? No bites at all?"

"I was too low and behind it for that. Couldn't reach. Tried. Failed."

Dean picked bits of grass and leaves from Jak's back and hair. "That was the hottest pipe I ever saw," he said breathlessly. "Thought you was done."

"I thought same," Jak replied, ruffling the boy's dark curly hair. "Like riding tree in flume. No control. Had to hang on. Follow. No other way."

"Good job you called out the warning, Mildred," J.B. said, putting an arm around her shoulders. "Otherwise I'd have blasted the snake and the girl would've been crushed."

"The young lady in question finds that the agony is somewhat abated. And she is feeling a little better." Doc was leading Rain Flower toward them. She was shaking, and blood seeped from under the nails of her right hand. Despite the darkness of her skin, it was all too easy to make out the number of purple bruises rising on arms, legs and body.

Mildred went to her, smiling, hands spread. "You all right, child?" she asked.

"Hurts all of me." But she brushed past Mildred as though she weren't there, making her way to where Jak was standing, kneeling and touching her forehead to the trampled grass. "Only god would be filled with heart blood." She hesitated, struggling for the word she wanted. "Courage."

"Shit," the teenager muttered. "Oh, shit!"

THIS TIME AROUND Rain Flower wasn't that worried about the ghosts of the long-dead Americans that were supposed to haunt the base. She followed close behind Jak, actually setting her own bare feet into the marks left by his combat boots. Her eyes never left him.

The cataclysmic battle with the giant mutie python seemed to have scared away most of the wildlife from the area, with the exception of the beautiful butterflies that proliferated everywhere in the jungle. Many of them had already caught the smell of death from the snake and were fluttering eagerly about it, covering the bleeding wounds to its eyes and head in a shroud of living, iridescent color.

There was a second ruined helicopter lying at the edge of the trees, its rotors all smashed. "Bell Kiowa," J.B. said. "Light observation machine."

Virtually all of the buildings of the predark base were totally wrecked, many showing signs of mortar fire or the effects of hi-ex.

"Wasting time here," Jak said.

"Then perhaps we could return to the village," Doc suggested. "My throat is in a similar condition to a sand snake's ass. Pardon my French, ladies."

Ryan had been looking around, worried at the silence in the green hell beyond the limits of the complex. But the noises of the forest were creeping back, reassuring him that there was no immediately threatening enemy.

"There's the big building over at the far side. We'll give that the once-over and then leave it be."

J.B. was delighted to have found the rotted remnants of a Russkie pistol, a 9 mm Makarov lying under a pile of glass from a shattered window.

"Proves there was a firefight," he said.

The biggest of the buildings—well over a hundred and fifty feet in length and more than half that in width—was also in the best condition. It had a roof, and all four walls were still standing, though virtually every window had been smashed.

The double sec doors hung from a single hinge, and as Ryan pushed at them, they fell down with a deafening clatter, sending an armadillo scuttling from its shelter just inside the main entrance hall.

Dean leveled his blaster at it, just controlling himself in time. "Thought it was one of the ghosts," he said, grinning nervously at his father.

The bullet scars on the walls were even more noticeable here, prompting Ryan to wonder whether this might have been a last-stand situation for the American defenders of the base. It was hardly likely that frontline, top-grade troops would have been stuck out here in the jungle, and an attack by ace-on-the-line Russkies had to have come as a lethal shock.

Rain Flower was deeply unhappy in the big building. "Home of ghosts," she moaned, teeth chattering, eyes darting nervously all around her. "No man walk here."

It looked as if the animal predators shared her unease. Or, more likely, the sec doors had been enough of a barrier to keep them out, because there were still several corpses in the last part of the complex.

"American and Russkies," J.B. pronounced, kneeling beside one dried bundle of sticks and grinning teeth in rags of uniform. The corpses lay here and there, most still clutching rusted blasters.

The firearms alone would have told their story, Kalashnikovs and M-16 rifles, the badges and rank markings on the uniforms merely confirming it.

Most of the leathery bodies showed bullet wounds, with broken ribs or fractured skulls, the uniforms often clotted with black patches of ancient blood. Two or three of them were still locked in the throes of hand-to-hand combat, their corpses tangled together, with rusting bayonets buried in dark brown bones.

J.B. looked around him. "Way I read this, the fighting was to the wire. Knives, eye to eye. Like the Russkies were right on the edge of winning control of the base. Then I figure reinforcements arrived in the choppers and the tanks, and the surviving defenders were saved. But so much damage was done that they evacuated the place on the spot."

"Leaving the dead?" Doc asked. "Surely they would have removed their own casualties!"

Ryan shook his head. "Not if skydark was right around the corner, Doc. Little we know about the last week before the nukings, and the months straight afterward, points to a bolt out of the blue. Followed by total chaos. Lightning from a clear sky. Russkies attacking way out here must've been part of a desperate contingency plan. By the time this firefight took place, the odds are that Newyork and Moscow and all the other big cities were already cosmic dust and rad ash. No time to think about bodies."

"No time to think, period," Mildred added.

"Worth checking out the rest of the place?" Ryan asked.

"Why not?" J.B. looked along the corridor, past a half-dozen scattered corpses. "Could be they pulled out so fast they left stuff behind. Stuff we might be able to use."

# Chapter Sixteen

The only part of the entire base that hadn't been destroyed during the fighting was a stores section at the rear end of the main building. It looked as though the skirmish hadn't reached it, as the walls were free from shrapnel or bullet damage. And there were no corpses at the back.

"Supplies and Armament," Dean read slowly, stumbling over the last word. "Means there's blasters and food, doesn't it, Dad? Could anything still be okay after all the years and the heat and the damp and all?"

Ryan looked at his son. "State of the blasters we've seen means there aren't likely to be any left here still fireable. And I doubt there's eatable food left after close on a hundred years. So don't lift your hopes."

Rain Flower was now so bold that she had attached herself to Jak, hanging on to his arm, staring nervously up into his face for a hint of a smile.

"We wait outside," the teenager said to Ryan. "Get some fresh air. This place stinks of death."

"Think I'll join you," Krysty told him. "Hate these predark tombs."

The other five went on forward, pushing through the door that led to the last part of the base. The door was stiff, creaking on unoiled hinges, and the air inside tasted of long stillness and inexorable decay.

J.B. stopped in the doorway, peering into the dimly lit interior. "Five gets ten there isn't going to be anything worth picking from here."

"There seems to be a store of chemicals over on these shelves," Doc called. "I rather suspect that they might have been used in mining or some other sort of industrial research."

J.B. went over to join the old man, taking off his glasses and polishing them on his sleeve. "Yeah. Iron oxide. Barium peroxide powder. Could be right, Doc." He stopped and repolished the lenses, his face suddenly alight with an unholy excitement. "Hey! Now let's see if they've also got some... Yeah, they do. And how's about..."

Ryan left him muttering to himself, going on to browse around the rest of the stores area. Ants had gotten into some of the boxes, crumbling them into dust, leaving the weapons inside exposed to the atmosphere.

Dean and Mildred wandered with him, staring at the lined shelves in the hope that they might somehow hold something worthwhile.

"No good," Ryan said. "Waste of time. Let's get outside with the others."

Mildred agreed. "Thought there might possibly have been some sealed first-aid kits that could have given us something useful. Like you say, it was all too long ago."

"Can I stay awhile longer, Dad?" asked Dean, who was on hands and knees, burrowing through the pile of dirt and sawdust under the shelves and tables.

"Five minutes is all. Five minutes."

"Doc and I have found something," J.B. called. "If I can remember how to put it all together."

"I think that my chemistry might come in handy for once," Doc said. "I sat in those desks for interminable hours on sunny afternoons when I would rather have been out throwing the pigskin. The utter tedium of science. Volumes of given gases and total internal reflection and osmosis and litmus paper and the lime-water equation. Seems so much wasteful gibberish to me now. Except that I think John Barrymore is on to something. Something that would take the leering smiles off the faces of those ghastly slavers."

"What is it?" Ryan asked.

J.B. waved a hand at him. "You go on outside, Ryan. We need to find bags to hold some of this stuff."

"And a strong sealed container to put it in after we've mixed it," Doc added.

"Long as we don't blow our own fool heads off." J.B. and Doc both cackled together at whatever it was that they were planning to try.

Ryan smiled at their enthusiasm, wondering what piece of arcane lore the Armorer had stumbled on, knowing from long friendship with J.B. that it was unlikely to be a waste of time.

The air outside struck at him like a moist blanket, and he whistled through his teeth. Mildred was right behind him. "Turkish-bath time, Ryan," she said.

Krysty was sitting with Jak and Rain Flower a few yards away from the building, leaning against a tumbled concrete pillbox at the side of a dark swamp.

"Where're the others, lover?"

"Dean's nosing to see if he can discover some long-lost weapon that hasn't rotted to rust."

Mildred wiped a bead of sweat from her forehead. "And John and Doc are playing at being little boys again. Discovered some big-deal secret."

"No ghosts?" the young native woman stammered. "You see there is no ghosts?"

"Nothing," Ryan replied. "Few folks that caught the last train west, close on a century gone." He saw the expression of bewilderment on the woman's face and explained. "Means some dead bodies. Gone to meet their gods, I guess."

"We should go back to village."

Jak stood. "Once agree. Been here long enough. Nothing to do or see."

Behind them, Doc and J.B. appeared from the wrecked entrance to the building. Both carried burlap bags that seemed to weigh heavy. The Armorer also carried a plastic bin, about three feet high and eighteen inches across.

"Got what you wanted?" Ryan asked.

J.B. nodded, grinning broadly, his fedora pushed back on his forehead. "Course, most of this stuff is likely way past its use-by date."

"Only about a century," Doc agreed, also grinning. "Still, plenty of chemicals retain their qualities for a good long time, if they're stored in sealed units like most of these were."

"What are you going to make?" Ryan asked. "My guess is that it'll either explode or flame. Or both. Can't imagine you, J.B., wasting time on anything else."

The Armorer rubbed the side of his nose in a secretive gesture. "Like Trader used to say, Ryan, patience is the greatest virtue."

"Yeah. Also used to say that a man who waited was a man who likely got himself chilled."

"Where's Dean?" Krysty asked.

"Inside," Ryan said.

Doc rested the bags in the grass. "Last time I saw the young imp he was burrowing under piles of rotted boxes beneath one of the benches. I think that he was hoping to come upon Flint's treasure."

"Who Flint?" Jak said. "One of slavers?"

Doc smiled at the young man. "Fifteen men on a dead man's chest, Master Lauren. The black spot. Cheese and Ben Gunn. Long John and the barrel of apples. The good ship *Hispaniola.*" He contorted his face into an actor's mask. "Them as dies'll be the lucky ones, Squire Trelawney. Right, Jim lad. Blind Pew going down screaming under the hooves of the revenue men."

He stopped as he realized that everyone but Mildred was looking at him as though he'd totally lost his mind.

"You want a lie-down, Doc?" Ryan suggested. "Over in the shade?"

"Dr. Wyeth, would you be so kind as to confirm to these unbelievers that I have not mislaid all of my marbles?"

The woman grinned wolfishly. "No idea what you're blabbering about, Doc. Always knew you were at least two sandwiches shy of a picnic but this—"

"You...!" He stepped toward Mildred, flourishing his ebony cane at her.

She backed away, still smiling. "All right, all right." She turned to the others. "The old goat was digging out references to a great kids' book called *Treasure Island*. Rattling yarn."

Everyone except Rain Flower laughed at the expression on Doc's face, mixing relief and anger.

"Dad!"

It was Dean, staggering out from the shattered entrance of the base carrying a big rectangular metal box, painted olive green, with a string of coded letters and numerals stenciled white on its lid and sides.

"What you find, son?"

"Look and see."

With an effort he managed to balance the corner of the box on the crumbling concrete of the pillbox, keeping it there with his chest.

J.B. lifted the lid, peering inside. "Dark night!"

Ryan looked over his friend's shoulder, seeing that it was a standard army-issue container of the kind that they'd seen in many old redoubts, virtually all of them empty.

But this box was more than half full.

With grenades.

They were of mixed kinds, some with flip-top firing mechanisms and the rest with two-step buttons, one to arm the gren and one to trigger the firing system.

They were all a dull metallic silvery color, with bands of different colors around their tops.

Ryan could remember some of the color combinations but not all of them.

"Scarlet and blue's the implode, isn't it?" he said, picking one from the box and weighing it in his hand. He examined the slightly pitted surface of the metal, seeing that there was a trail of thick liquid drying around the top, looking like it might have leaked from the fuse elements.

"Yeah," J.B. agreed. "Got a fine mix in here, Dean. One or two of everything. That one's a frag and that's a burner. Nerve gas in that."

"Is this a hi-ex?" Jak asked. "Seen some like this back in the swamps."

The Armorer took it from him. "Yeah, it is. Quite a fair bit of corrosion in some of them."

"They're greased," Dean insisted, steadying the box when it threatened to topple off its perch.

"No. Grease has dried by now," Mildred argued. "Not surprising after all these years. Bottom of the box is rusted clean through in this corner, as well."

"There's smoke and lights," J.B. said. "Think this one's a hi-alt gren. Remotes, delays and shraps. It's a good mix, Dean. You did well to find them."

"They were buried under a sort of pile of shelves that had been eaten through by ants and fallen down. Think we can use them?" he asked J.B.

"Against the Jaguar people and the slavers you mean? Don't see why not, though I'm a bit worried about the stuff leaking from some of them."

All of the friends had taken gleaming grens from the metal box, except for Rain Flower, who had moved several steps away from the group, fingers knotting in front of her, betraying her intense nervousness.

"Be useful," Ryan said. He held a frag gren, looking down at a colorless sticky liquid that was seeping from under the flip-top firing mechanism. "But..."

"But what, Dad?"

"But I'm a long way from being certain that they're still safe, son."

"Let's try one."

"Too much noise. Don't want to bring ourselves some unwelcome company, Dean."

"Could be trainers," Jak suggested. "Found some myself back home in bayous. Old armory. Thought found best weapons in Deathlands. All filled plastic. No ex-plas." He ran his fingers through his long white hair. "Found some ring pulls in same place. Writing gone off them all so didn't know what they were. Exciting."

"What were they, Jak?" Dean asked.

"Canned cabbage." He pulled a wry face. "All dissolved into kind of porridge. Threw away."

"We could test one of these, Ryan," J.B. said. "Heave one into the heart of the building. Walls and roof'll muffle explosion. Mebbe use a delay. It shouldn't make too much of a bang in there. Then we could all take a couple with us."

"For the time being, put them all back in the box," Ryan said. "Hang on to it there, Dean."

"Sure, Dad." His skinny arms grappled with the heavy metal container.

J.B. held on to a single grenade with bands of dull green and bright yellow, peering down at it. "Timers on these generally run around fifteen seconds as set. You can alter the setting for anything from ten seconds to ten hours but..." He squinted through his glasses. "Yeah, these have a base setting of fifteen seconds. I'll stick with that. Take it in and throw it down the end of the passage. Give me time to run back out there. Everyone take cover in case there's any broken glass. Here I go."

The slim figure vanished past the tumbled sec doors, fedora tipped jauntily to one side.

Dean struggled, refusing any offer of help, and managed to lay the box down in the grass, crouching with the others behind the ruined pillbox.

"Haven't seen a gren in ages, Dad," he said.

"Me neither. Found some a while back, and we used to have a decent store of them in War Wag One. Trader found them or bought them, somewhere up in the Darks, I think it was."

They all heard the sound of running feet and knelt behind the cover, Jak pulling the young native woman by the hand, reassuring her that everything would be double safe but there would be a double-loud bang.

Ryan knelt, hands over his ears, closing his eye, keeping his mouth open to try to minimize the effects of any blast, aware of Krysty pressed against him on the right side.

"Hope you remembered to kiss your ass goodbye," she whispered, making him smile.

J.B. came out of the doorway, springing hard, arms pumping, knees raised. He carried the Uzi, but he'd left the scattergun outside with Mildred.

He jinked to his right, heading toward the pillbox, his combat boots slipping a little on the damp grass. As he ran, J.B. was shouting out the timing, counting down the fifteen seconds.

"Nine and eight and seven..." He reached the concrete emplacement, breathing hard. "And six and five and four and three and two and one and go!"

Everyone winced in expectation of the explosion. Rain Flower had begun to cry, sensing the tension, even though she had no real understanding of what was happening.

"Go," the Armorer repeated.

"No go," Jak breathed.

Dean started to get up. "Can I go take a look, Dad, and see whether—"

"See whether you get your stupe head blown off, Dean?" Ryan interrupted. "No, on the whole I'd rather you stayed here with us for a little while. Until we know for sure if the gren's going to blow or not."

"Not, is my guess," Krysty said, peering uncertainly around the side of the metal box with the rest of the grens inside it.

They waited in the forest stillness. Ryan glanced at his wrist chron. "Thirty seconds, gone," he said.

"Sure it wasn't training gren?" Jak asked.

"Sure. Proper primer and it started to tick as soon as I triggered it." J.B. stood, straightening creases in his pants, brushing smears of mud from his knees. "Well, it sure seems like they're duds."

"Can't we try some more?" Dean asked eagerly, heaving the box back on top of the pillbox, barely keeping it balanced. "Some might work."

The Armorer shook his head. "No. Waste of time, Dean. See the corrosion and the leaking stuff."

"How about this one with purple and— Oh, shit!" The box started to slide, falling inexorably to the turf with a shuddering crash, spilling the grens all around the boy's feet.

Mildred was first to stoop and start picking them up, holding one of the timer grens with its green and yellow stripes, dropping it like a hot brick.

"It's ticking, folks! Fucker's ticking!"

# Chapter Seventeen

In fifteen seconds a first-class athlete could spring roughly one hundred and forty yards, with a reaction time to the pistol of the starter measured in fractions of a second.

Despite his honed combat reflexes, Ryan took nearly four seconds to register the horror of the situation and decide what was best to do.

By then Rain Flower had guessed instinctively that something had gone seriously, lethally wrong and was several strides away from the others, racing full pelt toward the emerald fringe of the forest.

"Run," Ryan shouted, grabbing Dean by the wrist, pulling him after him.

There was a moment of disorganized panic.

Doc took it into his befuddled old head that the best course of action was to pick up the ticking timer gren and throw it a long way in the opposite direction. But when Mildred dropped it, the lethal predark device had disappeared into the other thirty or so grens that lay scattered around the base of the concrete-fortified pillbox.

"By the—" he began, shaking his head in bewilderment, not making any attempt to run for safety.

Mildred saved his life. She spotted his confusion and spun and raced back to him, slapping him smartly across the cheek as she arrived, then tugging him by the ear. She let go only when Doc yelped in pain and started to chase after her, his face flushed in anger.

Ryan had glanced at his chron as soon as he realized what Mildred's warning meant.

Now, as he sprinted toward the welcoming cover of the florid shrubs and bushes beneath the trees, he was counting to himself, allowing for the timer having fifteen seconds to run before the ignition sequence was completed.

It was also at the front of his consciousness that the delay gren that J.B. had thrown inside the building had utterly failed to detonate. Bearing in mind the sorry state of most of the box, there was a better than average chance that none of the grenades would function properly.

But the odds weren't good enough for Ryan to slow down in his run for shelter.

Rain Flower was first in the lung-bursting chase to safety, followed by Jak and Krysty. Ryan and Dean were running together in equal fourth, followed closely by J.B. Despite their slow start, Mildred and Doc were charging along at the heels of the Armorer.

"Twelve seconds!" Ryan panted. "Everyone down, now!"

The ground dipped slightly a few yards before the beginnings of the jungle, and he dived for it, rolling over on his face, cupping his ears and closing his eye. He opened his mouth, counting to himself under his breath.

The delay gren went off on fourteen seconds.

The ground shook and heaved as if from a major quake, lifting Ryan's body clear of the grass for a moment, then sending him crashing down again. The hot blast tugged at his clothes and his hair, bits of stone and dirt stinging the exposed portions of his face.

The shock wave was colossal, and the surge of heat scorched his skin.

It seemed that the one gren had triggered all the others, sending them off within a nanosecond of one another, the whole box detonating virtually at once.

The noise was literally deafening.

Ryan lay still, pressed to the comforting earth, shoulders hunched, placing his hands over the top of his head to protect himself as best he could from the torrential hail of debris from the explosion.

Large stones and clods of turf began to patter around him, some of them hitting his back, none of them doing him any serious harm.

He had experienced the familiar sucking shock of an implode and recognized the characteristic stench of the burners and smokes going off. Shards of razored metal from the frag gren sliced through the air above him, ripping noisily into the leaves and branches of the trees.

His immediate worry was that one or more of the grens might have contained nerve gas.

As soon as the rumbling of the explosions had faded away, he risked a glance. Thick smoke was drifting from the wrecked pillbox, with flames glowing brightly at its heart. The wind seemed to be carrying it away from Ryan and the others, toward the main buildings of the base.

"Safe?" J.B. shouted.

"Better give it another half minute in case there's more of the delays. How about nervies?"

The Armorer considered Ryan's question for a few moments. "Don't think I spotted any. But I can't be sure. Yeah, be a bastard to get caught by one of them."

"Everyone else all right?" Ryan called. "Dean?"

"Yeah, Dad. Can't hardly hear you. Feels like my ears been filled with water. Hey, I'm triple sorry about that, but I never knew they—"

"That's all right, son. Krysty?"

She was close enough to reach out and squeeze his hand. "Near thing that," she said. "I'm fine. Got a load of mud and grass in my hair."

"Jak?"

"Deaf."

"The girl?"

"She's all right. Pissed herself in fear. Think have to carry her back the village. Doubt she'll walk."

"Mildred?" There was no answer for a moment. "Mildred, are you all right?"

"Sorry, didn't hear you properly. Yeah. I got a little blood from my ears but I don't think there's any permanent damage done. Close call, friends."

Doc's voice boomed out across the clearing. "The good doctor has a little blood from her ears? Is that what the good lady said? She is lucky to have any ears left. After her violent attack on my person I thought that my one ear had vanished into her fingers." He paused, dropping the mock-angry bantering tone. "I thank you for saving my life, madam. Most sincerely."

"Welcome, Doc."

Ryan looked up again, over the rise in the ground. There didn't seem much risk of more grens going off.

"Let's move it," he said. "Head away toward the main entrance. Need a hand with Rain Flower, Jak?"

"No. Manage."

Brushing dirt, leaves and pebbles from themselves, they all stood, staring nervously toward the smoldering crater behind them.

Ryan noticed that Doc had suffered one of his nosebleeds, crimson streaking his mouth and chin. He was mopping at it with his trusty kerchief. Everyone else looked well enough, though Dean was pale with shock.

Rain Flower was holding Jak by the hand, looking up at him from beneath lowered lids. She was trembling like an aspen in a hurricane.

Krysty's bright hair was dulled and had coiled itself tightly around her nape. Her green eyes blinked as she rubbed dust from them, but she still managed a smile for Ryan. "Never a dull moment, lover," she said.

ITZCOATL, WITH A NUMBER of his senior warriors, all of them fully armed, met them on the trail a quarter mile outside the village. "What was the thunder?" he asked, pointing at the bags carried by J.B. and Doc. "What have you removed from the temple of the Americans."

"Just some powder and stuff that we found over at the base. Think that we might be able to use it to help you." Ryan quickly changed the subject. "And the noise? Guess we might've woke up some of the old gods," Ryan replied. "But we won and they lost. They always lose."

The chief looked at Rain Flower, and he suddenly spit a long question at her in their own tongue. After a brief hesitation she replied at great length, gesturing first at Jak, then at Mildred, finally at Jak again.

Itzcoatl nodded slowly, his dark eyes returning to Ryan. "You angered the old ones," he said accusingly, "and nearly paid the blood price."

"Some old grenades got triggered and went off. It was dangerous but we escaped all right. It's nothing to do with any fireblasted gods!"

The chief responded to Ryan's burst of temper, pointing at him with his obsidian sword. "You have helped us but don't step over the line or you better watch your ass."

Ryan couldn't help smiling at the man's use of the old predark American slang. "Sure, Chief. Sure. We could use a good wash and mebbe some food?"

"Tonight there will be the ritual of winning the favor of the gods. The two Jaguar warriors and the slaver you caught will all help us in this. It will be a feast of celebration."

"But we can eat now?"

"No. Water only is allowed. It is part of the cleansing. We do not eat after the burying of our brothers. Not before they are joined by our enemies."

"Joined?" J.B. repeated. "Do that mean what I think it do, Chief?"

But Itzcoatl shook his head. "Tonight, before the setting of the sun. You will see all and understand all."

EVERYONE FRESHENED UP, using water from the nearby lake to wash.

Doc took the opportunity to clean his swallow's-eye kerchief, rinsing out blood and crusted sweat.

"The talk of this ceremony tonight," he said. "It likes me not, brothers and sisters."

"Sacrifice?" Mildred asked.

"Means they'll chill the three prisoners they've got, doesn't it, Dad?"

"We don't have to go," Krysty said, trying to dry her hair on an inadequately small towel of linen.

Mildred shook her head. "Trouble is, I only did Native American sociological grouping as my minor. But I know that all of the main cultures of Central and South America were seriously big on their rituals."

"Aztecs, Maya and Inca," Doc said. "I know something of them. During the long hours I spent in durance vile at the various safehouses of the white-coat time scientists, I had ample opportunity to catch up on my neglected reading. I believe that it was probably in the Victorian Gothic frame house in rural Maryland, or was it the military-intelligence mansion in the misty hills of Virginia . . . ? It matters not."

"Get on with it, Doc," Ryan said.

"Of course. There was a library there and I remember reading an excellent tome on this very subject."

"What subject, Doc?" Mildred asked, looking bewildered. "You've been rambling so far and so long that I've plain forgotten what it was you were talking about. Could it possibly have been the Mayan, Inca and Aztec civilizations?"

Doc sniffed. "I choose to ignore that pettish and peevish interruption. I dismiss it as being of less moment than the cheeping of demons in a dry gutter. The book was called *The Sun, the Pyramid and the Knife*, by a scholarly author whose name was... Let me see... Yes, Jedediah Alnwick. He gave great detail of the barbaric murders these people carried out in the name of their religion. Still, I suppose that it was ever thus."

"So?" Mildred said. "What's your point, Doc? Supposing you have a point at all."

"I remember that everyone was required to attend these sacrifices. *Everyone.* I think it might be unwise to reject any invitation."


THE AFTERNOON DRIFTED BY.

Dean fell asleep, giving his father and Krysty the opportunity to make hurried love beneath a long embroidered blanket that was trimmed with the colorful feathers of a bird of paradise.

After they'd finished, Ryan went quickly and washed himself in an unglazed pottery bowl. Neither of them had bothered to take off their outdoor clothing, simply unbelting their pants and rolling them down to the knees.

"That was nice," Krysty said, lying on her back on the bed, watching Ryan.

"Yeah."

"Though I reckon I'd always take a slowie over a quickie any day of the week. Any week of the year. Finished with the water, lover?"

"Sure. Yeah, I agree." Both of them were keeping their voices pitched low to avoid waking the boy, sleeping behind the beaded curtain.

"We going to help these people?"

Ryan sat on the bed, checking the action of the SIG-Sauer. "Don't see why we might not help them out a little on a raid of these Jaguar people. And if the slavers were to come calling . . ." He let the rest of the sentence trail off into the moist heat of the thatched hut.

"What's that stuff that J.B. and Doc were playing around with out back of their place?"

Ryan holstered the heavy automatic and stood, stretching. "I reckon it's likely going to turn out to be a primitive explosive of some kind."

"Someone's coming." Krysty quickly pulled up her pants and fastened the belt.

"I don't hear them," Ryan said.

"Didn't hear them. Felt them." She paused. "Now I hear them. Two men."

Ryan caught the sound of bare feet padding across the open ground toward their hut.

"Dean!"

"What is it?" the boy asked sleepily.

"Company."

The boy swung off his bed, appearing through the beaded curtain with his 9 mm Browning gripped in his right fist, looking as big as a cannon.

The men swept into the hut without bothering to knock or call out a warning.

One of them was a young boy, wearing a mask of a human skull, fleshless, with empty holes where the eyes should have been. The teeth were inlaid chips of turquoise.

But he was clearly subordinate to the other figure. Ryan had already learned enough of the color-coded regalia of the tribe to recognize that the man was a priest, a very senior priest.

His robes were black, and he wore a mask of a sable serpent's mouth, the sharpened teeth gripping the polished head of what looked like a large rat. Between its fangs there was a smaller skull, looking disturbingly humanoid.

The priest's own hair was long and matted with fresh blood that leaked down over his shoulders.

"You all come."

It sounded to Ryan like a command rather than a question. "Yeah. Krysty?"

"What, lover?"

"Go get J.B. and the others. Remind them we're all on double red."

"Sure." She vanished, the dark eyes of the natives turning to follow her.

"They quick," the priest said in a harsh guttural voice. "Before sun sleeps."

"Right. How long will this take?"

"What?"

Ryan shook his head, realizing that the priest's grasp of the American language was very poor.

While he waited, Ryan looked at the strange robe that the native was wearing. It was some sort of fine tanned leather, fitting well over shoulders and chest, though there were strange dangling protuberances hanging from near the top of his arms and from the hips on both sides.

Hearing the sound of voices as Krysty returned with J.B., Mildred, Doc and Jak, the priest turned and stepped into the doorway, where he was starkly illuminated in the scarlet glow of the setting sun, enabling Ryan to see clearly what the bizarre robe was made from.

It was made from the flayed skin of a fully grown man.

# Chapter Eighteen

"Those are the arms and legs, hanging down both sides. See the fingers and toes," Ryan whispered.

"Gaia!"

"I couldn't believe it when I saw it. The head's been cut clean off. Wondered at first whether the priest was wearing that, as well, like a kind of mask."

The woman mimed gagging. "Sickies."

"Guess it's their religion. Some kind of ritual that they wear the skins of their enemies. Like some of the Native Americans eating the hearts from dead enemies to sort of take their courage inside them."

"Still makes my lungs shrink. Gives an idea of what we're about to see."

Doc was at their heels. "And may the Lord make us truly thankful," he breathed.

THEY FOLLOWED THE PRIEST and his young assistant out of the main part of the village, toward the ancient pyramid that towered above the evening forest.

All the men of the village were gathered around the base of the stone mountain, the women and children ranged behind them. Ryan saw that many of the council of elders were dressed in their best ceremonial finery, with whispering beads, jeweled masks and swaying feathers.

He recognized Speaking Eagle and Smoking Crest, both wearing blue shrouds. Itzcoatl was in red, streaked with black. In the front line of the women stood Rain Flower, her eyes fixed to Jak.

Drums pounded and trumpets shrilled. The shadows were elongated, stretching from the trees while the setting sun dappled everything with crimson. Scented smoke drifted across the scene from iron braziers placed at each angle. There were several larger fires built on the flat top of the pyramid. More ghostly figures, wearing flayed human skin and sodden with blood, moved slowly from corner to corner in what seemed to be a stately dance.

"Looks like a scene from some big movie," Mildred said quietly.

"Too grim," Doc replied. "Oh, my dear lady, it is far too real and far too grim."

The priest turned and scowled, holding a bony finger to his lips. "Not speak," he snarled.

The boy led Ryan to a position of honor in the first line, alongside some of the older warriors, their scarred bodies showing the battles they'd fought. Krysty followed, the others at her heels. There was a susurration from the natives as Jak took his place, last of the friends.

All of them carried their firearms.

For a moment the large natural arena was totally still and silent.

Ryan could just make out the mirrored surface of the lake between the trees and huts, and he saw the sudden silvered splash of a fishing eagle diving into the deeps. It emerged empty-beaked, tiny drops of water tumbling from its flapping wings as it flew higher and caught the last rays of the sun.

Heads began to turn, and Ryan looked back toward the village, seeing the three prisoners being brought out by an escort of warriors.

The men were dancing in a ponderous ritual, two steps to the front and then one to the side, one back and one more to the other side, then two strides forward. The whole cycle was repeated to the slow beating of a slack-skinned drum, feet rising and falling in the endless rhythm of those beneath the earth, rising and falling.

Living and death.

Partly living.

To his great surprise, Ryan saw that the two Jaguar warriors were also dancing, following the pattern of the others, faces impassive, unsmiling. Their hands and feet were free, and sweat glistened on their bodies.

The swarthy slaver, still wearing the blood-soaked shirt that masked the deep wound to his stomach, was not participating gladly in the ceremony.

His hands had been tied behind his back, his feet dragging furrows through the dirt. Two warriors hauled him along between them while a third walked behind, keeping the prisoner moving with a spear tipped with the black stone.

He fought and struggled all the way, crying out in a strange, guttural way, with no words audible among the stream of tortured sound.

At a gesture from Itzcoatl, one of the junior priests strode forward and stopped in front of the white man.

He held a small tube in his hands and poured something into it from a pouch at his waist, lifting it and blowing into the prisoner's face.

Ryan saw that it was a pale powder, and it had the effect of calming the man.

"Drug?" he whispered to Mildred.

"That stuff they call *yauhtli*. Indian hemp. Narcotic. Takes away a little of the pain. Takes a lot of the fear and anxiety from the poor bastard. Helps him to go more gently into the endless night."

Now the dancers were nearly on top of them, heading toward the foot of the pyramid. At an unseen signal, all of the ordinary natives bowed down, foreheads touching the dew-slick grass. The priests and elders stood where they were.

In the sway of movement, Ryan found himself pushed against the chief, who turned to him.

"This is dedicated to Huehueteotl, who is the god of fire. That is why..." He gestured to the blazing piles of logs all around them and on top of the pyramid.

"The Jaguar people...? They seem to be going willingly to their deaths."

Itzcoatl nodded. "Right on, my friend. They have also been given *yauhtli*, which—"

"I know," Ryan said. "Makes the pain less painful."

"And it helps to go with the ritual."

Now the dancers had reached the foot of the pyramid and were performing a complicated interweaving step, circling around and around, in and out, hypnotically. The drums were beating faster, and the trumpets had been replaced by the delicate, warbling note of the pipes.

Then they began to climb.

As the men moved higher, they rose from the grayness of dusk into the last rays of the sun, which painted them scarlet and gold, catching the brilliant glitter of their necklaces and earrings, glinting off the polished stone of the daggers.

"By the Three Kennedys!" Doc whispered. "This is like being transported in a time machine, back, far back into the sixteenth century. And beyond. We are witnessing a ceremony that no white man could have seen for hundreds of years. It was believed long lost."

"They going to chill them, Dad?"

"Think so, Dean. But whatever happens, you're not to move or cry out. Understand? Our lives...all of our lives could depend on not behaving stupe."

"Sure, Dad."

The dancers were more than halfway up the side, climbing row after row of the steep steps with fluid ease. The wounded slaver seemed much more passive, waiting at the bottom, half supported by his guards.

A large log fell into the heart of the nearest fire, raising a flare of dazzling flames.

"Dark night!" J.B. exclaimed, taken by surprise. The light showed the white prisoner more clearly, revealing the reason for his inability to call out properly for help, showing the waggling stump of his amputated tongue, raw and bleeding.

Now he was being helped up the pyramid, a faltering step at a time. The watching natives had all stood, watching the progress of the ritual.

Time passed with a strange drugged slowness.

Ryan was becoming increasingly disoriented, his head weightless, feeling as though the solid turf were shimmering under his feet, like the scales of some gigantic reptile.

The smoke that swirled all around was tainted with the bitter scent of herbs, which he began to suspect might be seriously intoxicating. He tried to breathe in a more shallow manner, through his mouth, hoping that it might minimize the adverse effects of the native drugs.

Without realizing it, Ryan had closed his good eye, drifting away from the present, jerking back to life when Krysty nudged him in the ribs.

"Dropping asleep, lover," she warned.

Now all three prisoners were together on the top of the pyramid. Most of the dancers had stepped away, returning carefully down the shadowed steps to level ground. The sun was nearly done, illuminating only the very topmost layer of stones. It was beginning to get cool.

"Soon," Itzcoatl said softly.

Two warriors remained beside the white slaver, bracing him up as though he might have collapsed without their support.

Now the Jaguar men danced together, just the two of them alone, very slowly, hands on each other's shoulders, faces almost touching, eyes closed, lips moving as if they were whispering their farewells. The dark clearing was so still that the watchers below could clearly hear the faint slap of their bare feet upon the hewn stones.

Three of the priests now joined the dance, their long matted hair gleaming with fresh-spilled blood, their gowns of human skin whirling about them, dancing closer to the three prisoners, almost caressingly.

One by one they each lifted a prisoner on their backs, carrying them as if they were frail elderly relatives. Neither the Jaguar natives nor the slaver seemed to be offering any resistance to this.

They seemed to find the men weightless, dancing with an infinite lightness.

Slower and slower.

Slower.

"This isn't too..." Jak began, the sentence choking in his throat.

At a hidden signal the drums and the pipes stopped, and there was a single piercing note on the trumpet.

The trio of priests turned and dumped the prisoners off their backs into the center of each of the three main fires that topped the huge pyramid.

"Oh, Jesus!" Mildred exclaimed, turning her back on the ghastly spectacle.

But it wasn't over.

It had barely begun.

The screams of the three hapless men soared above the eagerly watching crowd as the flames frizzled and blackened their hair, blistering the skin from their bodies with fierce intensity. All of them tried to stand and move from the hearts of the fires, but more of the priests pushed them back into the blazes.

"Why do this?" Ryan asked Itzcoatl. "It's fucking barbaric to chill someone like this. Even if they're your enemies."

But the chief merely held up his right hand. "Peace, friend. It is not yet done. The fire god has only received a part of his tribute. The right word? Tribute?"

But Ryan ignored him.

Even a hundred feet below the crest of the pyramid the air was filled with the stink of roasting flesh, rising above the scent of the smoky herbs.

"They're rescuing the poor devils," Doc said, standing on tiptoe to study the ritual.

"Don't look," Mildred called. "I know what's happening next. I remember the black swords...."

Doc also turned away, staring blankly into the dark wall of trees.

The burned men were still alive, wriggling and crying out as they were dragged from the fires and pinioned in a firm grip, legs spread, arms held wide.

Each of the main priests was holding a short sword of polished black obsidian, lifting it toward the heavens. They cried out in a loud chorus, to which Itzcoatl replied in a firm, ringing voice in their own tongue.

The three swords flashed as one.

"Fireblast!" Ryan said, feeling vomit rising in his throat at the sight.

For a moment he was reminded of a method of execution called the flying eagle, where a sharp knife was thrust into the solar plexus and drawn up on the right and back again, then up on the left, like the wings of a bird of prey. Finally the ritual killer would stretch his hands into the deep, steaming gash, and rip out the victim's lungs.

This time the swords rose and fell, cutting open a massive wound in each prisoner's chest. The black blades, smoking in the cool evening, were dropped and each priest reached into the cavity and wrenched out the living, beating heart.

Dean's face was as white as ivory and he was swallowing hard, fighting for control, desperate not to let his father down in front of the entire tribe.

Now the sun was almost done with its day's journey, its last bright rays touching the tableau on top of the pyramid, the three dripping hearts held aloft to catch the light.

The natives around Ryan and the others cried out in a single word, which sounded like the name of their fire god, Huehueteotl.

Itzcoatl turned to Ryan. "It went well, did it not?" he asked, as calm as if he'd been watching a pie bake at a Kansas summer picnic.

"It was..." Ryan was aware that the scar that seamed down his face from his good eye to the corner of his mouth was flaming with his anger. With the greatest effort he controlled his rage, keeping his voice calm and neutral. "Yeah, it was interesting, Chief."

"There is more."

"What?"

"The bodies will be brought down after the hearts are thrown into the fires. And the priests will build new fires in the empty bodies, where the hearts lived. This will be the final way of giving them to the fire god. He will be pleased and wars will go well. We will be warmed in the cold.''

"And the crops'll grow,'' Mildred said. "Long as the creeks don't rise.''

Itzcoatl looked puzzled. "No. This is not for the growing gods. That will come when we—'' He stopped as though his tongue had been running away with him.

"When?'' Ryan asked.

"When we are ready.''

"Well, forgive me, Chief, but we've had a busy day and we've seen most of your service. Think we'll all go on back to our huts now.''

"It is not over,'' the chief insisted stubbornly. "You stick around.''

"No.''

"There is food after.''

"More rat's brains,'' Jak said.

"Yes, if you want them,'' Itzcoatl replied eagerly. "We thought you did not like them.''

"I don't,'' the teenager replied.

"Then what...?'' The smile disappeared. "Have we done something shitty and offended you, Jak? Was it me? Or another? Give us your command.''

"No. Nobody.''

"They will be punished. The spines of the agave cactus will be pushed into their flesh and then set on fire. Or they will be strangled. Or stoned to dying. Or we will pluck out their eyes.''

"I said not. Look, we're tired and we've had enough. All right?''

"If the gods wish it so.''

## GOLD EAGLE READER SERVICE™: HERE'S HOW IT WORKS

Accepting free books places you under no obligation to buy anything. You may keep the books and gift and return the shipping statement marked "cancel". If you do not cancel, about a month later we will send you four additional novels, and bill you just $14.80*— that's a saving of 12% off the cover price for all four books! And there's no extra charge for shipping! You may cancel anytime, but if you choose to continue, then every other month we'll send you four more books, which you may either purchase at our great low price...or return at our expense and cancel your subscription.

*Terms and prices subject to change without notice. Sales tax applicable in N.Y.

# FIND OUT INSTANTLY THE GIFTS YOU GET ABSOLUTELY FREE!

## LUCKY CARNIVAL WHEEL

▼ **SCRATCH-OFF GAME!** ▼

*Scratch off ALL 3 gold areas*

WINNER

LOSER

WINNER

WINNER

LOSER

LUCKY CARNIVAL WHEEL

DETACH AND MAIL CARD TODAY!

*YES!* I have scratched off the 3 Gold Areas above. Please send me all the gifts to which I am entitled. I understand I am under no obligation to purchase any books, as explained on the back and on the opposite page.

164 CIM AWG6
(U-DL-10/95)

NAME

ADDRESS | APT.

CITY | STATE | ZIP

Ryan nodded. "They do, Chief. They surely do. Can you send some of that *atolli* stuff to our huts, along with water? And we'll manage just fine."

"But the lighting of the fires in the bodies is the hottest potato, Ryan."

"No, Chief. Thanks a lot, but I reckon not. Thanks anyway. Some other time."

Ryan turned on his heel and led the others back toward the center of the village and their huts.

# Chapter Nineteen

Ryan awakened early, disturbed by the first fragile tendrils of dawn sunshine peeking through holes in the thatched roof of their hut.

He had slept well, though there'd been a disturbing dream about losing handfuls of jack in a room that was burning. Everywhere he looked for the money would burst into flames, scorching his fingers, making him jump back to safety.

He and Krysty had made slow, gentle love during the night, bringing each other to a shuddering climax with the skill of long practice.

Now she lay by him, hair spread across the woven blanket like living fire.

Outside, he could hear the sounds of a community rising to meet the day.

Women pounded grain and readied the mixture to make the breakfast tortillas. A dog barked sharply, once, and somewhere in the village a baby was crying. Fires had been lit, and lazy coils of smoke drifted through the beaded doorway of the hut.

The acrid smell of the smoke and the cooking of meat brought back the jarring memory of the ritual sacrifices the previous evening.

Everyone in their party had been quiet, shaken by the savage, brutish violence of the ceremony, and nobody had felt like staying up late.

Now it was time to rise and face another day in the jungle. Ryan lay still, flat on his back, wondering whether they should leave and make their way back to the gateway and jump out, return to Deathlands.

Despite the savagery of the killings, Ryan's sense of morality pressed him to try to do something for Itzcoatl's tribe, caught between a rock and a very hard place.

Between their warlike Jaguar neighbors and the slavers away to the north.

"I think we could help."

Krysty had spoken without opening her emerald eyes, without giving the least warning that she had awakened.

"Reading my mind again, lover?" Ryan said, grinning sideways at her.

"Not exactly. Last thing we talked about last night." She touched him gently on the chest. "Last thing but one that we talked about. So I realized you were lying awake and I figured it was a fair bet you were still puzzling over whether we should go and jump back to Deathlands or stay. I think we should stay a couple more days and see what we can do."

He nodded slowly. "Guess so."

FISH STEW WITH TORTILLAS followed by fruit started the day for everyone.

Itzcoatl, two priests, Rain Flower and a dozen older men joined the outlanders for breakfast.

"You feel better this morning, Jak?" the chief asked.

"Yeah."

"You are not used to the way we pay our gods?"

"No."

"You did not like it?"

"Not much," the albino teenager admitted, helping himself to a second helping of the stew, ladling it into his wooden bowl. "No, not much."

"It is our way," one of the priests said. Some blood remained in his hair from the previous evening's ceremony, though he'd obviously made an effort to try to clean it.

"Saying that doesn't make it right," Doc pronounced. "Every religion in the damned world thinks it's the one that's got it right. None of them has. You haven't. To butcher those three helpless, drugged men was murder in any language. And trying to gift wrap it in mumbo jumbo and ancient ritual... Well, truth is, it makes me sick to the pit of my stomach, Chief. And that's the fact of it."

Itzcoatl looked at him for a dozen heartbeats. "There is a word for going against the gods."

"Blasphemy?" Doc suggested, while everyone else remained silent.

"I think that is it. In our people there are many bad things. Murder is bad. To force a woman to love is bad. Stealing is bad. Witching is very bad. Blasphemy is a bad thing. A very bad thing. You could feel the noose tighten about your throat if you speak things against the gods."

There were warriors standing behind each of the Anglos, something that was already making Ryan uncomfortable. At their chief's words, the men had tensed as though they were readying themselves for violence.

Ryan decided that it was time to make things clear.

He stood in a single easy movement, drawing the SIG-Sauer, cocking it and pointing it at Itzcoatl's head at point-blank range. "Best you know what's going down," he said.

"If I die, then your blood will flow upon mine," the chief said calmly.

"This is one of the most powerful blasters in the world," Ryan replied. "I pull the trigger and you get a 9 mm full-metal-jacket round through the side of your head. Hole going in'll be about as big as that girl's little finger." He pointed with his free hand at Rain Flower. "Bullet going out would take half your skull and most all of your brain, Chief, and put it in the grass. All I'm saying is, don't try and threaten us and don't push us. Because we don't like it."

"I see that." His voice remained steady, his dark eyes locked to Ryan's face.

"I've seen more blood than any of you. Blood doesn't bother me. Death doesn't frighten me, Chief. He's been riding at my shoulder since I was two years old. Understand this?"

"Yes. Are you going from us?"

"Not yet. We talked it over and we'll give you some help against the Jaguar people. Mebbe against the slavers if the bones fall right for us."

Itzcoatl slowly reached up a hand and gently pushed away the muzzle of the gun. "We mean you no evil. Not to any of you. We want very much that you remain to help us. That you all help us. This is why you are the waited ones. The ones we have heard of in our stories."

"I WANT TO TAKE another look at the old base," Ryan said. "If there were grens and those chemicals, mebbe there was something else we missed. Never took a good look around the far side, behind that main building."

"Can I come, Dad?"

"Possibly."

Both Jak and J.B. were suffering from mild stomach upsets.

"I don't fancy walking around the jungle this morning," the Armorer stated. "Don't like the idea of diving into the bushes and trying to find some big soft leaves."

"Nor me." Jak was sweating with the bug, lying on his back on the floor, massaging his stomach.

"They all right, Mildred?" Ryan asked.

"I think so." She hesitated a moment. "Don't guess it's cholera or typhoid of any of those tropical nasties. Much more likely to be a touch of good old Montezuma's revenge."

"Never heard of that one," Ryan said. "That a predark sickness?"

The woman laughed, showing her fine strong teeth. "Just a fancy name for the shits, Ryan. They drink plenty of water, they should be fine." She paused again. "Unless, of course, the thing's already in the water. Still, it'll stop them from dehydrating. That's the main thing. Think it might be better if I hang around the village for today. Keep an eye on them. Just in case. I reckon it'll soon be over."

"I'll come with you, lover," Krysty said. "Like to walk off those bad memories from last night."

"I'll stay behind, as well." Doc looked a little tired, his skin pallid.

"You got the bug, Doc?" Mildred asked.

"I believe not, thank you. And if I have, then I might take the liberty of treating myself."

"Three of us, then," Ryan said. "No need to take any food. Only be gone a couple of hours."

Dean had stood and clapped his hands excitedly, then the delighted expression vanished from his face, like a carnival mask being ripped away.

"What's wrong?" Jak asked, sensitive to the changing moods of the others.

"Nothing. Come on, Dad, let's . . . go."

The boy's cheeks were suddenly the color of water-sodden parchment.

"I'm . . ." Dean's dark eyes showed sudden horror. His whole body tensed, and he pressed his thighs together. "Gotta go, Dad. Get off without me. See you later."

And he was gone, hobbling down the steps of the hut, leaving the wood-beaded curtain swinging and whispering behind him. Ryan watched his son as he made a desperate stumbling dash toward the outhouses.

"Sure he'll be all right, Mildred?"

"Sure."

"Not some disease that's going to—"

She held up a hand. "I told you, Ryan. You and Krysty get going right now."

"And remember about keeping a weather eye open for any bushes with suitable large, soft leaves," Doc said, cackling.


IT WAS A BEAUTIFUL MORNING.

"That dreadful humidity that was so overpowering near the redoubt seems much better down here by the lake," Krysty said. "Lovely summer day. Reminds me of the best of times when I was a girl back in Harmony ville."

"Be nice to go back and visit there sometime." Ryan stretched, looking at the jungle around them. The stepped, four-sided pyramid still loomed against the bright green of the trees, a doleful reminder of the previous night.

Krysty nodded, hooking her left arm through his right, striding out, hair flowing free across her broad shoulders.

"Think the others are going to be all right?" he asked. "Felt sorry for Dean, taken short like that."

She smiled at him. "Mildred isn't worried, so I'm not worried. They'll be fine. Nice to have the forest to ourselves. Just the two of us."

"It is."

The sun was a little way up on the eastern sector of the flawless blue sky. A flock of green-and-yellow parrots flew noisily into the trees at their approach, and one of the diminutive pigs that seemed to inhabit

that part of the jungle darted across the trail a few
yards ahead of them.

They passed a clump of enormously tall lilies, with
bright orange petals and a scent that filled the shimmering air. Butterflies danced among the bushes, in
every shade of the rainbow, and hummingbirds floated
in the air, long beaks dipping into the pools of nectar.

"Paradise," Krysty said. "Shouldn't say that. I
know I've said it before, and it always seems to get
drenched in blood the next moment."

Ryan stopped in midstride and pulled Krysty against
him, kissing her first on the side of the neck, then on
the cheek, finally on the mouth, the tip of his tongue
probing between her parted lips.

She responded and for several seconds they clung to
each other until they separated, breathless.

Krysty ran her fingers down his cheek. "Need a
shave, lover."

"That put you off?"

"No. What's that lovely old song that we heard in
that frontier gaudy? Fastwood Bar? Tall blond woman
at a beat-up piano. It had a line about taking me into
the tall grass and letting me do my stuff. Something
like that."

"Why not?"

They walked a yard off the trail, pushing through a
shrub with a dense mass of brilliant red flowers that
released a scent of fresh apples.

"Think this is safe, lover?" Krysty asked as she sat
in a pool of rich green grass.

"You mean are you going to get pregnant?"

She laughed, sliding her pants down to her ankles. "You know what I mean."

"I don't hear anything, except the normal noises around here." He was sitting by her, unbuckling the SIG-Sauer P-226 and placing it close to hand. "Reckon the time to worry is when you suddenly don't hear those noises. Mean something's coming that's double-bad news."

Krysty reached and held his swelling erection in her strong fingers. "Only thing coming's this and it's triple good, lover," she whispered.

Ryan rolled over in the grass, kissing her, his tongue pushing again at her warm lips, his arms around her, feeling an overwhelming need for her body.

Their lovemaking was slow and gentle, both taking their time, exploring each other's familiar bodies, smiling into each other's eyes.

"Soon," she whispered.

"Wait, wait, wait..."

He could feel the muscles inside gripping him, beginning to flutter as she neared her own climax. Ryan was slightly slower than her as she came, but his own orgasm was powerful, making him arch his back, unable to restrain the moan of pleasure.

There was a long stillness between them, lying side by side in the crushed grass, the warmth of the sun fierce on their exposed bodies.

Something moved through the bushes behind them and Ryan pulled up his pants, reaching for the butt of the automatic. Krysty followed his lead, standing and buckling her belt.

"What is it, lover?"

"Doesn't sound anything too big, but it's going fast away from the east."

"Best get on and take a look at the base."

Ryan sniffed. "Yeah. If it hadn't been for you and your excessive demands we could've been there a good half hour ago."

She raised the middle finger of her right hand with exquisite delicacy and timing. "Below contempt is what you are," she said, answering the smile that played on Ryan's lips, her green eyes dancing with amusement. "Just get real, Ryan."

THE CRATER left by the explosion of the grens was a ragged circle of scorched earth and torn grass beside the frag-shattered remnants of the defensive pillbox. Ryan peered into the hole, fifteen feet across and five or six feet deep, looking at the layer of scummy mud at its bottom.

"Lucky," he said.

Krysty was at his side. "If it hadn't been one of the slow timers, they'd have been picking bits of us out of the top of the trees. Look like someone had emptied a butcher's shop all over the jungle. Yeah, we were lucky."

They walked through the base, paying particular attention to the part of the complex where Dean had discovered the old armament. But there was nothing there, just rotting shelves and worm-eaten closets filled with rusting and burst tins, all of them without labels.

Overhead they heard the sound of a large flock of birds, flying low and fast from the east. Krysty wiped away layers of grime and looked out of a splintered window but was too slow to make them out properly.

"Think they were herons or something like that. Long legs and big wings."

There was a smaller section farther back, past the store that held the containers of chemicals. A corroded shortwave radio was set on a tilting desk, with a corpse seated at it, slumped forward, earphones on his head over the earless skull. One bony hand was reaching for the controls.

Ryan pointed wordlessly at the small-caliber bullet hole through the back of the head and the splinters of dark brown bone that were scattered all over the desk.

"Took him from behind," Krysty said. "Probably calling for help."

Ryan moved across the room, the heels of his combat boots crunching among the shards of dusty broken glass that covered the floor.

"There's that big tank I saw from yesterday," he said. "Could be gasoline."

"No use to the natives. Bet there's not a wag within five hundred miles of here."

"Still..."

The tank was twenty feet long, cylindrical on top, twelve feet in circumference. It had once been painted a rich deep orange, but nearly a century of tropical humidity had reduced it to a watery yellow, the black-stenciled letter-and-number code now almost totally illegible.

Ryan and Krysty made their silent way out of the military catacomb, into the bright sunlight again. They paused, drinking in the fresh warm air, after the strange dank chill of the concrete buildings.

"Look." Krysty's word was hardly a whisper.

A magnificent jaguar, its glossy coat as black as midnight, stepped out of the wall of green on the eastern flank of the base, where the razor wire had fallen into total decay. Its great head turned and looked at the two human invaders of its domain, its golden eyes blank and unfathomable.

"What a fabulous animal," Ryan breathed, hand on the butt of the SIG-Sauer. "See why the natives worship it, can't you? Walking death."

"Looks uneasy, lover."

The jaguar kept looking over its shoulder, behind it, as though it were being pursued. The tip of its long tail was brushing back and forth over a carpet of dead leaves, and its sharp ears were pricked.

"Slavers," Ryan said.

"Something bothering it," Krysty agreed.

A crowd of gibbering monkeys appeared, swinging through the highest branches, chattering angrily at the jaguar and the man and woman below them.

But in moments they were gone, moving westward.

After a few seconds the big predator followed them, padding silently off and disappearing into the striped darkness of the forest.

Ryan shook his head. "Something going on," he said. "Seems to be rattling the whole forest. Could be slavers, I guess. Keep on double red."

He walked over to the yellow tank, squatting by a round handle, trying to turn it and failing.

"Want a hand, lover?"

"Yeah. Rusted shut for a hundred years. Get both hands on it and give it your best shot."

"Want me to use the Gaia power?"

"No!" His eyes burned into her.

"All right, all right."

"You know what it does to you, using that power. This isn't the time or the place."

"Fine." Krysty held up both hands. "You want to do this yourself, Ryan?"

He stepped back, banging a fist hard on the side of the tank, which resounded with a sullen clanging noise. "Full of something, isn't it?"

"Gasoline?"

He stopped and braced himself against the handle again. The muscles knotted in his forearms, chest and shoulders as he put all of his strength into it.

"Moving," he grunted.

"Hold it." Krysty knelt and put a finger under the faucet where a thin trickle of oily liquid was seeping out. She touched it to her nose. "Yeah. Gas all right. Shame we don't have the wags to use it."

Ryan tightened the handle again, wiping sweat from his forehead. "Predark gasoline's worth more than its weight in jack back in Deathlands," he said. "Modern rough-processed stuff's nothing like as good. Doesn't compare."

"Think the slavers might have wags, lover?"

"I somehow doubt it. Terrain like this, the highways must be long gone and overgrown."

"Guess so."

"Trader would've loved finding this. Times he said that only himself and Gert Wolfram and the mutie they called the Magus were ever any good at finding the old gas.''

Krysty looked around, her head back, closing her eyes, almost as though she were tasting the air.

Ryan caught the movement, and his hand went to the butt of the blaster.

''Trouble?'' he asked.

''Yeah. Trouble.''

# Chapter Twenty

"The jaguar. Monkeys. Birds." Ryan punched his right fist into his left hand. "All of them moving west. All of them moving away from something."

"What?"

"Fire?"

"No smoke. Wind's coming at us from that direction. If it was a big fire, we'd smell it."

"Anyway, this isn't like the barrancas of the Southwest. Dust dry, ready for a spark to fire the tinder. This is all so wet, I doubt you could start a decent blaze, even with all the gasoline in this tank."

"So, what? Muties?" Krysty asked.

"Mebbe. Slavers? Wrong direction. Wrong direction for the Jaguar people, as well."

Krysty shook her head. "I'm getting a feeling like I never had before."

"Tell it."

"Like looking into the midnight sky, in the mountains, watching all the stars. Countless diamonds. The eyes of angels, is what Uncle Tyas McCann used to call them, drawing your soul out into infinity, far, far out."

"You mean you feel like stars are falling? Something like a chem storm? Nuke junk from deep space finally dropping back to Earth?"

"No. Not like that, lover. But sort of..." Krysty stamped her foot in frustration. "Gaia! I can't describe it. Can't focus on it. Every time I try, the image kind of slips away through my fingers like limitless grains of sand."

"Volcano? Could be that, Krysty. Some sort of quake or eruption."

"I guess it could. Don't know."

"We'd best take us a look." Ryan started to walk toward the base perimeter and the rotted coils of wire. "If it's coming this way, we could all be in danger."

"It's slow."

"How's that?"

Krysty nodded. "Yeah. I'm sure of that. Whatever it is, it's not coming at a dead run."

"Still need to take a look."

She hesitated. "I don't know if that's such a real good idea, lover."

"Can't not go." It was a simple, flat statement. "You stay here and I'll go."

"No. No, if we go, then we go together."


THERE WAS rapid confirmation that something was badly wrong east of the base.

There was a narrow hunting trail that Ryan started to follow through the towering trees, Krysty right behind him, her own Smith & Wesson double-action 640 Model cocked in her right hand, fingers close to the trigger.

Almost immediately they started to encounter all manner of forest life, all, without a single exception, moving in the opposite direction.

West.

First came the faster animals, beginning with a dozen different kinds of deer, most less than three feet at the shoulder. But a herd of a dozen mutie bucks came thundering along, forcing Ryan and Krysty to jump for cover. These creatures stood ten feet at the shoulder and had horns close to six feet in length.

None of the deer took any notice of the two humans, darting around them, some taking to invisible pathways through the lush vegetation.

There were the tiny pigs, with even tinier piglets, squeaking and squealing on their frightened way.

Twice more they saw jaguars, proud, elegant beasts, princes of the jungle, now reduced to skulking, scampering animals, running west, belly down, tails curled submissively, golden eyes darting nervously from side to side.

A bird like a peacock strutted by, but its long ornamental tail drooped sadly, the brilliant feathers trailing through the mud of the pathway.

More monkeys dived among the overhead vines, several of them stopping and urinating in the direction of Ryan and Krysty, who were able to dodge beneath the umbrellalike leaves.

The ground shook with the thunder of hooves, and Ryan turned and dragged Krysty off the trail again.

It was water buffalo, a herd of twenty or thirty of them, with long, curved horns that ended in vicious spikes. They were charging along, jostling one another, flanks streaked with mud and white salt, red eyes wide open in terror.

Ryan and Krysty pushed through some thorn-bushes, taking shelter behind the wide trunk of a walnut tree, pressing against it as the herd raged by.

"What the dark night's got them going like that?" Ryan said, as he and Krysty emerged once more onto the trampled track, watching the last of the buffalo vanishing toward the west.

OVER THE NEXT HOUR OR SO, it seemed to Ryan that he and Krysty were like salmon, swimming desperately against torrential rapids, battling over slick rocks to try to reach the spawning grounds higher up the river.

Every living thing was moving west, in the opposite direction to them.

Birds flew noisily above them, and snakes slithered quickly through the sun-browned grasses.

And there was still neither sight nor sound of the enemy that had produced this terrifying flight.

"Has to be a fire," Ryan insisted. "Or some hunters with a long line of beaters driving every creature ahead of them."

"Be the biggest hunt I ever saw, lover." She stopped again, using her sleeve to wipe sweat off her forehead. "I can't believe it."

"And if it was a fire..." He sniffed. "What wind there is in this hothouse is blowing in our direction, from the east. Can't catch a hint of any smoke at all." He looked at Krysty. "Can you feel anything more?

We must've walked about eight or ten miles from the village by now."

She shook her head, running fingers through the fiery, sentient hair, which was coiled tightly around her nape. An hour or so earlier and it had been tumbling free across her shoulders.

"Nothing more. And the way my hair feels make it seem like there's some bad trouble somewhere along the line. Could be within the next mile or so."

"But we've heard nothing. What kind of disaster can cause panic at every level, and not be heard or smelled or seen? Fireblast! It beats me."

"Seems like most everything that's running's already gone past us," Krysty said.

"Yeah. Except for him." He pointed up to a long-toed sloth that was still making its leisurely way from branch to branch, about forty feet above them, its hooded, milky eyes watching them disdainfully.

There was also an occasional rustling noise from deep among the undergrowth, showing that some of the smaller forest denizens were scuttling for safety. But they were becoming fewer and farther between.

They passed a deep natural basin in the red stone, bare of vegetation, looking as if it had once been part of a river course but had been bypassed and left high and dry. It was about two hundred feet across and thirty feet deep. The trail wound straight for it and crossed it, between higher walls of the same rippled rocks.

Ryan sat on its edge, flipping stones into the bowl while he sipped from the canteen. Krysty passed the time by climbing one of the cliffs, scrambling her way to the very top and shading her eyes eastward, standing like a hewn statue for several seconds.

"Anything?" he called.

"No," she replied, sounding rather doubtful. "The trees grow thinner and it turns into more like meadowland. But there's a sort of heat haze shimmering over it and I can't make out too much." She laughed as she started to descend again. "Looks like the whole earth's moving."

THEY WERE WELL PAST the middle of the day.

Now the jungle was weakening its hold, as Krysty had seen from the top of the sandstone ridge. The hardwood giants grew smaller and more scattered, with patches of green land showing between them, and they passed by several areas of swamp.

"Quiet here," Ryan said, unconsciously dropping his own voice against the stillness.

"Seems like everything's gone now."

Ryan stopped, shaking his head. "Look, lover. This is becoming triple stupe. There's something out there that can clear a whole bastard jungle of all its life."

"Think we should back off, as well?"

"Mebbe we should."

"We've got blasters."

Ryan smiled grimly. "Depends on what we're up against. I can think of times that a blaster was about as much use as pissing into the wind."

"True." She shuddered suddenly.

"What?"

"Felt like someone was walking over my grave. Real cold chill sort of feeling."

Ryan rubbed the side of his nose, considering their options. "Go back and bring J.B. and the others? Posse of the warriors, as well?"

"If it can frighten jaguars and panic a herd of buffalo, then would we have the firepower?"

"Think it might be something that we've never encountered back home in Deathlands?"

"Possibly, I suppose." Her face had grown pale, her emerald eyes standing out like blazing jewels. "You mean ghosts or zombies or something like that?"

"I don't know, lover. That's what's so bastard difficult. If we knew, we could mebbe fight it. Remember what Trader used to say?"

"About what? Trader had a saying for every event known to man, didn't he?"

"Faced with a real threat, he used to ask what steps we should take."

"And?"

"And he'd answer his own question."

Krysty smiled at him. "Come on, lover. I'll bite. What steps should you take when faced with a real danger?"

"Fucking long ones."

THE PATH HAD DIPPED into a narrow valley, with a small stream running along its bottom, overgrown with clumps of pallid Spanish moss.

They had agreed that they'd continue east for another thirty minutes, then review the situation again. That half hour was almost up.

"Trees are thicker," Krysty observed. "Getting dense, like mangroves."

"And ground cover's longer. These tiny flowered bushes. Flowers like wax models. They're like miniature versions of the good old daisies back home."

"A little." She stooped and picked some, staying crouched as she smelled at them. "Delicious. Like cinnamon cookies, fresh baked."

Krysty held them up toward Ryan, for him to savor their smell, then cried out sharply.

"I've been stung. Gaia!"

It was such an everyday event in the forest, where every kind of flying insect and tick was hostile, that Ryan took no notice of Krysty's cry, taking the flowers from her and raising them to his nose, sniffing in the delicious scent.

"Lovely," he said.

But he realized suddenly that the woman was in some serious distress, hopping around on one foot, tugging her pant leg out of the top of the high Western boot, slapping at her leg. "Little bastard!"

"Wasp?"

"Don't think so. I've— Gaia! Another one's bitten me, Ryan."

He looked down in the grass, trying to see what it could've been, when he felt an electrifying stab of pain just above the top of his own combat boot. Like a bad bee sting, with more burning, more acid.

"Fireblast!"

"Got you, too?"

"Yeah." Then he saw what it was, glimpsing pinpoints of fiery light among the lush blades of grass, flickering movement by his feet.

"It's ants!" Krysty exclaimed, seeing the insects at the same moment.

Both of them felt more bites and moved quickly away, beating at their legs.

"Keep out of the way. Must be a nest," Ryan said. "I'll just take a look over the crest of the hill. See if I can spot what's scared everything out of the area."

He made no connection between the unseen horror and the dozen or so bright red ants that were bustling through the grass, seeming to home in on Krysty and himself.

Not until he ran to the top of the ridge and looked over.

Then he knew.

# Chapter Twenty-One

It was one of the most amazing sights that Ryan had ever seen in his life. He stood on top of the shallow hillside, looking down the other side, where the trees had thinned out even more, leaving what should have been a swath of fresh green grass.

Instead, there was a carpet of shifting, whispering crimson, stretching back down the other side of the slope for more than a quarter mile.

As Ryan stared at it, he felt two more bites. One of them was near the top of his thigh, and he winced at the pain, realizing that the first scouts of the aggressive tidal army of ants were already surrounding him, infiltrating his clothes, seeking bare flesh to attack.

The numbers of insects ahead of him was incalculable.

Millions.

Billions.

The figures didn't matter. Not when you were faced with an unstoppable army of voracious killers.

Ryan glanced down at the ground seeing that there were forty or fifty of the ants darting over his boots, working their way up the legs of his pants.

Cursing under his breath, he knocked most of them off, running quickly back to join Krysty, who was crouched fifty yards away, dividing her attention between the waving grass around her and the cluster of small red lumps on her right leg, all of them just below the knee.

"Get out of here," he panted.

"Just putting some spittle on these bites. Sometimes helps them. Sort of dilutes the acid poison in the bites." She glanced up at him and saw the shock etched deep in his face. "What is it, lover?" Realization dawned on her. "That's what it is! What's freaked out every living thing in the whole jungle. An army of ants!"

"Yeah. Army isn't the right word. Doc's good with words. There's a universe of them out there, covering a square mile or so of ground like a red carpet."

"Coming this way?"

"Right."

She quickly pulled on her dark blue boot and tucked in the leg of her trousers, taking care not to leave any gaps. "These are the recce party?"

"Guess so, lover."

"Can I see the rest?"

"We need to get our bolts greased and hurry back to the village. Warn them."

Krysty stamped her feet on a group of ants that had found her. "Must be vibration that attracts them. I have to go take a quick look, Ryan. For myself."

"Skirt around to the right there." He pointed to the highest point of the ridge.

She ran quickly, moving as lightly as she could, with Ryan at her shoulder.

When they reached the top of the hill they stood together, staring down at the awesome sight. Her hand reached out and took Ryan's, squeezing hard.

"Shit-scared, lover," she whispered. "I swear to the green gods I never saw anything like this."

"Nor me."

"How fast they going?"

Ryan shook his head. "Probably sort of slow. They must be eating all the time, on the march. Only two or three miles a day. But..." He looked behind him. "They've got a straight ace on the line for the village."

"Time for people to move if we warn them."

"Sure." Ryan looked carefully around and spotted a squad of the red ants moving toward them. They didn't seem to be physically mutated, being well under an inch long. But their fierceness and eagerness in hunting was something new. "Sure the people can move, but look way back, where they've been. Stripped the land bare for a half mile across."

"Over there!" Krysty pointed to her right.

The forest wasn't utterly deserted.

A young water buffalo calf had been left behind. Perhaps it was sickly or maybe it had wandered too far when the rest of the herd fled.

Now it came wandering from some dense foliage, with strands of vegetation dangling from its jaws. It seemed totally insensible to its danger.

Ryan drew the SIG-Sauer, intending to fire a shot to warn it away from the advancing column of ants. But he hesitated a moment and then holstered the blaster. "No point," he said. "It's too young to make it far.

And the noise of the bullet might bring them all over us. Silencer doesn't work like it used to.''

The animal was very tottery on its long, skinny legs, staggering like a newborn colt, moving toward the nearest edge of the ants.

''They've sensed it,'' Krysty said, watching as a long arm split off from the broad central column, reaching out like living fire toward the hapless animal.

The buffalo calf stopped suddenly, peering at the ground in front of it with a concentration and surprise that would have been amusing.

If it hadn't been so tragic.

''Got it,'' Ryan said, checking behind them to make sure that none of the marauding insects had yet reached them, not wanting to find themselves isolated up on the crown of the ridge. ''They'll take it now.''

The buffalo gave a short, sharp yelp, tossing its head back, its skinny little tail waving futilely, as though it had been stung by a gadfly. Then it took a number of unsteady steps to the side, head going up and down, its body beginning to twitch. Tiny red streaks appeared up its legs, across its belly and flanks, as the ants climbed onto its body.

''Run,'' Krysty said to the doomed animal.

''Too late.'' Ryan looked behind them again. ''Hey! Little bastards are on to us. Better get moving out of here.''

''Just a second. Why doesn't it . . . ?''

Now the calf was obviously in agony from dozens of the burning bites.

"Come on, lover, quick," Ryan warned, snatching at Krysty's right arm.

"It's down."

The young animal fell, its legs kicking out wildly. It was as if it had fallen into a fast-flowing river of lava. The moment it went down, the ants swarmed all over it, covering its body inches thick, biting and stinging it on the mouth, in the ears and on the eyes, blinding it.

Krysty gasped in horror. "Just like that," she said. "Down and done in half a minute. About as quick as those mutie piranhas we once saw."

They ran from the ridge together, planting their feet hard in the long grass, crushing dozens of the bright red insects beneath their boots, heading toward the village.

They moved at a steady pace, alternating between a slow run and a fast walk, crossing the strange deep bowl of bare rock, continuing west. The trees grew thick about them as they rolled back the long miles.

The sun was well past its zenith when they finally caught sight of the flat-topped pyramid that stood just beyond the outskirts of the village.

"Can we just stop for a couple of minutes?" Krysty panted. "Think I'm getting too old for all this running around. Sweating like a pig."

"Me too. Didn't Doc say that only horses sweated?"

Krysty grinned, wiping her face on her sleeve. "Right. And men perspire. But ladies simply glow."

They both laughed at the saying, so typically peculiar and old-fashioned and Doclike.

Ryan squatted on his haunches. "Notice now some of the noises of the jungle kind of returned as we came closer to the village?"

"Yeah. Seems normal here at the moment. Right. Think I can go on and arrive without looking like a mobile puddle of greasy candle fat."

A SHRILL BLAST on one of the war trumpets greeted their arrival at the main gates of the village. Speaking Eagle was the first person of any authority to see them. He realized from their appearance that something had happened.

"Jaguar people?"

"No," Ryan replied, shaking his head.

"Men with whips?"

"Not them, neither. Look, we don't want to have to tell this story a dozen different times. Just the once. It's triple important." Ryan spoke slowly, as he'd already found that the native didn't have the best grasp of the American language. "Call Itzcoatl and all your main men. I'll get J.B. and the rest of my friends. Meet in the main hut in five minutes from now."

The man nodded slowly, his eyes fixed on Krysty's sweat-sodden shirt. "I tell," he said. "The story you will speak to us is a bad one?"

"Yeah. It's a bad one."

THEY SAT TOGETHER on the bed in their hut, the others gathered around.

The attack of dysentery had vanished as swiftly as it had struck, and everyone was feeling fine.

"What is it, Dad?"

"Slavers?" the Armorer asked.

"Stickies?" Jak queried. "Haven't seen bad muties here. That it?"

"Perhaps some mythical beast from beyond the blasphemous deeps of time and space?" Doc offered.

All the voices overlapped with their questions, and Ryan held up a hand for silence.

"Quiet," he said. "Going out for a council of war with the natives in a couple of minutes. Give you all the details there. But I can tell you quickly what it was. No interruptions. Questions and stuff can come later."

He glanced across at Krysty, who gave them the answer in a single word. "Ants," she said.

Ryan gave them a brief outline. "Not big mutie ants. Ferocious scarlet little boogers." He pulled up his shirt to show the half-dozen scattered bites, now turned into yellow-peaked lumps, each about the size of an old quarter.

"Want me to try and get something for those?" Mildred said. "Probably got herb poultices that'd help."

"No. Let it be for a bit. They sting and burn and itch all at once." Ryan tucked in his shirt again. "Main thing is, there's a whole army of them. Must cover more than a mile, and they're eating their way toward us."

"Eating everything in their way." Krysty told the others about the way the jungle had emptied of life. And of the water buffalo calf and its lonely, agonizing death.

"They're still several miles off and it'll be dark soon. Anyone know if ants travel at night?"

Doc raised a tentative hand. "I might be proved wrong, but I rather doubt it. I imagine that they'll form themselves into a sort of camp. Protect their queen and all the grubs and babies. Must be a whole species on the move. An entire colony burning their way through the forest. I've read tales of this happening. I vote for no travel at night."

Ryan nodded. "My guess, too, Doc. In that case we've got a little time. And we can mebbe use that time to try and come up with a plan." He glanced at his chron. "Five minutes is up. Let's go and talk this over with our hosts."

THE NATIVES WERE APPALLED at the ant army that was moving toward them. As soon as Ryan broke the news to them, they began to chatter and argue, several of them standing and pointing toward the east.

Itzcoatl silenced the panic by clapping his hands and making a strange hissing noise between his teeth. He spoke American for the benefit of Ryan and the others.

"This is very bad. The sacrifices the other night were wasted. Something must have been done wrongly and the gods have become angry with us. All things are pushing against us on all sides. The gods wish to destroy us."

"But first they make you mad," Doc whispered to Dean, looking disappointed at the blank bewilderment on the boy's face.

"We can only run," Itzcoatl said.

He turned to Ryan. "How long before the small biting ones reach us here?"

"Difficult to tell, Chief."

"Are they in trees," Smoking Crest asked, "or in grass?"

"Grass. Sort of swampy kind of region, where the trees are thinned out."

Krysty interrupted him. "Best description is that big red-stone basin. They'll know that."

"The spit bowl of the fire gods," Itzcoatl said. "We know it. Have the ants got that close?"

Ryan looked at the sun, which was low on the horizon. "Answer me a question. These red ants, when they up and move like now, do they march at night?"

Itzcoatl looked around the council table, waiting for some of the older warriors to answer him. Finally a man called White Jaguar spoke.

"Not in dark," he said. "Only in light."

Ryan nodded. "Then the ants should reach that deep bowl in the rock during the middle of the next morning. Mebbe a little sooner."

"They will be in our pockets by the middle of the following day," Itzcoatl said. "Where they move, the ground dies. Where their shadows fall, the flowers crumble. We can do nothing. Nothing stops them."

"Water?" Jak asked.

"Oh, yes, Jak. A fast river will stop them. They will send the scouting ants up and down until they find a fallen tree or a place to cross. We have no river in the way of them."

Everyone sat silently, regarding the disaster that was moving remorselessly toward them.

"Might they just stop?" Mildred asked. "Or change the direction of their march?"

Itzcoatl shrugged. "Only if the gods will it. But their eyes are against us."

Doc suddenly spoke. "You said you'd found a lot of gasoline, Ryan?"

"Sure."

The old man's milky blue eyes were alight with eagerness. My father's friend, Leiningen, was a plantation owner in the jungle. He was faced with an army of ants."

"And?" Ryan prompted.

Doc grinned wolfishly. "And I will tell you how he solved the problem."

# Chapter Twenty-Two

The whole village worked through the night—the warriors, the priests, the elders, the children and the women.

At first it was Itzcoatl who was in charge of the desperate operation, but he simply didn't have the logistical skill for anything on this scale.

He handed over control to Ryan, who ordered, chased, shouted and kicked to get his way, organizing the village into a number of squads, each of them with a specific task, each with a different member of the group of friends to take command of them.

Dean was given a group of the youngest children, whose task was to collect all the available honey from the village's stores and carry it in pots, through the dark jungle, until they reached the chosen spot.

Mildred went around the entire settlement with Rain Flower, gathering any meat from the houses, as well as the offal and rotting carcasses from the village midden, dragging the stinking mass of pork, beef, monkey and dog along the same trail, to the same place as the honey.

Krysty went quickly through the forest with Ryan, establishing a base at the center, where the plan would be carried out. Doc followed at a slower pace, accompanied by several of the older warriors, who were to carry out the finer details of the scheme.

J.B. and Jak took all of the other males, and some of the young women, directly to the ruined army base. Itzcoatl went with them, explaining that the fear of the place as the abode of hostile spirits meant that there might be a reluctance on the part of some of his people to go near the military complex.

Particularly at night.

RYAN WIPED SWEAT from his forehead, straightening and looking toward the east. "Not long," he said.

Already there was the first lightening of the sky, heralding the arrival of the false dawn. In less than an hour it would be full light, and the column of ants would be on the move again, heading directly toward them.

"You sure that this guy Leiningen was telling the truth about what he did?" Krysty said, addressing Doc, who had wandered up to join them, the ferrule of his swordstick rapping on the soft red sandstone.

"I had no reason to doubt him."

Mildred joined them, looking exhausted. "The smell of some of that meat would have made a gator puke," she said. "Still, we've built it. Now we wait and see if they'll come."

Eyes wide with exhaustion, Dean walked unsteadily to join the others on the rim of the basin. He was licking his fingers, and his face was smeared with a layer of honey. "Ready as we'll ever be," he said.

Krysty glanced across to where Itzcoatl was deep in conversation with his council of priests and elders. He was waving his hands vigorously, constantly pointing toward the east. The chief caught Ryan's eye and broke off from the talk, walking slowly to join the Anglos.

"We have done all you said." He glanced toward where Jak Lauren was still at work, shepherding the natives who were responsible for the first wave of gasoline. The albino's hair flamed like a beacon of snowy fire in the predawn gloom. "If the gods labor with us, then we cannot fail."

Doc patted the native on the shoulder. "The plan worked before. And I vow that it will work again. How can it fail with such an effort from everyone?"

"I hope the forest gods are not pissed at us for doing this thing."

Doc laughed, his voice booming into the stillness, attracting glances from everyone around the rim of the basin. "The ants will come this way. They will find the trail of wild honey that has been laid out near where they have stopped for the night. They will follow that and then catch the odor of the rotting meat. As sure as mighty Phoebus Apollo drives his chariot on the heels of the goddess of the moon who's called... I disremember that. It matters not a jot nor a tittle. The ants will be lured here into this basin of rock, where they will discover the feast of a lifetime."

"And they will all come to dine," Itzcoatl said excitedly. "They *will* come."

"Sure," Ryan said. "And then all the carrying of gas across those miles of forest'll be worth it. We pour it down on them and then..." He clicked his fingers.

"Wop bop aloobop, a wop bam *boom!*" Mildred sang, clapping her hands.

"And it'll be over," Ryan said confidently, managing to hide his serious doubt that Doc's plan would really work.

THE THING THAT EVERYONE noticed first about the break of dawn was the stillness. An oppressive silence hung to the tops of the trees behind them like an almost palpable entity, a silence that clung around the waiting men and women like an unwrapped shroud.

"The ants are still there," Ryan said, speaking for the sake of breaking the quiet.

"The whole jungle knows it," Jak said. "Want me to go check them, Ryan?"

"No."

"I could go, Dad."

"No. Everyone's done their part. Now we just keep still and quiet and wait to see if Doc's right."

The old man sniffed. "So, I'm to bring home the bacon. I mean, carry the can, if things turn awry, am I?"

Mildred patted him on the back. "I'll be first to tell you so, Doc. In between running away from here, very fast in the opposite direction."

He shook his head, not joining in the joke. "I can't share your amusement, Dr. Wyeth. I fear that failure here will mean the end for all these poor people."

Ryan pointed a finger at him. "Bullshit, Doc. If you hadn't come up with a plan, they'd have been lost, anyway. It should work. It will work."

ITZCOATL HAD WALKED OVER to join them. He had a
fan with a turquoise handle, made of bird of paradise
feathers, and he used it to swat away the hordes of flies
that had been attracted by the stinking mess of rotten
meat and honey that filled the bottom of the natural
basin of rock.

"The ants do not come."

"Give them time," Ryan said. "We don't know how
close they are to this place. How early they start in the
morning. How far they got last night. We don't know
any of this. We just have to wait and be patient."

"I will send a recce man. He will tell us where the
ants are and if they are come here."

Ryan considered the idea. "Guess so," he said.


IT WAS A MAN in his thirties with the stocky build and
powerful upper body of a wrestler. His body was almost naked, painted with white and yellow stripes that
formed a complicated pattern across his chest.

"His name is Crushing Bull. He is ready for war,"
Itzcoatl said. "This is war."

"He speak American?" J.B. asked.

"No. Very little."

"Then tell him that a dead hero is no use to us. He
has to keep clear and not risk his life. Then run and tell
us what news there is of the ants."

"I will tell him," the chief said. "But that is not the
way of courage of my people. To look and run away
with no prisoners or dead enemy or wounds on your
own body to show how brave you have been. Not our
way."

"Tell him anyway," the Armorer insisted. "We need to know if they're coming and how far away they are, so we can all get real ready."

"I will tell him," Itzcoatl promised.

CRUSHING BULL had been gone for a little over twenty-five minutes. Ryan glanced at his chron. "Could be the ants have gone off on a different route."

Doc shook his head. "Unlikely, friend Cawdor. Once set on their course, very little will divert them."

"I honestly don't know whether I hope that you're right or wrong, Doc."

There had been a quiet buzz of conversation around the basin of red, raw rock, but it ceased at that precise moment, ceased when everyone heard the shouts.

"Coming," Jak said.

Itzcoatl turned to the Anglos and smiled, showing his filed, inlaid teeth. "All is hunky-dory. Crushing Bull runs to us with good news."

Mildred shook her head sadly. "Not all good news, Chief. Man making those shouts is in great pain. Listen. You can hear naked agony in the voice."

The yelling was closer.

Everyone scrambled for a vantage point, shading their eyes against the rising sun, peering toward the edge of the forest that lay to the east.

Krysty was at Ryan's side. "The man's dying," she whispered. "Can feel it."

One of the warriors gave a guttural cry, pointing with his hunting spear.

Then they all saw him.

He was running as if he was under water, arms and legs pumping in slow motion, head thrown back, the tendons in his neck strained like whipcord. His dark body was patterned with patches and streaks of bright red.

"Ants got him," Ryan said.

Crushing Bull was dying in front of them, from hundreds of vicious acid bites, his blood boiling in his veins. He was almost blind, barely able to shout through the swollen lips. His tongue protruded, purpled and bleeding, and blood ran down over the tattoos on his chest.

"He says they are only a half mile behind him," Itzcoatl said, unable to control his own shaking voice. "And they come this way. This way."

Crushing Bull was down, slumping to hands and knees, less than two hundred yards away from them. But nobody made any effort to try to go to the aid of the helpless man.

Ryan unslung the Steyr rifle from his back, working the bolt action and levering a 7.62 mm round into the breech. He brought the walnut stock to his shoulder and drew a bead on Crushing Bull through the laser image enhancer, glanced sideways at Itzcoatl, who nodded once.

Ryan's index finger tightened on the trigger of the powerful rifle. There was the sharp crack of the explosion, and the stock kicked against his shoulder.

At that range, on a motionless target, it wasn't likely that Ryan could miss.

The bullet struck the crouching man between the puffed, bleeding eyes, kicking him over on his back, blood, brains and bone splattering the ground behind him. The native's legs kicked two or three times, then he was still.

"Thank to you," Speaking Eagle said.

"Best way." Ryan ejected the brass cartridge case, which tinkled on the bare rock. One of the youngest of the warriors dived in and snatched it up, tucking it into the small leather pouch around his neck.

"It will be good magic," Itzcoatl said.

"Sure." Ryan looked around. "Well, we got the news. Best all get ready."


FOLLOWING RYAN'S ORDERS, everyone crouched behind the rear wall of the rocky basin, out of sight. He had told them to keep completely still, so that the lead ants didn't pick up on any vibrations through their delicate antennae.

The mess of honey-covered meat did its stuff.

The first outrunners appeared, barely visible, tiny spots of fire among the vivid green of the lush grass, picking their cautious way closer to the rim of the sandstone, followed by dozens more.

Hundreds more.

Thousands.

Then millions.

"By the Three Kennedys!" Doc breathed. "I swear that the sight is just as Mr. Leiningen described it. An army that covered the ground like a living blanket of flame."

"Everyone keep still," Ryan warned.

To Itzcoatl he said, "Pass the word quietly through your people that nobody is to move until I give the word."

"I hear and obey," the chief muttered, sending the message through the waiting natives.

"Think they'll smell the gas?" J.B. asked.

Ryan considered a moment. "Wind's right for us. Blowing light from the east. Carry it away from the ants."

The tantalizing odor was driving the swarming insects frantic. The mass was rolling forward, overwhelming the scouts, flooding into the basin to gorge on the feast that had been planned for them.

"Wait," Ryan said, sensing restlessness among the watchers. "Soon."

For the countless horde to fill the bowl of sandstone took more than an hour. But by then the whole place was a seething mass of tumbling, crazed ants.

"Itzcoatl?"

"Yes?"

"Make sure that your people understand that they must move away before I set the fire. They can watch, but it must be from a safe distance."

"I have told them. They understand this. We are not stupid, you see."

"Sure."

Ryan stared down at the insects, trying to judge the moment. The torrent seemed to have slowed to a stream and the grass was visible behind them, showing that most of the army had already followed the scent of the meat and honey.

"I think now," he said.

Itzcoatl raised his fan and gave a great shout, the sound echoed by cheering from all around the rim of the basin, a noise that didn't seem to have any effect at all on the gorging mass of fire ants.

Every container from the village had been used, gourds and buckets and bowls, all filled to overflowing with the precious predark gasoline from the yellow tank. Now it was tipped over the edge of the steep-sided basin. Splashing down, darkening the color of the rocks, soaking the top layer of the ants.

"Quicker!" Ryan yelled. "Moment they suspect a trap they'll be out of here!"

The air filled with the heavy fumes of gasoline as gallon after gallon poured down the sloping sandstone.

The attack seemed to have thrown the ants into total confusion. They were milling around, most of them still eating on, oblivious to the rising level of the liquid. But a significant number seemed to be grouping together, heads in the air, antennae twitching.

Ryan called across to Jak and Dean, who were on the far side of the basin. "How much more gas?"

"Less than quarter!" the albino shouted. "Going fast. Another two minutes'll do it."

Ryan bit his lip. It would obviously be stupe to expect to chill every one of the ants, but it was vital that they didn't allow a significant portion to escape from the trap. "One minute!" he shouted.

"Some of them are coming this way," Krysty said. "And lots of the others have stopped eating. Drowning in the pool of gas."

"I know." He checked the chron again. "Forty seconds!"

He reached into his jacket pocket for a small pack of self-lights, carefully removing one and holding it ready in his right hand.

"There's thousands of them, heading fast toward the top, Ryan."

Doc's shout decided it. Ryan looked up and waved both hands over his head. "That'll do. Everyone out of the way." He looked at Itzcoatl. "Tell them!"

There was instant chaos. Some of the natives continued to tip containers of gasoline down onto the milling insects. Some threw down empty gourds and bowls, and others simply started to run, giving a frightened ululating cry.

Ryan waited a few moments, until the calmer spirits prevailed and everyone was moved away from the rim. He had kept a plastic can of gas for himself and he now carefully poured some over the edge, watching it wash away the leading group of fire ants that were climbing fast toward the top.

Ryan flicked at the self-light with the corner of his thumbnail.

And nothing happened.

He tried again, this time rewarded by a flicker of pale yellow flame. Ryan dropped it into the pool of gas, seeing it catch, the fire almost invisible at first in the bright morning sunlight. Then it grew stronger, lapping down the trickle of gas toward the bottom of the natural bowl of stone.

There was the thunder of a massive explosion as the lake of gasoline caught in a single moment of devastating power that made the rocks quiver.

The orange flames and the pillar of noxious black smoke rose more than a mile into the air.

# Chapter Twenty-Three

They were back at the village well before noon.

Ryan stopped and turned around, looking eastward at the dark finger of smoke that still pointed toward the sky, ragged at the top where the easterly wind was tugging at it.

"Good one, Doc," he said.

The old man put a finger to his chin and simpered prettily, like a vaudeville soubrette. "Why, thank you, kind sir. Thank you kindly."

"Sure it got all of them, Dad?"

"I told you before that I thought that it wouldn't possibly burn every single ant. But we took out way over ninety percent of them. There haven't been many massacres in history that didn't leave a single survivor.

"The Alamo," J.B. said.

"And the Little Bighorn," Mildred suggested. "Unless you count the horse, Comanche."

THERE WAS A CELEBRATION, though it was short on meat, virtually all of the village's supply having gone to lure the ants to their fiery deaths.

But there was ample fish and great vats filled with *atolli,* the spiced gruel of maize, honey and chili. Everyone sat on the floor at the tables, helping themselves with their fingers. Pitchers of *octli* were passed from hand to hand, drained by the men and refilled by the women.

Mildred and Krysty were the only two females allowed to sit at the table, presumably because of their friendship with the god, Jak Lauren.

"The danger is now gone and the god light shines upon us again," Itzcoatl proclaimed, looking pointedly at the white-haired teenager.

"Don't want to be a spoiler, Chief, but you've got two other dangers." Ryan ticked them off on his fingers. "The Jaguar people and the slavers. Both of them could mean the end of your village, as sure as if it was being overrun by the ants."

The native's smile vanished like ice off a river at the spring greening.

"Those are words with the color of blood," he said. "We must think on them."

"Sure."

The meal was virtually over, several of the natives lying in the dirt, hopelessly drunk. Doc was sitting across from Ryan, and the old man's speech was more than a little slurred. He had embarked on a long and bizarre anecdote about a young friend of his from the long-ago past, someone who had survived quite extraordinary adventures. The last part that Ryan heard was about how the friend had begun to run a paper down at the end of the Florida Keys. But nobody appeared to be listening to the endless story.

Some of the younger warriors had begun to play a strange game in the open square of the village.

They had a sort of ball made from a tightly knotted length of leather cord, and the object of the game was to keep this ball aloft without the use of hands at all, just feet, legs, heads, hips and shoulders.

Ryan watched, fascinated by the skill and cunning displayed by the young men as they threw themselves around the dusty patch of flat ground.

Jak had also been watching.

"I'd like try that, Chief," he said.

Itzcoatl gaped at the idea of a visiting god wishing to demean himself in a childish game. But because Jak was clearly the visiting god of salvation of their legends, he could do nothing but give a nod of permission.

Ryan felt exhausted after the labor of the previous night, when nobody had any sleep. He watched as Jak walked, as light as air, to join the young men of the tribe.

Then he had to have dozed off as he jerked awake to find Krysty nudging him.

"Look, lover."

The whole village seemed to be standing around the square, silently watching Jak.

The teenager had the finest coordination of anyone Ryan had ever seen, making him a lethal opponent at any form of hand-to-hand combat. Now, relaxing after the tension of the night and the dawning, he was dazzlingly unstoppable.

"He's kept that ball going for at least five minutes," Krysty said.

Jak stood on one foot, perfectly balanced, keeping the leather ball in the air with his other foot. Occasionally, for variety, he flicked it onto his left shoulder, then the right, up to his head where he kept it balanced, almost hidden among the sweeping flood of white hair.

As Ryan watched, the teenager kicked the little ball high in the air, diving into a double forward roll and catching it perfectly at the nape of his neck, snapping his head back to send it soaring again, while he did a standing back somersault and caught the ball on his chin, balancing it there.

Everyone gave a great roar of approval, applauding his brilliance, the cheers led by Itzcoatl and the adoring figure of Rain Flower.

Mildred leaned across the table to whisper to the others. "Now nothing's going to convince them that our Jak's not a true-born god."

Krysty smiled at yet another acrobatic leap from the young albino. "Least them worshipping him doesn't seem to have any downside."

"So far," Doc grunted.

AFTER THE MEAL, almost the entire population of the village crashed out, trying to make up for some of the lost sleep. Itzcoatl posted sentries on a rotating basis. Other than them, the settlement was quiet.

Ryan hardly needed to suggest to his companions that they should follow suit. Dean was visibly out on his feet, and Doc had to be helped to his bed.

Two hours later Ryan woke up, feeling pressure on his bladder. He rolled out of the sack and went to piss against the fence behind the hut, returning past his sleeping son to find that Krysty was also awake.

"Wrong time of day for shut-eye, lover," she said. "I can't work out whether it's too early or too late. Definitely one or the other."

"Agreed. Want to come for a walk?"

"Why not?"

It took only a few moments for her to pull on the Western boots. Afternoon sunlight chinked through the beaded curtain, bouncing off the chiseled silver toes.

"Taking the rifle?"

Ryan considered it. "No. Won't go far. Anything comes at you out of the deep forest is likely to be a target for close-range shooting."

They walked out of the hut and across the deserted square. One of the priests, his hair matted with fresh blood, was standing by the gates to the village. "Go with open eyes," he warned. "Everything is danger and death."

"Sure." Ryan half waved at the black-cloaked figure. "We'll take care. Everyone still sleeping?"

The dark eyes narrowed as the man struggled to understand. "Ah, sleeping. Some women in fields, working. Most men sleeping. Sleeping is good."

As they passed through the gates, Krysty touched Ryan on the arm. "There you are," she said. "Story of woman's lot throughout history."

"I don't know nothing about history, lover."

"It's *anything*, lover. Not *nothing*. You don't know *anything* about history. I can't argue with that. Mebbe you need more book learning than you already have."

"That'll be the day, pilgrim. That'll be the day."

THIS TIME THEY WALKED south from the village, along one of the network of wide trails and narrow pathways that mazed all around the area.

The sky was still virtually clear, and the column of smoke had vanished from the eastern horizon. There was a cluster of thunderheads building to the north, away toward the silver mine that used the native slaves.

Ryan and Krysty passed a few of the local women, who giggled, smiled and hid their faces as they walked by. They were carrying reed baskets of fruit and vegetables.

Behind them, there came the distant, muted sound of a shrill trumpet from the village, marking a change of shift for the field-workers.

"If it wasn't for being permanently at war and being threatened by the slavers, these people have a real good life," Krysty said. "Everything they need at hand."

"Including a swarm of red fire ants." Ryan grinned. "But I know what you mean. Only thing I find hard to handle is their human sacrifices."

"That's true. Mebbe it isn't paradise. Mebbe nowhere's paradise."

THEY CAME TO THE tilled fields, about a half mile from the heart of the village, surrounded by a stout fence against animal predators, with its own water supply in a small stream that ran through.

"Maize, beans and sweet potatoes," Krysty said, looking along the neat rows.

The women had stopped at their arrival, looking uncomfortable in the presence of the white friends of their new god. One of them they knew already. Middle-aged with rings in her ears that had stretched the lobes to her shoulders, her name was Ibis, Atototl in their language.

She came toward them, smiling, her lips moving as she rehearsed her little speech.

"Welcome, Ryan and Krysty," she said. "This is where we grow much of our food."

"Isn't there a risk that the Jaguar people might come and steal it?" Krysty asked.

Ibis looked shocked. "No! They are bad but not too bad to steal food. Only..." She struggled for the word she wanted, finding it. "Witchcraft. That is baddest. Throw stones to death for witchcraft. But steal food is also badder."

"But you are at war. You kill each other when you can," Ryan said.

"That is blood for gods. Different." She shook her head pityingly. "You from outside do not see well."

"Guess we don't," Krysty admitted. "Are there other places where you work?"

"That way." She pointed past the stream. "River where some women catching fish."

"Mebbe we'll go take a look," Ryan said.

Ibis looked worried, again fighting for the words she wanted to express herself. "A girl says she had gone after deer with snapped leg. Before sun was past the top of the sky. Her only. Heard noise and hid in bush. Says she saw many men with whips and many Jaguar people. More than fingers. Much more."

"Slavers raiding the Jaguar village?" Ryan asked. "Is she sure about that?"

"Say so. Says she is not seen so much of the...slavers before."

Ryan looked at Krysty. "Mebbe we ought to go check this out. If there's a sudden increase in the number of the slaves that they need for their silver mine, they could easily come calling on our village. Let's check it out."

Krysty nodded, touching the woman on the arm, by her coiled silver bracelets, making her jump. "Best you get all the women together and go back to the village. Tell Itzcoatl what you told us and also tell Jak. The god should know of this. Tell the god, Jak, that we're going to recce."

"To wreck?"

"No. Say we're going to take a look. That's all. You understand?"

"Yes. We go back village and tell of slavers. You will be follow them?"

"Right." Krysty turned to Ryan. "Let's go, lover."

"LOOKS LIKE WE COULD BE in for rain," Krysty said, gesturing toward the thunderheads that were gathering height and strength toward the north.

"Reckon that when it really rains in a jungle like this, you need to keep your mouth closed to stop from drowning. Coming our way, too."

"I can hear the river. Must be where they're doing the fishing. We can warn them and send them all back safe to the village. Away from any slaver patrols."

"Sure."

"Just so long as they understand American."

Ryan grinned as they reached a point in the trail where it zigged and zagged steeply downhill, with flowering bushes on either side, their scent like fresh grapes.

"If they don't, we just point toward the village and look fierce and angry and shout a lot."

Krysty was in the lead, pausing at a sharp bend where they could look down, two or three hundred feet of sheer drop, to a fast-flowing river that ran from a feathery waterfall a little way up the valley. There were a number of brown-skinned women, some of them naked, throwing thin nets into the frothing pools. Even from that height, it was possible to hear the sound of their unrestrained laughter.

"Slavers come by here and they'll think it's Christmas and Thanksgiving all rolled into one," Krysty said. "Sooner they leave for the village, the better."

Ryan nodded. "Paradise in the Bible had its snake, didn't it? This place has all kinds of snakes, and not many of them crawl on the ground."

They were three-quarters of the way down the narrow track before any of the women saw them. At first there was a moment of hysterical panic as they ran in all directions, screaming and dropping their nets, until one of them recognized Krysty's flaming red hair, and the tall man with the patch over his eye, and calm was restored.

Most of them made an effort to grab at their loose cotton dresses, while others, mainly the younger ones, made no effort to hide their nakedness.

Several actually flaunted their bodies, smiling at Ryan and touching their own breasts, allowing their wet fingers to wander down across their bellies to the dark curling hair at the junction of their thighs.

"Think you could strike it lucky here, lover, if you play your cards right," Krysty whispered.

"Sure, sure." He clapped his hands and beckoned for the women to gather around. They did so, some of them so close that their wet bodies left damp patches on his clothes. Some had collected the nets and others had picked up the willow baskets filled with silver-scaled fish.

"Anyone speak good American?"

Several hands went up, and he selected an older woman who'd had the grace to dress herself in her cotton shift. She wore a necklace of tiny pieces of pink quartz and had a single silver stud through her nose.

"There are slavers, men with whips...close. Understand?" She nodded, eyes widening with fear. "You must all go back to the village very quickly."

"Where they?"

"Close."

The woman turned to the others and spoke a string of rapid words, pointing first to the surrounding forest and then back to the village.

"Quickly," Krysty urged.

Most of them were ready to go, but some went around the riverbanks to retrieve clothes, creels and nets.

Ryan was just thinking that it had gone safely and well when the bushes across the river parted and out stalked death.

# Chapter Twenty-Four

"Fireblast!"

Ryan had been deeply worried that the group of slavers might be close, waiting silently in the dense undergrowth to try to ambush them.

The last thing he expected to see was the giant jaguar that he and Krysty had seen earlier.

It was a gigantic brute, with a smooth-as-silk black hide, its long tail moving slowly from side to side as though it had a hungry life of its own. Its jaws were open, the needled fangs dripping saliva. Below the sloping forehead, the golden eyes looked around with an elegant disdain, its whole manner showing that it had seen nothing that caused it any fear.

"Should've brought the Steyr, lover," Krysty whispered at his elbow.

"Think the SIG-Sauer'll be enough blaster. Mebbe we won't need to use..."

The words died in his throat as he saw a dreadful sight. One of the young women, looking to be less than fifteen, had been sleeping in the long grass at the edge of the jungle. Now, the cries of the others had awakened her and she sat up, rubbing her eyes, less than a dozen feet from the huge mutie carnivore.

The jaguar threw its head back and gave a roar of triumph, so loud and menacing that Ryan felt all the short hairs curling at his nape.

The young woman turned around and saw her doom, almost close enough to touch, and gave a weak, pitiful cry for help. Then her eyes rolled up white in their sockets and she collapsed back in the grass in a total faint.

The rest of the women had all fallen to their knees, most with foreheads pressed to the dirt, all chanting in their own tongue.

The jaguar still hadn't moved toward its helpless prey, its tail moving faster, its eyes fixed on Ryan and Krysty. There was the momentary hope that it might have fed recently and might turn around and leave the riverbank.

With infinite slowness, Ryan had half turned, so that his body concealed his right hand as it inched toward the butt of the holstered automatic, feeling the familiar chill of cold metal against his palm.

There was a flash of lightning and a crack of thunder from the north, with its promise of a storm closing in on them. But right now that didn't concern Ryan.

The blaster was clear of the leather, and the jaguar still hadn't made a threatening move toward the unconscious girl. But it had lowered its rear quarters in the unmistakable pose of a cat readying itself to pounce.

The range was at least fifty yards across the foaming river, the rushing water making it much harder to judge the range and angle of the target.

"Make it a good one, lover," Krysty whispered.

Everything happened at once.

Ryan drew the SIG-Sauer and leveled it at the big cat, finger ready on the trigger. The jaguar began its spring at the helpless girl, jaws gaping, claws extended, and the woman with the pink necklace threw herself at Ryan, hitting him just behind the knees, knocking him to the grass. The blaster went off as he fell, the 9 mm round slicing uselessly through the upper branches of a palm tree.

Despite his combat-trained reflexes, Ryan was taken totally by surprise. He rolled onto his left side, lashing out with the barrel, catching the native a cracking blow across her forehead.

She moaned and fell back, blood seeping from a deep cut over her left eye. Ryan pushed her away and came up into a crouch, knowing that he was going to be way too late.

The jaguar had seized the young native woman between neck and shoulder, bringing its massive jaws together in a hideous crunching of bone. Crimson spurted from the wound, soaking her pale yellow cotton dress. She came around for a moment and slapped and kicked at the jaguar, but the mutie beast held her with its implacable power. It shifted its grip higher, teeth snapping on the skull, crushing it with effortless ease.

Krysty had drawn her own blaster, aiming the 5-shot .38 and opening fire. But the Smith & Wesson had only a short two-inch barrel and the bullet went wide.

The noise startled the beast and it began to back away, sliding toward the forest's cover on its haunches, dragging the corpse of its victim effortlessly behind it through the muddied, bloodied grass.

Krysty fired three more shots, spaced and aimed, and at least one of them hit home.

The jaguar howled, snapping at its shoulder, where a tiny red rose bloomed in the soft black fur. For a moment it dropped the corpse, then recovered itself and vanished into the undergrowth, snarling in a high, angry whine.

Ryan was on hands and knees, frozen for a moment, before replacing the SIG-Sauer, unfired, into its holster. He stood and sighed.

"Fuck that," he said. "You got it."

"Only winged it. Range and everything was all against me. Head-on, it wasn't much of a target with the girl's body hanging in the way."

"I know. Did well to wing it."

"Why didn't you shoot?"

"No point." He looked around at the other women, who crouched, heads down, still chanting what he guessed was some kind of a prayer. "I could have saved her if it hadn't been for this bastard stupe." He kicked at the semiconscious woman by his feet. "Get up!" he shouted. "It's gone. Over. Girl's dead!"

In the struggle the woman's necklace had broken, and the tiny shards of pink stone lay in the emerald grass. She opened her eyes. "Did you kill jaguar?"

"No. Thanks to you, it got away."

"I wounded it," Krysty said, busily reloading her own blaster. "But it got away and took the body with it. Probably already eating it." She spit in the dirt, aware that she had lost her usual calm. "Gaia! Why did you do that?"

"Jaguar is god. Any man or woman picked by jaguar is picked by gods. It is..."

"An honor?" Krysty suggested sarcastically.

"Yes. Good word. Honor. Dies for honor. Could not let you shoot jaguar. Like shooted god. Bad luck many days of life. Very bad luck."

"It was bastard bad luck for that poor little girl," Ryan said furiously. For a couple of pieces of small jack he would have drawn the SIG-Sauer and put a bullet through the woman's head. But he managed to control himself.

One by one the rest of the natives rose to their feet and stared out into the forest, then turned to gaze at Ryan, Krysty and their wounded friend, who had finally struggled to her feet and stood wobbling, looking defiantly at the two Anglos. "Any woman will have been happy to die with the jaguar. You from outside do not understand this. Do you?"

Ryan shook his head. "No. Glad to say I don't." There was another vivid flash of pink-purple lightning and a deafening peal of thunder that followed almost simultaneously. He felt the first heavy spots of the storm strike him in the face.

"Are you going after the animal?" Krysty asked. "At least get the child's body back before it's eaten?"

"No. Jaguar eats spirit. All is good. Help in taking fish. Just as Jak will—" She stopped speaking at another, even louder crack of thunder, almost on top of them. "Rain bad. Go back now."

She turned and rejoined the other women, all of them walking toward the village, vanishing within yards as the spots of rain became a torrential downpour.

In less than thirty seconds, Ryan and Krysty were drenched to the skin, as wet as if they'd jumped straight into the middle of the river.

Visibility was down to fifteen feet.

"Got to get shelter!" Ryan shouted, having to clutch at Krysty and put his mouth close to her ear for her to catch what he was saying above the noise of the storm.

"Sure. Rain's hurting my head."

It was true. The raindrops were so large and so incessant that the beating on top of the skull was actually painful.

They took cover under a massive teak tree, pressing themselves against the trunk, keeping out of the worse of the direct rain. The storm seemed to be squatting astride them, the sound and fury filling the forest.

Krysty put her arm around Ryan, for comfort against the raging of the elements. "Bad one!" she yelled, aware that he had nodded, but unable to hear his reply.

It was as vicious a chem storm as they'd known.

The lightning was so constant and blinding that Krysty closed both eyes, Ryan pressing the palm of his hand over his good eye. The air quivered with thunder, and the jungle seemed to be saturated with the bitter taste of ozone.

Twice in five minutes the ground around trembled as a lightning strike brought down one of the giant trees that surrounded them. Every now and again the rain would ease for a moment, enabling the couple to see the alarming rise in the level of the river. It had turned into a frothing, muddy maelstrom that was already lapping at its banks.

"Gonna have to move!"

Krysty could just feel Ryan's words, rather than hear them. She squeezed his hand to show that she had understood him. "To the village?"

"Unless river bursts and we get flash flood. Close to it now." A rumble of thunder surrounded them, so intense that Krysty put her hands to her ears, expecting to find them bleeding. Ryan tried again. "If rain eases again, we'll run for it."

THE RAIN DIDN'T EASE again. If anything it pounded down with renewed vigor. Ryan checked his wrist chron by the constant silver glow of the lightning, finding that the storm had been raging for only twenty-five minutes, a time that seemed an eternity.

Once the river went, it would be highly dangerous to remain where they were, but to have moved from cover earlier during such a cataclysmic tempest would have been suicidal.

Krysty tugged at his hand. "Look!"

The rain swirled around in an impenetrable blanket, but it parted for a moment, showing that the inevitable had happened. The river was no longer confined between the banks and was spreading steadily across the clearing toward them.

It seemed that the heart of the darkness had passed, and the lightning was no longer a constant. There were gaps between the flash and the rumble, showing that the storm was moving away from them.

"Let's go!" Ryan yelled. Still holding on to Krysty's hand, he led the way through the rain, moving quickly in a stooped run, away from the flooding river.

Away from the village.

A NARROW HUNTING TRAIL doglegged up the side of the valley. It was more like a muddy river than a track, and climbing it was slippery and difficult. Orange water streamed down from higher up the hill, filling the deep ruts. Half the time Krysty and Ryan were on hands and knees, battling their way toward the top.

A large fir tree had been struck by lightning and lay across the trail, its bark smoldering.

As Ryan started to climb over, the earth shifted below it and the tree began to slide toward the edge of the trail and a sheer drop to the flooded river.

With an effort he pushed off, his boots slipping on the sodden bark of the tree, managing to roll free before it toppled over the brink and vanished into the veil of rain.

He lay flat on his back in the slimy mud, water pouring over him. Wiping dirt from his eye, he blinked up at Krysty.

"You all right, lover?"

He grinned, his teeth white through the mask of yellowish mud. "If this is all right, then I guess I am."

EVERY TWIST AND TURN of the track seemed to take them farther from the village.

The lightning was now two or three miles away, the thunder subsided to a sullen background roar. But the rain continued to fall with remorseless intent.

Both Ryan and Krysty had a highly developed sense of direction, but the winding, bending track and the overpowering presence of the storm were so distracting that within less than an hour they found themselves lost.

"We're not really lost," Ryan insisted. "I'm fairly sure that I know which way the village is. Just that I'm not at all sure that I know how to get back there."

"I think it's in that direction," Krysty said, pointing a finger into the ceaseless rain, a little to their left and behind them.

"Yeah. About what I figure, also. But there's been no side trail off to the left at all, and we still seem to be climbing higher and higher."

"I reckon we're moving away, lover."

Ryan nodded, water dripping from his dark, curly hair, now matted to his skull. "Best we stop until this stops. Then we should mebbe backtrack. Hope the river's gone down. Get across it and then straight home again."

"What if the river stays high?"

"Then we go upstream until we find a place that we can get across."

She smiled at him. "Thing I love about you, Ryan Cawdor, is your permanent optimism."

He grinned back at her. "Thing I love about you, Krysty Wroth, is the way you pretend to believe my permanent optimism. Really helps."

"Thanks, kind sir."

THE STORM finally moved on, the sheeting rain sinking to a wearisome drizzle that reduced visibility and dripped from the mournful trees.

"Been hours," Ryan said, wiping moisture from the face of his tiny wrist chron and peering at the liquid-crystal display. "Be lucky to get back tonight."

"Think they'll send out a search for us?"

"Doubt it. Not yet. J.B. will have seen the storm and heard about it from the women. He'll guess that we probably got ourselves caught up in it. Had to shelter. Evening's coming on. They won't worry until around the middle of tomorrow."

Krysty sighed. "Could've used a quiet night in bed. Still, least we can probably find somewhere dry to hole up. Climb a tree, lover? I don't fancy staying on the floor with all the wildlife around here."

# Chapter Twenty-Five

Ryan's best guess put dusk roughly a half hour away.

Already the sky was darkening, and to the far west there was only a faint sliver of scarlet from the setting sun. The jungle was growing quiet as all the living creatures readied themselves for the night.

Some to be hunters.

Most to be the hunted.

"Least that bastard rain's finally packed in," Krysty said. "I don't believe that I'll ever get dry. My skin's turned into one large pink prune."

"I'm hungry. Should've picked some fruit while there was still plenty of light."

They'd reached the top of the steep ascent, coming out onto a plateau that ran into a hogback ridge and was now widening slowly toward what they guessed was probably another river, or a tributary of the same flooded river that had barred them from returning directly to the village.

The trail was very narrow, parts of it washed away by the storm, twisting and turning under low branches. About two hundred yards ahead of them was a huge flowering bush that marked the junction of several trails. Beyond that there was a pool, covered with a thick smear of bright green lichen, and the obvious signs of a number of campfires having been lit near to it.

"Looks like folks stop there," Krysty said. "Does that make it a good place or a bad place for us?"

"Cat could jump either way. If we were in Deathlands, then I'd likely say we should risk it and camp for the night. But it isn't and I don't."

"So, where? It's starting to get kind of cool. Some sort of shelter would be good."

He looked around them. "We'll go down to that joining of the trails. There's a biggish tree there with wide branches and good foliage. Don't know what kind of tree it is. Never seen one like it before."

Krysty stretched, rubbing at the small of her back. "Doesn't sound like a goose-feather mattress, lover. Sure you can't find us a good motel?"

"Where the best surprise is no surprise," he replied, quoting the old predark slogan of a motel chain, a saying that Trader had adopted to his own use.

"Right." She flapped a swarm of tiny gnats away from her face. "Be good if these little pissheads could go away and sleep someplace for the night. And leave us alone."

Ryan took her in his arms and kissed her hard on the lips. "It'll be fine," he said, when they finally broke apart from each other. "Just fine."

IN THE TROPICAL FOREST, darkness fell like a dropped cloak. One moment they could see the glitter of a scarlet light off the still surface of the pool. Next moment it was blacker than the inside of a beaver hat.

Ryan had led the way down the slippery track to the flowering bush. It carried enormous clusters of white-and-orange petals that gave off a faint scent of pepper and lilac. The tree that stood at its heart was easy to climb and had broad branches that were just as accommodating as they'd seemed from higher up the trail.

There was no point in climbing to the top.

If anything got into the tree, it was better to know about it straightaway. If it could climb to them, it could easily climb all the way to the trembling, feathery top.

"We both sleeping?" Krysty asked, easing herself out, full length.

Ryan thought about that one. "How do you feel?"

"Bushed."

"Me too. Odds are that we'll wake if anything comes by. Let's both snatch some rest now and then play it as it lays later in the night."

"Fine by me."

Ryan was surprised at how exhausted he felt. It made sense that the sleepless labors of the previous night, against the ant army, would take its toll. But he'd rested some and would have expected to feel sharper.

"Mebbe gettin' old," he muttered to himself as he slipped into his own personal darkness.

There was a confused dream.

He stood in what he figured was a predark railroad terminal, with dozens of platforms, glittering steel rails stretching away into the distance. Ryan knew that he was supposed to be meeting Krysty and Dean there, and they were going to travel to one of the ancient steam locomotives.

But he didn't know which platform, didn't know the destination, didn't even know where he was.

A tall man with silver eyes, in a deep blue uniform dripping with gold braid, was tugging at his sleeve, asking him for his authority to travel.

"Don't have—" he muttered.

He snapped from sleep as Krysty laid her hand softly across his lips. He could feel her hair brushing at his face, the breath from her voice whispering in his ear.

"Think it's slavers, just below us. Lighting a fire. Look, there."

Ryan rolled off his back, making sure he kept his balance in the tree. "See them," he breathed.

They had to have brought dry wood with them, as all the surroundings were still sodden from the rain. But there were bright flames showing in the blackened place on the grass by the perimeter of the pool.

Ryan could just see shadowy figures, moving around the edges of the growing fire, but it was still too dark to make out any of them clearly. All he could be sure of was that they were certainly Anglos and not natives.

The night was still and quiet, and he could make out a babble of words, some of it in the language he guessed was Spanish or Portuguese, most of it in a bastardized American. But it was impossible to hear properly what was being said.

Krysty moved softly through the branches of the tree to crouch at his side.

"I count ten of them," she said.

"If you say so. Your night sight's always been much better than mine."

"Could be eleven."

Ryan patted her on the arm. "Doesn't much matter which. With handblasters we aren't likely to start a firefight. Way too many of them."

"We wait quiet."

"Sure. Might even hear something of where they're going and what they're doing."

The next fifty minutes or so were desperately frustrating, with the delicious scent of cooking meat drifting through the trees. The fire burned brightly enough for Ryan to make out some of the original gang of slavers that they'd encountered. The orange flames danced off the gold teeth of the grossly fat Manuel, and showed the leader of the heavily armed group, reclining and fanning away persistent insects with the ribboned panama hat. Rodrigo Bivar.

"They staying the night, lover?"

"Likely. Can't see any reason for them to move on from here."

"If we sleep, I just hope you don't snore."

"Best we stay awake."

The meal was over, followed by noisy belching and farting from the slavers.

"Think they must've had beans," Krysty breathed. "Glad the wind's blowing the other way."

Now that the eating was done, the general conversation slowed and it became easier to hear the individual voices. Bottles were being passed around the group of ten men, which rapidly had the effect of loosening tongues.

"Too much fuckin' hard work, my old amigo, Rodrigo! *Mucho mucho!*"

"You get plenty jack, Jésus. I don't hear you make the big moan about that."

There was an immediate and muddled chorus of shouting, most of which seemed to favor Bivar, the leader of the slavers. But there was a distinct splinter group supporting the skinny man called Jésus.

"Yeah, we work off our asses and the boss men at the mine take all the silver and we get the sweat."

"We get paid." Bivar stood, swatting at a stubborn mosquito with his hat. "We get paid good. For chasing flies out of their stinking villages. That hard work, brothers? I think not. Big pay and low risks."

"We have lost men. Too many in the last days," complained another member of the gang.

"Sure. There was José by the water trough."

Another voice cut in. "Garcia and Alfredo out there in the fields."

"Miguel outside the old mission, by the ruins of the great house."

Bivar laughed. "Listen, stupes! We just removed a little ugly fat, is all. Lean animal travels fastest and wins all the fuckin' prizes."

"Them Jaguar people didn't give us too much shit," someone shouted from the side of the fire. He was a stout man, with a long mustache, wearing a jacket sewn with pearls.

Bivar spun and pointed at the speaker. "Sure, Diego. Sure, you speak the truth, all right."

Ryan noticed that Bivar was now wearing a Model 66 Smith & Wesson Combat Magnum revolver in a holster at his right hip. It was an enormously powerful .357 revolver capable of blowing a hole in six men in a line.

"But why we have to take out the whole village, *Jefe?* Always we leave a little corn in the fields for next year."

The fat Manuel grinned, flashing his gold tooth in the firelight. "We left the old men and bitches and babies to make the ground rich."

The cruel joke was greeted with a burst of laughter from everyone.

Krysty whispered to Ryan. "They chilled or captured the whole of the Jaguar village?"

"Sounds that way."

"Least Itzcoatl and his people are likely safe from that danger."

Ryan shook his head. "If they picked that particular peach off the tree, then it sounds likely the demand's outstripping the supply."

"Oh, yeah. You reckon they might pick on our village for their next raid?"

Ryan eased his position, stretching out his right leg. "Getting a charley horse," he said.

"But what..."

"Quiet, lover. We'll hear plenty more by listening than by talking."

"The dagos got a big strike up north there," Bivar said, strutting around, hands on hips, preening himself like a dunghill cockerel. "And we help them."

"Why they not look after the slaves better?" asked someone who was sitting with his back to Ryan and Krysty.

"If they do, then they don't need us, you stupe fuck! We want them to keep whipping them natives from dawn to dusk and all the fuckin' way back again."

"Hey, Rodrigo?" Jésus said, standing and reaching for the bottle, taking a great gulp from it.

"What is it?"

Ryan nudged Krysty, but she'd already noticed that the leader of the slavers had casually reached down and thumbed the retaining cord off the hammer of his blaster, on the blind side to the man called Jésus.

"I think you mebbe don't listen to Jésus anymore. You say there's old Jésus and he works pretty good and he do like I say and all that shit. But good old Jésus he got things to say as well as the others."

"Get to the point, my old amigo." The hand was now resting on the butt of the Smith & Wesson Magnum.

But the other man was so far gone with liquor that he didn't seem to hear the question, swaying back and forth, the bottle forgotten in his hand. Singing a snatch of "Adelita," he shaded his eyes and stared out past the ring of fire, into the forest beyond, seeming to look straight at Ryan and Krysty. Both began to draw their blasters, not wanting to make any sudden movement that might give them away.

"I ask you a question, Jésus," Bivar said insistently. "What you look at, loco?"

"Thought saw something in trees." He shook his head. "Mebbe I don't see so good with the smoke in my eyes. Hey, I was saying we did too much work."

"We got more men," Bivar said. "Twenty-five of us now. Take some stopping, amigo. We done them Jaguars. Now we go in a couple days and take out that place where they got the big stone hill place."

"The pyramid," Krysty whispered.

"Yeah. They're going against Itzcoatl next. Poor devils won't stand a chance against twenty-five well-armed men. They've all got either rifles or handblasters. Must've traded for them with the guys who run the silver mine."

"Can we stop them?"

"We can try. First thing we have to do is get out of this place safe."

Around the fire, the confrontation between Rodrigo Bivar and Jésus was continuing. The two men faced each other across the bright flames of the cooking fire.

The drunk slaver was waving the bottle toward his leader. "How come you don't drink like us, *Jefe?* You think you better than us? Stinkin' pride."

"Why don't I drink? Because I don't want to let no thief in my head that's going to rob me of my senses. And the other question? Better than you, Jésus? An aborted blind goat is better than you, amigo."

There was a roar of laughter from the men, drowning out the sound of the empty liquor bottle being smashed to the ground by the furious Jésus.

"You fuck-pig shit-eatin' bastard son of a whore!"

Jésus fumbled at his belt for a large automatic, but his drink-sodden fingers let him down.

Bivar drew and leveled the Smith & Wesson and shot the man through the guts, a finger's width above the belt buckle. Jésus sat down near the edge of the fire, a look of mixed shock and stupidity on his face.

"Hey, you wound me, *Jefe!*"

"Wrong, amigo." Bivar aimed the massive revolver again and put a second .357 round through the man's sagging mouth. "I kill you."

# Chapter Twenty-Six

The fire died down to a pile of gray ashes, sprinkled with tiny eyes of crimson.

The slavers obviously felt secure and didn't bother posting a guard on their camp. Most had fallen asleep, drunk, after throwing the corpse of Jésus into the pool. Bivar had stayed awake longer than any of them, walking around the slumbering embers of their fire, wrapped in a long cloak.

Though Ryan and Krysty were both bone weary, sleep was out of the question for either of them. It was vital that they remain alert, lying still on the wide branches of the sheltering tree, waiting for all of the slavers to drop into sleep. And the chance of escaping.

Finally, his white panama hat gleaming like a beacon in the pale moonlight, Rodrigo Bivar lay down and wrapped himself in a blanket.

Hidden in their tree, Ryan and Krysty didn't make a move for close to a half hour.

"Now?" he finally breathed.

Krysty hesitated. "I can feel him sleeping, lover. But it's real shallow. Most of the others are well away. Have to move like mice over eggshells."

Ryan went first, crawling back along the branch, the SIG-Sauer ready in his right hand, gently lowering himself onto the main trunk of the tree. Climbing cautiously down, he stood in the center of the lilac-and-pepper-scented bush, helping Krysty as she scrambled to join him.

"Still okay?"

She nodded. "Terrible feeling of blood and smiling and pain from the gang," she whispered.

They eased their way through the flowering undergrowth, keeping the bulk of the tree between them and the gang of slavers, edging into the deeper cover of the jungle, then going back along the steep winding trail.

They eventually found themselves at the place where the angry river had burst its banks during the chem storm the previous day. The moonlight showed them the flattened grass, glistening with slimy mud and water. But the river itself had slunk back into its course like a whipped cur, opening the way for them to return quickly and safely to the village.

"Nobody following us?" Ryan asked, pausing by the side of the fast-flowing stream.

"No. Nobody."

THE CHALLENGE CAME in the guttural clicking tongue of the village folk.

"It's Ryan and Krysty, coming back with some big news. Let us in."

There was a long pause. Ryan's keen hearing caught the sound of a high-pitched whistle and the pattering of naked feet. He could just make out the head and shoulders of one of the guards above the fence, joined by another man.

"It is Smoking Crest here. Are you the spirits of the ones gone before?"

"No. We're the ones who got caught in the storm and the flash flood and now we're back and we're cold and wet and hungry. All right?"

One of the heavy gates began to open, stopping when there was a gap of only a couple of feet. The voice of the native, Smoking Crest, came from the darkness.

"There are two of you. One Eye and Red Hair."

"Yeah. Can we come in, or are you going to keep us out here until bastard dawn?"

"The women came from the rain. Said the jaguar had taken a bride."

Ryan was losing his temper. "Fireblast! We know all this. It wasn't a bride. The animal fucking chilled her. And we know something even more important."

"The men with whips have destroyed the village of Jaguar people."

Ryan was taken by surprise. "Well, yeah."

"We have heard this."

"How?"

"Hunters."

"Your people?"

The native appeared in the gap, beckoning to them. "Yes. Before rain, there was smoke from fire from flames. Hunters went and saw it. Some dead. Old and very little."

Ryan nodded. "We'd best speak to Itzcoatl and the main men of the ville here. We saw the slavers."

"Saw them?"

Ryan walked into the village, Krysty at his heels. Dawn was coming, and he realized that he'd gone almost three days and two nights with virtually no sleep.

"The others up?" Krysty asked.

The native shook his head, taking a half step back, away from the red-haired woman. "No."

She tapped Ryan on the arm. "No good, lover," she said. "I have to crash for a couple of hours."

"Right. Me too."

He turned to the native. "We are very, very tired. We will sleep for three hours." After seeing the blank look on the man's face, he added, "Until after full sunrise."

"Yes. Do you wish food?"

"That'd be good. Some tortillas and fish and some fresh water to drink."

"It will be doing for you."

"Thanks. Oh, and when they wake, can you tell our friends we're back safe."

"Yes."

He walked through the quiet village, past the remains of the cooking fires from the previous night, into their hut, going to check that Dean was all right.

The boy was fast asleep, an embroidered blanket crumpled around his knees. Ryan gently tugged it up to his son's shoulders, stooping over and kissing him gently on the forehead.

"Good night," he whispered.

Dean smiled in his sleep, half rolling over, sighing to himself.

IT SEEMED AS IF fifteen seconds had raced by from the moment Ryan's head hit the bed until the moment when Dean was shaking him by the shoulder.

"Come on, Dad."

"What?" For a nanosecond Ryan felt his fist clench and his muscles begin to operate, ready to strike out at the face that was leaning over him.

"It's me, Dad."

"I know that."

"Only you looked sort of scary for a minute there. Like I was king of the stickies and you..."

Ryan swung his legs over the side of the bed, seeing Krysty was already pulling on her Western boots, running her fingers through her tangled hair.

"Yeah, sorry, son," he said. "Just that my sleep banks are a bit low."

The boy nodded. "We were worried when you two didn't come back after all that rain."

Ryan tightened the laces on his combat boots, blinking owlishly at the plate of cold tortillas and fish stew that stood congealed by the bed. "Never touched the food," he said.

"Nor me, lover. Not when the magic lady of the sand came galloping by us."

"Instant shut-eye."

"Sure was."

They smiled at each other, both standing at the same moment. Cool, clear light came filtering through the beaded curtain across the front doorway of the hut.

"Everyone else up?" Ryan asked.

At that instant the curtain rattled and Doc walked in, flourishing the ebony swordstick. "Here I am, my dear, dear friends. The famous Burlington Bertie, who rises sharply at ten-thirty. Burlington Bertie from... Where was it? From Bow. Beau Brummell? Surely not." He shook his head. "I lost my train of thought there, perhaps propelled by a switch of the points into a deserted siding. Anyway, the word out on the highways and byways of this charming ville is that we are all up and waiting to hear your stories. Positively agog for it."

"Be right there, Doc," Krysty said.

The bead curtain parted and in came Itzcoatl, his face and body smeared with jagged lightning patterns in vivid vermilion clay. Two of the older warriors accompanied him, both wearing unstrung bows across their shoulders.

"We know that slavers have raided the village of the Jaguar people. Terminated them. Totally fucked them from the eyes of the earth."

Ryan nodded. "That's what we heard. Seems likely that they'll be coming for you real soon."

"When?"

"Who knows?" Ryan shrugged. "We were lucky to hear as much as we did. Seems the mines are busy and they need slaves. More and more, quicker and quicker."

The chief nodded slowly. "If the Jaguar people could do nothing to save themselves, then we got no hope."

"Bullshit!"

"You think that we can be saved? We have talked about it and we can see one chance."

"What's that?" Ryan asked.

"We can run. Drive the animals and take our small... What is name of things we have?"

"Possessions?" Krysty suggested.

Itzcoatl smiled at her. "That is the word. We take our possessions and run far into the jungle. Run so far and so fast that slavers leave us alone. Then we build a new village and hope gods find us."

Ryan sighed. "I'm not sure that you can find a place where the slavers won't track you down."

Itzcoatl's smile slipped away. "Not?"

Ryan shook his head. "Not."

"How not?"

"You have good trackers?"

"Of course. The trackers from this village, aided by the gods, are the best in all the valleys and mountains."

"Sure. Could they follow a wounded deer through the deep forest?"

Itzcoatl grinned and threw out his chest proudly. "Yes, many times, yes. Even the most crawling baby could do such a thing with eyes closed."

"Then don't you think the slavers could follow the trail of a hundred men and women and children and dogs and cattle and pigs and all their possessions?"

The chief considered that for a long time. "Running not good?"

"I think a man who runs for a day simply keeps himself breathing for another day. He holds off death for a while. Not escapes it."

Doc nodded. "There is the tale told of the man in... let us say in the ville of old Boston, who was walking through the marketplace when he was horrified to see the figure of Death, who looked startled to see him. Knowing this was a dreadful omen of his own demise, he immediately went home, packed his possessions and ran as fast as he could. Many hundreds of miles to another city where he felt he would be safe. The new town was called Baltimore. And there he walked in the streets, feeling safe. When, to his horror, Death came for him. And Death looked very surprised, explaining that he had been taken aback seeing my friend in Boston the day before. Because his appointment was for today, in Baltimore.''

Itzcoatl had followed the story with rapt attention, nodding and grinning broadly at the ending. ''I understand it, Doc. A man can not escape his own fate.''

''That's it, my dear fellow. That's it, absolutely spot on, Chief.''

Outside, the drums had begun their rhythmic beating, interrupted by a blaring trumpet.

''The food is prepared and we can talk,'' Itzcoatl said. ''Do you have any plan for us, Ryan?''

''Wait and see. Food first and then we can talk. Right now I could eat a water buffalo, horns and all.''

THERE WAS VERY LITTLE fresh meat, as the village hadn't recovered from using it all to combat the ants. But there were earthenware platters of tortillas, and plenty of fish with some sliced duck and a haunch of venison, slain the previous afternoon by a group of hunters.

''You want *octli?*'' asked one of the oldest of the warriors, sitting cross-legged across from Ryan, offering him the thick, milky drink from a white glazed jug.

"No, thanks. Need to keep a triple-clear head for the next few days."

He realized that there was a sudden silence, and that everyone around the low table was looking in his direction, waiting for him to speak.

He took another bite from a duck leg, chewing slowly to give himself a little time, finishing it and taking a sip of water.

"Right," he said.

# Chapter Twenty-Seven

"What was it called?"

J.B. pushed back the fedora and scratched his forehead. "Damned if I can remember, Millie."

"But you are still completely confident about the exact quantities that constitute the thermite mixture, are you not, John Barrymore?"

"Sure I am, Doc," J.B. said, adding after a significant pause, "Least, I'm *nearly* completely confident."

"We running risk being blown up?" Jak asked, looking around to make sure that an escape route was open toward the safety of the forest.

The Armorer acted as if he hadn't heard the question. "I remember the book was real excellent and it was by some predark writer called Abbey."

"Science book?" Krysty asked.

"No. Kind of history about some good folks trying to stop the big companies from destroying the land. I found it in a ruined mall in the Shens. No cover on it. Couldn't decide if it was fact or fiction."

"Which is which?" Dean asked.

"Fact means it's true and fiction means it's made up," Mildred replied.

J.B. straightened, dusting his hands, looking down at the small metal cylinder that was half-buried in the damp earth in the clearing on the edge of the village. "There. Two-thirds mixture and one-third igniter."

"What's in it?" Ryan asked. "All stuff that you found in the old base?"

Doc beamed. "But of course." He ticked off the items on his long, bony fingers. "Forty pounds of iron oxide flakes. Like rust. Couple of pounds of powdered magnesium. Ten pounds of barium peroxide. Thirty pounds or so of powdered aluminum."

"And the mix?" Krysty asked.

"I vow that it could not be any simpler, my dear Krysty. Three parts of the iron with two parts of the aluminum equals thermite. It's as simple as that."

"What's the other stuff for?" Dean was staring, fascinated, at the narrow tube of metal as though he expected it to explode at any moment.

"Igniter," J.B. replied. "One part magnesium goes with four parts of the barium powder."

"Five hundred degrees centigrade," Doc said slowly, his hands folded in front of him as though he were reciting a part of the Athanasian Creed.

A twist of fuse stuck out the top, and J.B. knelt again, holding a pack of self-lights in his hand. "Ready or not," he said. "Here we go."

Everyone backed away, keeping about thirty yards between themselves and the small thermite bomb. Beyond them was a hesitant circle of watching natives, led by the tall figure of Itzcoatl, wearing his ceremonial green robe, and most of his senior councillors.

The self-light flared, its tiny red-and-gold flame almost invisible in the strong morning sunlight. A wisp of smoke came curling from the top of the fuse, and J.B. ran, crouching, to join the others.

"How long?" Ryan asked.

"Ten seconds," the Armorer replied. "Off goes the igniter and then the thermite itself."

The white serpent of powder smoke grew stronger for a moment, and everyone started to duck, when it went out. Went out and stayed out.

There was an audible hissing sound, then silence.

"That it?" Jak said.

J.B. bit his lip in annoyance. "Yeah, Jak. Looks like that's it."

"Know what went wrong, John?" Mildred asked.

"I have a feeling that . . . I'm not sure. Don't want to make myself look a fool a second time."

"Back to the drawing board," Doc added.

Ryan slapped J.B. on the back. "Never mind. Leave it a while now. Plenty for us all to do in the village to get ready to receive our guests."

THAT HAD BEEN at the center of Ryan's plan.

"They'll expect to more or less take us by surprise," Ryan had said at the breakfast meeting. "Probably won't know we're here. Probably won't worry even if they know we're here. Just look to come in like always."

"But they might suspect we could stage an early deterrent strike," J.B. said.

"One thing they won't expect is for us to try and trap them here. Actually here in the village, the honey

pot they think they're walking in to raid." Ryan
pointed slowly around the table. "We'll turn this place
into a fortress. Not to keep them out. To let them in
and keep them in." He banged his fist into his palm.
"That's the heart of the plan."

RYAN HAD CALLED his private council of war with his
own six friends.

"Time's the problem. I don't know how long before they make the move against us here."

"Us?" Jak said. "Village is us?"

Ryan nodded. "Sure. For the time being, the village is us. Unless anyone here wants to break and
run?" Nobody spoke. "Fine. So, we are us."

"Main thing is to work fast," J.B. said. "My guess
is that they'll take a couple of days to regroup. Spend
some time in their camp. Clean their blasters. Sharpen
their knives. Rest. And they'll have to make contact
with their own masters at the silver mine. Confirm
orders. Yeah, three days."

J.B. WAS IN CHARGE of the conversion of the village
into a sophisticated mantrap. It was vital that everything should look like it always did. Nothing should
arouse the suspicion of the slavers.

Itzcoatl said that in big raids the Anglos generally
came in on horseback, which pleased the Armorer.
"We can hit animals more easily with pits and nets.
Build some internal walls. They don't have to be high
to block off freaked horses. Give shelter for us to do
some shooting."

The actual armory of the natives was disappointing, consisting only of a couple of old Portuguese Savage pistols and three Mauser-Vergueiro rifles, with virtually no ammunition.

J.B. checked them and dismissed them out of hand. "Been neglected for a hundred years. Breeches worn and every part's looser than a sow's tits. Good chance that they'll blow out and take a hand and half the face off anyone using them."

He explained to Itzcoatl that it would be more efficient if everyone used their bows and their blowpipes, used the time to make plenty more arrows."

"And more poison," the chief added.

"Poison?"

Mildred was with J.B. at that moment. "You mean, like curare?" she asked.

Itzcoatl looked puzzled. "I do not know that name," he said. "Never known it. The poison comes from a mix of the blood of a secret plant."

"Sap," Mildred said.

"I do not know that word, too. What bleeds when you cut into this plant. It is fed to a dog. Dog goes…" He pulled out his hands wide like a straight stick.

"Stiff," J.B. suggested.

"Stiff," Itzcoatl agreed. "Dies with eyes open and bloody and jaw wide. We keep body until it has gone rotten. Very quick. Quicker than ordinary dying. Boil body and keep boiled until only little sticky water is left. Use that wiped on points of arrows and darts from blowpipes." He rubbed his hands together, grinning, showing his filed teeth. "Is very good."

Ryan agreed with his old friend's judgment, and the men of the village busied themselves with making dozens more arrows while the priests and older women brewed up vile-smelling caldrons of the poisonous gruel.

And there was endless practicing, as J.B. sought to improve the already impressive marksmanship of the warriors.

The younger men and most of the women were set to digging traps and trenches, stringing up nets across the two main trails into the village, rigging them under Jak's supervision so that they could be pulled by hidden ropes at a moment's notice.

And in his spare time, J.B. worked with Doc on getting the recipe right for the thermite.

The fourth demonstration came toward the evening of the second day since Ryan and Krysty's safe return to the village. Like the other attempts, it was held a short distance from the perimeter fence, on a strip of level ground between lake and forest. Another of the small metal tubes was buried for three-quarters of its length in the dirt, with the curling end of the fuse protruding an inch from its top.

The second and third tries had both been total failures, with nothing more than the wisp of white smoke from the fuse, followed by stillness.

This time, only Ryan and Dean bothered to come and watch, the rest of the friends busy with the work of readying the settlement for the slavers' attack. A couple of the older women had also wandered by, stopping to watch the four mad Anglos at their incomprehensible games.

J.B. scratched the self-light, and the wavering flame was applied to the fuse. He waited until the white smoke told him that the potential bomb was lit, then scampered away to join the others.

"Fingers crossed," Doc muttered. "I am sure that we have the proportions correct this—"

There was a flash of brilliant silvery white light from the metal tube that lasted less than a hundredth of a second, almost blinding the watchers. The two native women both screamed and clung to each other for support.

But after the flash, there was nothing.

"That it?" Dean said, rubbing at his eyes, not bothering to hide his disappointment. "Might scare them slavers for a whole bit of a minute."

J.B. shook his head, walking toward the smoldering patch of scorched grass. "That was just the igniter mixture going. But it didn't set off the thermite."

Doc brushed a fly from the corner of his mouth. "Let us look on the bright side, my friend John. As the great Welsh philosopher, Daffydd ap Thomas, remarked, one must overcome the large defeats and cherish the small victories. We are getting there, John. Oh, yes, we are getting there."

BY DUSK OF THE THIRD DAY, everyone in the village was starting to get restless.

Dean summed it up after they'd eaten supper and gone back to their own huts. "Whole place is antsy, Dad. Getting so they almost want Bivar and his gang to come so they can get it all over with, one way or the other."

Ryan sat on the bed, pulling off his muddied combat boots. The belt with the SIG-Sauer and the panga lay on the floor at his side. Krysty had gone to the lake to wash and cool off after the hard work of the day, leaving the father and son together.

"You think they're frightened, Dean?"

"No. Not scared. They seem to think that having Jak with them means that nothing can go wrong. And all the rest of us, as well. I keep overhearing them talking about the will of the gods and all that shit."

"Not shit to them, son."

"Guess not."

"Thing worries me is the way everyone keeps snatching quick worshiping looks at Jak, when they think nobody's watching them. Bothers me that they still hang on to this belief that Jak's the chosen one that their religion talks about. The god with the pale skin and hair like white fire that'll come and rescue them and make them all right forever and ever."

"Amen," the boy said.

"This business with the slavers could easy go wrong and twist in our hands like a broken knife. I get the feeling that Itzcoatl and his priests are going to want someone to point an accusing finger at."

"And that'll be Jak."

"That'll be Jak and us, son."

RYAN AND KRYSTY MADE LOVE that third night, savoring the exquisite pleasure of each other's body, the silken feel of skin over taut muscle, the mixture of stillness and movement, using hands and fingertips and tongues on each other, relishing the delight of giving delight.

Ryan gasped as he thrust deep into Krysty, his face pressed to her neck, while her arms tightened around him, long nails working patterns across his shoulders.

After they had reached the divine heights of a simultaneous orgasm, they lay quietly in each other's arms.

She kissed him on the cheek. "Very good, lover," she whispered.

"Me too."

"Do you think they'll attack us soon?"

He took a slow breath. "Mebbe tomorrow. Who knows? But we still got tonight."

# Chapter Twenty-Eight

The fourth day opened dull and overcast, with a hint of drizzle in the air.

There was no communal breaking of the night's fast, everyone eating in the shelter of the huts. Ryan asked the four others to join him, Krysty and Dean in their main room, sitting around eating the fresh-baked maize bread, ladling out helpings of the fiery red beans and chili.

"Today?" Jak asked.

Ryan held out his hands. "It wasn't yesterday. Could be tomorrow. Might be today."

"How about sending scouts into the forest? Try and break their trail." J.B. was polishing the dampness from his spectacles as he spoke.

"No." Ryan reached for a mug of water. "Slavers snare them and make them talk, and we're all dead meat."

"Everything's just about as ready as it can be, isn't it?" asked Krysty.

"Yeah. I hope they come soon. Trader used to say that being combat honed only lasted a day or so. Then everyone starts to lose that sharpness."

"The adrenaline edge," Mildred said. "It's true. Like if a big sporting event gets postponed, even for an hour, the competitors start off flat and stale."

"Itzcoatl remarked that he would like some repair work done on the clay wall of that fishing dam, a mile or so north." Doc wiped his mouth, overlooking a smear of chili on his chin. "Said that he could send the younger children and a couple of the older women to keep an eye on them. If there's any sign of trouble, they would melt away into the trees."

Ryan looked at the old man. "You got a daub of food on your chin, Doc."

"Oh, my apologies." He scrubbed away with the sleeve of his antique frock coat. "What about the children and the dam? Itzcoatl was insistent it needed doing after all that torrential rain the other day."

"Don't like it. J.B., what d'you think?"

"Don't much like it, either. Problem is that if we go and guard them, we won't be much good against the whole mess of slavers. They're going to be vulnerable."

Ryan nodded. "Still, it's their village and their dam and their children. I guess we tell him that we aren't happy but leave it down to him."

"I could go with them, Dad."

Ryan considered the idea and nearly allowed his son to go, but finally decided against it.

LATER THAT MORNING Ryan was checking the walls and traps with Doc and Jak, when Itzcoatl joined them. The chief looked concerned, squinting from one of the Anglos to another, finally addressing Jak.

"The two women who took food to the children up at earth wall that holds water have not come back."

"How long?" the albino asked.

Time was a problem. Itzcoatl bit his lip. "Been gone longer than should have been going."

Ryan caught Jak's eye. "Worth a check. Want to go take a look and report back here?"

"Sure. Want come, Doc?"

The old man looked at the sky. It had brightened since the early dawn and the sun had broken through wisps of high cumulus cloud.

"Why not?" he said.

JAK LED THE WAY NORTH, careful not to set too fast a pace. Even so, Doc was struggling as the sun rose higher and the humidity increased.

"Upon my sacred soul, laddie! I have the fear that you might turn around and see a heap of clothing containing a few old bones and a puddle of perspiration."

"Want go village?"

"No," Doc replied, mopping at his streaming forehead with his kerchief. "Never let it be said that a Tanner gave up on anything." He waved his sword-stick angrily at a large hornet that had been threatening his nose. "Aroint thee, vile beastie!"

"Not far now," the teenager said encouragingly.

"You think there might be trouble, Jak?"

"Who knows, Doc."

"QUIET."

Doc took it to be a statement rather than a command. "Indeed it is, dear boy. In my time in Death-lands I have come to learn that such a stillness can oft betoken danger. You think that the slavers might be close by?"

"Might be, Doc. Stay in side of trail and keep tri-ple-red watch."

The sun was close to being directly overhead, and the temperature had risen way above the hundred mark. Doc drew the big Le Mat from its holster and cocked the hammer over the single 18-gauge round.

"Surely they wouldn't have harmed the children, Jak. Would they?"

"Never underestimate potential of butchers to carry out trade."

The trail was narrowing, rising slightly alongside a stream. The earth damn was less than a hundred yards ahead of them, but there was no sound of life up there.

"Look," Jak said, pointing above the topmost branches of the surrounding trees to the black, cir-cling silhouettes moving against the blue sky.

"Vultures." Doc hawked and spit in the long grass. "Disgusting creatures with their lean, pouched necks and bloodshot eyes." He stopped abruptly, realizing what they portended. "Oh, by the Three Kennedys, let them not . . . not all . . ."

As they walked the last few yards, they disturbed more of the disgusting predators, sending them flap-ping heavily away from their fresh feast.

The corpses lay everywhere, scattered like dis-carded toys, arms and legs tangled in heaps. The two old women were at the edge of the trees, naked, legs spread obscenely wide.

"Two younger women brought water not here," Jak said. "Taken them."

"All the slavers?" Doc cleared his throat, speaking in a hushed whisper. "Was it all of them, friend Lauren?"

Jak had been looking at the trampled tracks in the moist clay below the dam. "No, Doc. Three or four. Scouts. Could still be close. Some these wounds still bleeding."

"I see that."

It was a pathetic sight. One or two of the older boys had been gunned down, but most of the rest looked as if they'd been herded together, then had their throats slit like helpless cattle. There were seventeen dead children, all told.

Doc lowered his head. "I was not angry since I came to France until this instant," he muttered.

"What?"

"Nothing, Jak, nothing. The impotent rambling of a helpless and useless old man."

The albino stopped suddenly, head on one side, like a bird. "Listen."

Doc dabbed the tears from his gnarled cheeks and screwed up his eyes as though it might help him to listen better.

The albino had drawn his big satin-finish Colt Python. "Close," he breathed, pointing with the six-inch barrel into the undergrowth to their right.

He began to move, as light as a hunting panther, Doc following him, trying to keep quiet, though his knee joints creaked like rusted hinges.

Even Doc could see that they were following a trail of broken bushes and flattened grass. There was a length of bright dyed material hanging on a snapped twig that he recognized as having been worn by one of the food-bearing women.

Jak held up a hand, stopping with one foot raised, setting it gently to the ground. He beckoned Doc nearer, putting his mouth close to the old man's ear.

"Very close. See big tree, reddish trunk? Yeah? Behind that. We're goin' to take them, Doc. You ready?"

Doc nodded, face set like granite at the prospect of instant revenge for the mindless, brutish massacre.

They both hesitated as they heard an unmistakable sound from ahead of them, a short, agonized cry, followed by the pattering of what could only be blood, then the drowning, gargling noise of a death rattle. And a burst of harsh laughter.

Without a moment's thought, Doc pushed by the teenager, striding around the tree, blaster ready.

There were four slavers, four swarthy white men, with long, greasy hair, all wearing shirts and pants of stained once-white cotton. Two of them were busily pulling up their pants as Doc raged into sight. There was a dead woman from the village lying huddled and naked in the fetal position, her throat opened from ear to ear, blood streaking her thighs.

There was another naked young woman, blood pumping slowly from the severed artery at the side of her neck. Her feet were kicking as though they were tangled in blankets, and her arms were out straight, the fingers clawing at the damp mud, digging long furrows in her dying spasm.

*"Qué?"* one of the men said curiously, his murderous little rat's brain taking time to work out that the appearance of the silver-haired old man holding a cannon of a blaster could be a danger to them.

Doc squeezed the trigger on the Le Mat.

The scattergun charge starred out across the fifteen feet or so that separated him from the group of slavers.

It hit the nearest slaver in the stomach, almost cutting him in two. He staggered backward as his entrails slopped out of the gaping hole in his stomach, tumbling in yellowish coils about his bare feet.

The man tried to scream but it was way too late, and he went soundlessly down into the dark.

Jak's chosen weapons were his beloved throwing knives, honed and balanced to perfection. But this was a time for the .357 Python.

The slim teenager leveled the big handblaster and fired twice, shooting past Doc.

The first bullet hit one of the half-clothed men in the center of the chest, kicking him backward, arms spread, his pants falling to his ankles, tripping him as he went down.

The second round smashed into the shoulder of the third slaver, spinning him. He started to scream, falling into a crouch, trying to hold the wrecked joint together with his other hand.

Doc knew there wasn't time to fiddle with the gold-engraved Le Mat and change the hammer over to the revolver's chamber with its nine rounds of .44s.

He holstered the blaster and drew the slim rapier blade from its ebony hiding place, dropping the cane in the grass as he ran to the fourth man.

The slaver saw his doom upon him and he reached for the stained revolver in his belt. His mouth sagged open in the beginning of a yell of terror.

Doc straightened his right arm and lunged at the slaver's face, aiming for the gaping mouth with its stained teeth like tumbled tombstones. The point found its target with a perfect swordsman's skill.

The Toledo steel drilled through the slaver's tongue, pinning it to the roof of his mouth, then drove back, through the top of the throat, severing the spinal cord beneath the skull, cutting all the neural links between the brain and the body.

Doc twisted his wrist, freeing the rapier, watching with an obsidian stare as the man fell dying at his feet, eyes rolling in their sockets, blood pouring from mouth and nose.

"Touché," he said grimly.

Three were dead or dying and one was wounded.

The man with the shattered shoulder was rolling back and forth, mewing like a kitten, tears flooding down his pock-scarred cheeks.

"Help me, help me...for the love of God, señor..."

"You should not have waged your war against women and children," Doc said, his voice colder than Arctic pack ice. "A fatal mistake."

Jak stood by him, holding the Colt Python at his side. "Done them good, Doc," he said.

"We were too late, my boy." Doc was weeping, soundless tears running off his stubbled chin. "We arrived only to exact vengeance for the dead innocents."

"Better than nothing." The albino looked around the clearing. "Four scouts sent out by Bivar. We got all four. Make the son of a bitch wonder some."

"Please . . . The pain . . ."

"I don't want to bother with the Le Mat, nor do I wish to sully my steel with his foul blood. Would you do me the honor of allowing me the brief loan of your revolver, Master Lauren?"

"Gladly, Doc." He handed the heavy blaster to the old man, who had holstered the Le Mat and sheathed his rapier, having wiped it clean in the grass.

"I tell you things about Rodrigo," the wounded man yelped, kneeling in front of Doc.

"Like what?" Jak asked, gesturing to Doc to hold off with the blaster.

"He going attack village."

"Which village?"

"One with big-point building."

"When?"

The man grinned, showing a single gold tooth, carved to a point, at the front of his mouth. "You mebbe let me go? I don't do nothin'. Men like you and me, we don't fall out over few children and old sluts."

Doc pushed Jak aside. "Men like you and me?" he repeated unbelievingly. "You dare to link your depraved and vile person with us? As you would say . . . adios."

He leveled the big gun and squeezed the trigger, blowing the man's face away into a mask of blood and slick bone. Aiming at the twitching corpse, he put another bullet into the pulped skull, stilling the movement.

"First one did it," Jak said reproachfully.

"Second one felt even better," the old man replied, handing back the Colt Python.

"Might've talked more."

Doc shook his head. "No, Jak. I don't believe so. He would have lied to try to save his worthless skin. And that's all. There is nothing he could have told us that we don't already know. We have merely left the world a slightly cleaner place."

"Now what?"

Doc swung his swordstick in an arc about the place of death. "We go tell the mothers and the fathers that there is some burying to be done."

# Chapter Twenty-Nine

"Had provisions for two days," Jak reported.

"Means that they were scouts on a recce." J.B. looked at Ryan. "Bivar'll expect them back the day after tomorrow. Allow them a day. Then he'll come in."

Ryan counted on his fingers. "He'll probably still be moving toward us during those two days. Means that he'll likely arrive here in a minimum of two days."

"Maximum of three," Jak said.

"Anything else interesting in their saddlebags?" Krysty asked.

Jak pointed to the table in the hut. "That bag blasting powder. Doc says it is."

"I recognized it by the feel and the smell. An uncle of mine had done some prospecting out in the Superstitions in the sixties. Always after that elusive lost seam of the Dutchman." Doc smiled to himself at the two-hundred-year-old memory. "Needless to say, he never found it."

J.B. clapped his hands softly. "Might just be what we need to trigger the thermite, Doc. Done well."

"No. If Jak and I had departed a little earlier and traveled a little quicker—but he was slowed by some tardy cripple—then we might truly have done well and saved more than a dozen young lives from a vicious bloodletting."

The village was in mourning.

When Doc and the white-haired teenager returned with their grim news, Itzcoatl had dispatched a working party of thirty heavily armed men to retrieve the bodies and bring them back to their homes for ceremonial interment.

The companions had kept well out of the way of the massive grief.

Now they were all gathered in Ryan and Krysty's hut, discussing whether the happenings of the day made any difference to their plans, eventually deciding that they didn't.

"IF BIVAR HAD COME BY this afternoon or evening he could have walked right in and taken the whole place without a single hand being raised against him."

Krysty stood in the doorway of the thatched building as the rituals for the dead were still going on. The sun was almost down in the far west, beyond the lake.

Ryan joined her, resting his hand gently on her shoulder. "It's like we've said before, lover. You find a new place and it seems like it could be paradise. Bite into the apple and there's a stinking great worm."

"Best we can do is try and leave something better than we find it. Only thing we've ever been able to do."

THE DRUMS had been pounding a slow, mournful rhythm since the bodies of the women and children had been returned to the village, going on into the hours of darkness, making rest almost impossible, though it hadn't stopped Dean from falling instantly asleep the moment he got into his bed.

"Those damned drums," Ryan said, standing in the doorway, framed in bright moonlight.

"You ever take a good look at them, lover?"

"The drums?"

"Yeah."

"Not really. Why?"

Krysty pulled a face. "Like those robes the priests wear for the rituals."

Ryan turned. "No! You mean that those drums are made from flayed human skin, as well?"

"Right. The horrible thing is that you can see recognizable human parts on them. Nipples and navels. And arms and legs dangle down the sides."

"Fireblast, Krysty! Times in the last few days I've wondered whether we were doing the right thing staying on here to help. Now I'm even less certain than I was."

"But the god Jak is happy to help them against the slavers, isn't he?"

"Guess so. You going to try and sleep?"

"Might be able to set myself into a trance. Way Mother Sonja taught me."

They heard boots on the veranda outside the front door of the hut, followed by a light rap on the wall.

"Who is it?"

"Me," J. B. replied. "You able to get off to sleep with those bitchin' drums?"

"Dean's asleep," Krysty said, "and I'm going to try and ease myself off, as well."

"Doc's snoring like the last of the thunderbirds in our hut," the Armorer said. "Mildred keeps dropping off for a few minutes, then waking again."

"How about Jak?"

J.B. look behind him. "Not sure. Kid went out an hour ago and hasn't reappeared yet. My guess is that he and Rain Flower might have something going together."

"Mebbe he'll settle down here in the ville and have lots of little godlings," Krysty said, grinning.

J.B. shook his head. "Don't see the lad settling down again for a while. Not after the pain of the disaster of last time."

He turned to Ryan. "Good moon out there. Wondered if you fancied a short recce into the forest?"

"Hell, why not? Want to come, Krysty?"

"No thanks, lover. Bed sounds good to me. And they can't keep on drumming all night."

"HAVEN'T BROUGHT ANY of your thermite bombs with you, have you?" Ryan asked, as the two old friends quietly picked their way along the moonlit path toward the north.

"I know that we're on the brink of getting them to work. Mebbe if we top off the igniter with that blasting powder that Jak and Doc brought with them. Could do the trick. Not too much time left for experimenting."

The night was still, with occasional rustling among the undergrowth betraying the movement of the nocturnal denizens of the emerald jungle. The moon was close to full, throwing sharp-edged shadows and turning everything to shades of black, white and silver.

"Like old times," Ryan said as they walked together, one on each side of the trail.

"Been a while since the two of us went off for a recce together," the Armorer agreed. "Seemed times when we did nothing else for Trader."

"Think he made it?"

J.B. turned, his eyes invisible behind the gleaming lenses of his spectacles. "Day I get to spit in his empty eye sockets is the day I accept Trader's gone from us."

"It looked bad, that last glimpse that I had of him on that beach."

"Dark night!" J.B. laughed quietly. "You think that 'bad' is enough to chill Trader?"

Ryan grinned. Since there wasn't likely to be much long-range shooting, he'd left the Steyr back in the hut, despite its Starlite night scope, relying on the SIG-Sauer and the panga to see him through against danger.

J.B. had elected to take the Uzi, carrying it slung over one shoulder, ready for instant use.

They both went for their weapons when a large carnivore that looked oddly like a striped jaguar slunk quickly across the path, only a dozen yards in front of them. But it passed out of sight with only the most cursory, dismissive glance in their direction.

"Must mean there's not too much movement close by," J.B. observed, pausing to look behind them.

"Sure. If the slavers were on the road tonight, the forest would know it before we did."

"Remember that time we were on night recce through the Smokeys?"

Ryan stopped. "Mean the run-in with those inbred sickos that brewed liquor that took the paint off the war wags?"

"No, not them. Ones that used throwing axes."

"Oh, yeah. Take your head clean off your shoulders before you even knew that you'd been hit."

"So they said."

"Yeah, I remember them. You recall that summer patrol in West Texas? We were walking through thick woodland, you and me, on a night just like this."

"We came across an old mill. Wheel was rotted and moss covered, but it still turned in the flow of a fast stream. Made a grinding noise like a wag crushing an old auto."

"There was that family living in the mill, wasn't there? About a dozen of them, and not a single hair on the head of any of them. All bald."

J.B. laughed. "You asked them why, and the old woman said that you didn't see grass growing on a busy highway."

"We both thought she was making a kind of small joke, and we started to smile at her."

"And the shit hit the fan."

Ryan slapped his leg. "Bastard skeeter! Yeah, knives and straight razors and a couple of flintlock pistols appeared out of thin air."

"Time we got out of the place, there was blood dripping through the floorboards onto the dirt."

"We sure been some places and seen some things," Ryan mused. "Guess we've had our share of luck."

"Good and bad."

"Right. You're right, J.B., we've had some of both kinds of luck."

The Armorer wiped sweat off his face with his sleeve. "How about that business with the limping man, the missing brindled dog and the triple-fat woman who swore that she was able to take three—"

He stopped abruptly as Ryan suddenly held up a warning hand. Both of them stepped silently off the trail into the brush, crouching and waiting.

J.B. inched up behind Ryan. "Gone quiet," he whispered. "What did you hear?"

"Didn't hear anything."

"Then...?"

"Smelled smoke. Cooking fire. Just caught the faintest taste of it. Ahead of us. North."

"Must be them."

"Sure."

"Go in closer? Take a look?"

Ryan glanced at the sky, checking where the riding moon was, looking at the gathering bank of cloud moving toward them from the north.

"Got to be slavers."

"Guess so," J.B. replied.

Ryan was simply thinking aloud, using his oldest and closest friend's combat knowledge and wisdom as a sounding board for his own ideas.

"If it's them and it probably is, then they've moved a lot closer to the village. Only two, three hours away. Means they might be coming as early as dawn."

"Sooner," J.B. corrected. "Fires might be dying. Eaten earlier. Ready to move right now. Might even be closing in now."

"So we look."

"Yeah, Ryan. We look."

BIVAR WAS LYING on his back, staring at the star-sprinkled sky, listening to a young half-breed boy singing a melancholy song about a guerrilla fighter running the ridges of his homeland, eventually dying alone and friendless.

Ryan and J.B. had crawled within a dozen yards, taking advantage of thick brush. The slavers were secure in their numbers, not bothering to place any guards on watch. Altogether, Ryan counted thirty-six men around the big fire.

"Could spray a mag from the Uzi and take out eight or ten," the Armorer whispered.

"They likely know the jungle better than us," Ryan objected. "We two get chilled and the village'll fall."

"You're right."

"I'm always right, amigo," the one-eyed man said with a grin. "You should know that by now."

"Hell, I knew it all along."

The ending of the song was marked with a ripple of applause, led by Bivar himself.

"That was real pretty, Juan. I reckon we should be turning in soon, *compadres*." He waved a hand at the rumble of discontent. "Big day tomorrow. Up before dawn and hit the honey nest around first light. Just a few sluts cooking tortillas. Men all snoring like hogs in a dunghill."

Ryan nudged J.B. They'd heard all that they wanted to hear, learning what they wanted to learn.

"Time to go." Ryan jerked his thumb in a southerly direction through the moonlit woods, toward the village.

# Chapter Thirty

Rodrigo Bivar sat a palomino mare, standing in the stirrups, staring all around him. It was a fine morning, though some high clouds gave a warning of the possibility of rain later in the afternoon. The dawn sun was low on the eastern horizon, away to the left.

The flat-topped pyramid was about a hundred yards ahead of the attacking party, the bright morning light showing the ominous black stains that streaked the topmost stones.

Bivar pushed back the brim of his panama hat, wiping sweat from his forehead, checking that all thirty-five of his men were still in a raggedy line behind him.

His head ached from the copious amounts of pulque that he'd downed the night before.

It had been a pleasant enough ride through the opalescent early dawn, enjoying all the sights and sounds of the wakening emerald jungle.

One of his men had shot off a ripple of bullets at a strutting bird of paradise that had emerged across the trail in front of them, spooking half the horses in the column. If Bivar had been able to get hold of his own Combat Magnum, he'd have blown the cretin out of his saddle.

But he was too busy fighting for control of his own horse, which had reared on its hind legs, nearly spilling him onto the trail.

They were now so close to their destination that even the biggest triple stupe among the gang would know better than to fire a blaster and risk giving the natives any warning of their arrival.

Bivar felt real fine, top of the world, ready for anything, despite the small nagging doubt about the disappearance of his scouts.

They were four good men, men he'd trusted with the mission of going on ahead to recce the village. It had bothered Bivar a little, meeting that small group of outlanders. They had the cold-eye look of mercies, hired guns. But two of them had been women, and one was only a young boy. Not the sort of group that would bother with the village or the dirt-poor natives.

"But still . . ." he said aloud.

THE VILLAGE WAS READY.

J.B. had already set up a number of watchers, linked by line of sight, that could wave a message down the line to warn of the arrival of the gang.

Now that message had come, and the whole community was bowstring taut.

Ryan and the Armorer had spent nearly three hours with Itzcoatl and the elders when they returned from their own scouting mission. At the last minute Ryan had asked Jak to come along with them, explaining what he wanted. It turned out to be a good move, as the natives paid the utmost attention to everything that the young albino said.

He'd hammered home the vital importance of holding off any aggression until Ryan gave the signal by opening fire. "Must have them in village. Right in. Anyone shoot too soon and they run. Could be end for everyone."

At Ryan's suggestion the older women and the youngest surviving children left the village before dawn, following almost invisible hunting trails that wound south and east toward a cave hidden behind a waterfall.

The rest of the settlement was hidden in their appointed places, armed with what weapons had been available—almost no blasters, but plenty of arrows and blowpipe darts.

"Will we win?" Itzcoatl asked.

"Winning, losing..." Ryan said. "Just comes down to being caught on the wrong side of the line."


"WE GO IN, *Jefe?*"

Bivar rubbed at the side of his nose, where he'd been bitten by an insect during the night. He turned and called to Manuel, his second-in-command. "Here, amigo."

The fat man heeled his own horse forward to the head of the column, grinning at his chief, the gold teeth glinting in the sunlight. "Something wrong?"

"I keep thinking about the four men we sent out scouting. What happen to them?"

"They got tired and went for some funnin' someplace, I guess. Who fuck knows, *Jefe?*"

"Four of them. No message. No nothing from them. That sort of bothers me."

Manuel looked around. "We just gotta collect a full hand from this village. Is all."

Bivar sighed, wishing that he didn't have the throbbing sick headache pounding away at his temple like the bastard drums that so many villages used.

"What happen to the drums?" he said, feeling his background suspicions rushing headlong forward.

RYAN LOOKED across the deserted open square, checking that there was nothing to arouse any doubts. Bivar had to be used to riding into villages where everyone rushed in panic into hiding. But there was still something wrong.

He turned to J.B. "Those bastard drums!" he exclaimed. "Fireblast!"

The Armorer picked up on him. "Course. Should be beating with the trumpets and all. If Bivar comes in and hears nothing, then we could be going down the tubes."

"I'll tell the chief, right now."

MANUEL LIFTED A HAND to his ear. "Seems like I hear drums pretty good."

"They only just started," Bivar complained. "Seems kind of strange."

"They only beat them and play those trumpets when the day's started."

"Guess so." Bivar lifted his hand, then called out to try to attract the attention of his chattering horde. "Head 'em up! Ride 'em out! Let's go!"

"SEE, RAIN FLOWER," Itzcoatl called, pointing half-way up one of the tallest trees in the vicinity.

The woman stood on a branch as broad as a two-lane blacktop, waving a length of bright orange cloth.

"Here they come," Ryan said.

THE GATES TO THE VILLAGE stood wide open, show-ing a few of the huts and a trio of abandoned cooking fires. But there was no sign of any life.

And the drums had stopped.

Bivar reined in the palomino. "Mebbe we wait and watch. Send in six or seven to look around the place."

Very faintly, but very audibly, someone in the ranks behind him made the clucking sound of a chicken.

He spun, seeing that a number of the men were smirking, while others looked rigidly ahead. "You think I'm scared to go in? Do you? Anyone think that, then he come and tell me." He waited a few seconds, hand on the butt of his pistol. "I think mebbe it's not me that is the chicken. But we don't wait. We go in. Follow me and keep all your eyes open."

He set his spurs into the flank of the horse and led his men through the gates.

"They been doing some work, *Jefe,*" observed one of the slavers a moment later. "Look at them walls."

"Sure. I see them. They been working hard. Shame it's all for fuckin' nothing," Bivar said, laughing.

Now that they were actually inside the village, his doubts had evaporated. The fact that it seemed de-serted didn't worry him at all. There'd be plenty of them in the trees, as easy to trail as a three-legged sow. And once you got a few of the peons, you only had to use the flame or the steel on them to bring the rest out of the forest.

Bivar gestured for his men to form a rough half circle on both sides of him, covering the whole open area of the village. Smoke from one of the fires blew toward him, making the palomino skittish. He cursed it, striking the mare between the ears with his clenched fist.

He hadn't bothered to draw his blaster. Since there was nobody around, there didn't seem very much point.

When he was sure that his men were ready, he called out, "Hey, peasants, you lost your *cojones?* Come out, come out wherever you is."

His voice echoed around the open area.

"I think they all gone, *Jefe.*" Someone giggled, his voice thin and high with nerves.

"I try again." Bivar shouted louder, "Hey, you come out and you don't get hurt! Stay hidden and we get mad."

RYAN LOOKED along the row of huts, catching the anxious eyes of Itzcoatl. He grinned at the native to reassure him, putting his finger to his lips to reassert the need for quiet.

At his side, J.B. was blowing on a length of slow fuse that he and Doc had made, ready to apply it to the first of the line of thermite bombs.

Ryan watched Bivar, who seemed to be losing authority with some of his men. "I give you one more chance!" the slaver yelled. "Then me and my amigos start doing some shooting."

Ryan stood and showed himself, eye raking the group of thirty-six slavers, ready to duck back behind cover at the first sign of a threat.

Bivar leaned forward on his saddle horn, smiling with what seemed genuine amusement. "So, the outlander! I should've known, when my men didn't come back to me. Yeah, I should've fuckin' known."

"They got to be dead," Krysty said, matching the slaver for calm. "And real soon you all get to join them."

J.B. was beside Ryan, and he whispered a warning. "Watch him with that hat. He take it off and likely uses it to mask drawing his blaster."

Ryan nodded almost imperceptibly, concentrating on Bivar. "You got one chance."

"And what's that, amigo?"

"You all get down. Drop the blasters. Strip naked and you'll be walked through the forest for three or four days. Come back and you're dead."

Bivar stood again in the stirrups. "Hear that, brothers? This gringo say we're all trapped. Us, by him."

He turned to Ryan. "But figure you got your friends with you. The women and the little boy. I tell you, amigo, I'm real fuckin' terrified by you."

"You should be," Ryan said. "You got no choice, Bivar. Unless being dead is a good choice."

The men were getting restless, with hands dropping to the butts of their blasters, and Ryan could almost taste the bitterness of anger.

"This goes long enough," Bivar spit. "You think these pissy little walls keep us out? Well, they fuckin' don't, *compadre*. Because we already in."

"The walls weren't built to keep you out, Bivar. They're here to keep you in, so we can cut you all down."

"Like a lot of big oak trees? You hear that one, my friends? This man with no ax is cutting us all down to the ground. We like to see that, huh?"

"Shoot him, *Jefe*," Manuel muttered.

Bivar waved a hand at his lieutenant. "Real soon," he whispered, talking out of the corner of his mouth. "How come he so certain of himself? Where the fuck the others?"

"Don't matter," Manuel insisted. "Just terminate him and it don't matter."

"Yeah."

Bivar took off his elegant panama hat in a generous, sweeping gesture, half bowing toward the lone man, bringing it back across his body.

"Soon," J.B. breathed.

"This run too long. You give me two choices. I give you one choice, my one-eyed friend. Mebbe you like to know what that one choice is?"

"Not particularly," Ryan replied. Though he stood behind the wall, looking calm and relaxed, every muscle of his body was taut and tense.

"I tell you." Now the hat was over Bivar's lap, covering his right hand and the butt of the Smith & Wesson 66. "Bring your people and every one of these shit-suckin' natives out here before I count to ten, or you all die. That's the choice of Rodrigo Bivar. One, two, three, four..."

At the count of four his hand moved quickly under the cover of the panama and emerged with the big blaster, and he started shooting at Ryan.

# Chapter Thirty-One

At the first fraction of a movement from the slavers' leader, Ryan was already in motion, his honed reflexes saving his life yet again.

He hadn't needed the warning from J.B. Anyone who took off his hat when you were facing him down was going to use it as cover or as a distraction.

So eager was he to blast the cool smile off the face of the tall, powerful gringo that he actually blew a hole the size of a .357 round clear through the elegant rim of his ribboned panama.

The bullet went close, striking the top of the wall within inches of where Ryan had been standing, blasting a hole in the adobelike mixture, sending splinters of stone whining through the morning air.

The firefight lasted less than fifteen minutes from that explosive moment.

The first of the defenders to open fire on the slavers was a tall native whose name was Carrying Moon. He had an arrow notched to his long hunting bow and aimed at the leader of the attackers. But Bivar's horse shifted nervously at the sound of its master's shot, and the arrow missed its mark.

However, it buried itself in the neck of the man beyond Bivar. The arrow was loosed with such ferocious force that it entered just above the right shoulder, the barbed point continuing on to protrude several inches through the left side of the slaver's throat.

After that first death, there were so many others.

THE UZI CHATTERED, ripping into men and horses, sending them all down in the trampled dirt in a kicking, screaming maelstrom of blood.

Mildred had appeared at a window of one of the huts, standing in the classic pose of the professional shootist, side on, right arm extended, sighting with both eyes open along the barrel of the Czech ZKR 551 6-shot target revolver. She pumped the Smith & Wesson .38s into the heart of the gang, picking her victims with patient calm, making sure that every shot counted.

Six bullets and six men dead, all taken through the head, skulls exploding in a mist of gray-pink brains and fragments of bone and matted hair.

The other members of the group of friends were all playing their part in the carnage. Krysty stood on the other side of Ryan, with Dean next to her. Doc was on the far end of the line, having fired off the scattergun round of the engraved Le Mat, muttering under his breath as he fiddled about changing the position of the firing hammer. Jak, hair blazing like a distress flare, stood with legs apart, pumping lead into the slavers from his own Colt Python.

And the natives had appeared from their hiding places, using arrows and darts.

It was a perfect ambush.

BIVAR WAS LOST in a turbulence of mindless horror.

All around him men were dying, their horses screaming in fear and falling. Old Pedro had been alongside him, leaning from the saddle and yelling out a question. Then his face had blown up like a watermelon under a jackhammer, and Rodrigo's own head and shoulders had been soaked in a hot, salty brew of blood and brains.

Bullets hissed past him, thudding into flesh, sending blood gouting into the clean air.

He was firing his Smith & Wesson Magnum into the ranks of their attackers, but he had no idea whether any of the rounds actually hit anyone.

An arrow feathered itself in the shoulder of his horse, making it buck and rear, bloody froth around its jaw. Bivar leaned over and snapped the shaft with his left hand, knowing that the barbed tip, probably poisoned, would be working its mischief in the animal's chest.

To his right, there was someone he didn't recognize, his face a mask of flowing crimson, a tiny dart protruding from the socket of his left eye.

Some of the men were trying to control their terrified mounts, seeking a way out of the maze of low walls. But every turn brought them face-to-face with more of the natives, heading them off from the gates, which were closed behind them.

A bullet snatched the panama hat from Bivar's left hand, the ribbon unraveling as it dropped to the bloodied dirt.

Garcia fell when a young woman darted in among the hooves with a sharp gelding knife and sliced through the girth, tipping the saddle and dumping Garcia out the side door.

Despite his own pressing danger, Bivar watched in fascinated horror as one of his oldest *compadres* staggered to his feet, dazed by the tumble, reaching for his revolver, which had been jarred from the holster by the fall.

He was attacked by a half-dozen women, pecking at him with cooking knives and hacking with kindling axes, beating at him, severing fingers as the man began to cry out and wave his hands to try to defend himself.

Then he was down, vanishing in the dirt as the women crowed their triumph.

The last thing that Bivar saw of his friend Garcia, who'd had a fine light tenor voice and knew the names of all of the animals and birds of the forest, were his castrated genitals flourished high in the crimsoned fingers of one of the cackling older women.

RYAN HAD MOVED QUICKLY along the back of the front line of huts, an occasional bullet whistling dangerously close through the reed walls, ripping away a section of the thatch. His SIG-Sauer was cocked in his right hand, and he ran in a crouch, stopping twice to glance out at the battle.

As he'd hoped and planned, it was far more of a massacre than a battle.

The thirty-six slavers had been taken totally by surprise, cribbed into a confined space with no clear areas to turn their horses or work up any momentum against the defenders. The fresh-built walls were just high enough to deter a horse from attempting a jump off a short run, and already two of the newly dug pits had claimed victims.

There was one to his left, and Ryan sidetracked himself to check it. Two old natives were flanking it, so doddery that they could barely notch an arrow to their bows.

A horse lay in the pit, impaled on some of the sharpened stakes that lined its bottom. One of the slavers was standing on top of the dying animal, struggling to reload his blaster. One leg was crooked, with a jagged end of white bone sticking through the torn material of his cotton pants.

Ryan's face slit in a wolfish grin. It looked as if nobody there was going to do any killing. As he watched, one of the old men tried to loose an arrow, but it slipped off the string of the long hunting bow with a dull thunking sound and fell harmlessly into the staked pit.

"Let me," Ryan said, pausing a moment and shooting the slaver through the top of the head. The distorted bullet drove through the cranium, pulping the brain, past the eyes and nose, emerging through the roof of the dying man's mouth, giving him a final transient burning sensation on his tongue as he went down into endless night.

The two ancient natives both laid down their weapons and clapped their gnarled hands, beaming broadly at Ryan, who bowed in return and moved on.

BIVAR SCREAMED IN AGONY, as an arrow pierced his thigh, missing the bone, drilling clean through, pinning him to the palomino.

Ryan emerged around the side of the farthest hut in the line, with only the lake behind him. A half-dozen warriors were supposed to be there, covering any attempt at escape into the water. But the slaughter in the square had lured them from their posts, and the end of the village was completely deserted.

His informed guess was that more than half of the slavers would have bought the farm in the first three or four minutes of the assault, which meant that a part of the plan had worked.

But it didn't mean that the fight was over and won.

As if to confirm that, Ryan spotted three of the slavers, on foot, running toward the lake. He stood in the shadow of one of the huts, and they hadn't yet seen him.

One had a broken stump of an arrow protruding from his upper arm, just above the elbow, dark blood staining his cream shirt. Another had a gaping wound across his thigh, looking like a slash from a machete.

All three carried their blasters, darting toward the miraculous possibility of safety, constantly glancing back over their shoulders.

The men were less than thirty paces away, coming fast, the one with the bleeding leg limping heavily.

Ryan gripped his right wrist with his left hand, aiming at the leader of the escapees, bracing himself against the kick of the powerful automatic.

Without saying a word he opened fire, chest shots, the safest option against moving targets. It didn't matter much whether you were a couple of inches high or low or to either side. High and you took out the throat. Low and you had a gut shot, which was likely to be a killing hit with a 9 mm round fired from the P-226.

Either side of the breastbone and you were still wiping out some of the ribs and probably the lungs, and possibly the heart, as well.

You hit when you missed with a chest shot.

Ryan's first shot was dead center, splintering the sternoclavicular joint apart, shredding the man's lungs with fragments of lead and bone.

The second man, with the wounded arm, was quick, snapping off a shot toward the muzzle-flash in the shadows.

Being quick didn't mean being good.

He missed by a country mile.

Ryan's second bullet wasn't quite as central, straying a tad high. But it was close enough, hitting the slaver through the Adam's apple, snapping his neck as efficiently as a good hangman and blowing out most of the throat.

The third man tried to turn, but his injured leg betrayed him and he went over in the slippery dirt, falling awkwardly, dropping his blaster.

Ryan was just able to check himself from squeezing the trigger on the SIG-Sauer a third time, wasting a round over the top of the tumbling man.

"Save me, Jesus!" the slaver screamed, on hands and knees, peering toward Ryan, who put the third full-metal-jacket round through his forehead, drilling a neat hole from front to back. The impact lifted a flap of skull into the air, anchored by the scalp and the long, greasy hair, so that it flopped back down again, like a crooked toupee. The man rolled soundlessly onto his side in the trodden mud and didn't move again.

"Guess Jesus wasn't listening to you, friend," Ryan said.

DESPITE THE WOUND, Bivar was rallying his men for a desperate charge for safety.

"Time for the thermite, Doc!" J.B. yelled.

"Hope this is the time it works," shouted Mildred, who was kneeling behind a wall, calmly reloading the target revolver.

Doc thumbed the self-light and applied it to one end of the fuse, while J.B. did the same to the second length of cord. Both men watched as they fizzled and spluttered into life, snaking fast through the dust and smoke.

The old man held up crossed fingers.

Ryan stayed where he was, watching the last stages of the firefight.

Bivar had gathered the survivors around him, ready for a last stand, waving his blaster in the air, taking potshots at any of the villagers he could see.

Unnoticed by the slavers, but spotted by Ryan, two threads of white smoke fizzed through the trodden, bloodied dirt, worming their way toward the group of frightened horsemen and their desperate leader.

The blasting powder triggered the igniter mix of barium and magnesium. There was a brilliant flash of light from the first bomb, brighter than the noon sun, followed by another and another, as each mine in the row went off.

Ryan waited.

The dazzling display completed the spooking of the horses. Without exception they kicked and reared, crying out like gelded men, high and thin. Virtually all of the riders were unseated, including Bivar, though many struggled to hang on to the reins of their terrified mounts.

But the bombs were only halfway done.

The igniter mixture finally caught the main charge of aluminum and iron—the thermite mixture.

It began to burn at more than five hundred degrees centigrade, hot enough to set fire to the earth itself.

The line of fires, bubbling like the heart of Hell, completed the rout of the slavers.

The horses ran, blind with fear, knocking into walls, one or two dragging their riders with them, leaving them scattered around the village like broken marionettes, bloody, bruised and fractured.

A fresh volley of bullets, arrows and tiny poisoned darts flooded in against the dozen or so survivors, taking out half of them.

Most were on their knees, holding up their hands in surrender, wreathed in the blinding smoke from the thermite bombs. Itzcoatl shouted above the bedlam, ordering a cease-fire.

Ryan holstered his SIG-Sauer and began to pick his way through the dead and dying men and animals, eventually deciding to walk back along the rear of the huts, close to the perimeter fence.

Where he was attacked by Rodrigo Bivar.

# Chapter Thirty-Two

Bivar lunged out of the beaded back door of one of the smaller huts, holding his Smith & Wesson 66 in his right hand. He was limping heavily from his wound, clothes blackened with thermite smoke, crimson spotting his shirt and face, matting his long black hair. His eyes were so wide and blood veined that it looked as if they were about to burst from their sockets, and his mouth sagged open.

"Bastard!" he croaked, firing twice at Ryan.

The range was less than fifteen feet, but the slaver was off-balance, in the last stages of desperate exhaustion. Both bullets missed.

Ryan was in the act of drawing his own handblaster when the slaver chief threw his empty Combat Magnum at him, two pounds of blued steel.

Ironically his aim was much better with the empty blaster than with the full one, and it struck Ryan just below the elbow on the right arm.

The pain was so sharp that Ryan's first guess was that one of the bones was broken, and his fingers opened in a neural spasm, dropping his blaster at his feet.

Bivar was quick, faster than a man on the ragged edge of defeat had any right to be.

Even before Ryan's SIG-Sauer hit the dirt, he was closing in, holding a black-hilted switchblade in his right hand, lunging toward the one-eyed man's belly.

Ryan backed away, reaching clumsily with his left hand for the taped hilt of the panga, drawing it just in time to parry a second attack.

"You kill my men, you fuck bastard," the swarthy man panted, his lips peeled back off his teeth in a lupine grin. "I get over fence and way into trees. And leave you with your guts spilled!"

Ryan didn't waste time, energy or concentration on responding. One of the truest things Trader ever said was that if you came to talk, then you talked. But if you came to fight, then you got on with it.

The slim-bladed knife danced out again, as fast as a desert rattler, and Ryan was just able to parry it with the clumsier eighteen-inch blade of the heavy cleaver. He had trained himself to shoot and fight left-handed, but he was only too aware of his limitations.

He was conscious of the background noise of the firefight subsiding around the front of the huts, but his universe had narrowed to a couple of yards of worn grass and the silver point of Bivar's knife.

The slaver was breathing hard, his breath stinking of wild onions, fogging the air between them. But his eyes were like a cornered shithouse rat, fiery and crazed.

He kept up a stream of foul-mouthed abuse at Ryan, calling his paternity and his manhood into question.

But the one-eyed warrior ignored him. He flexed the fingers on his numb right hand, aware that a little feeling was creeping back and he was recovering movement, which meant a bad bruise, but no break. It was difficult using the weighty panga left-handed against the switchblade, like dueling against a rapier with a cutlass.

Bivar was skillful with his blade, holding it low in front of him, point upward, in the classic knife man's pose, ready for the thrust to the groin and lower stomach, the most difficult of all to parry.

Ryan was being forced backward, step by step, toward the fence, yielding ground to the dazzling attack, barely holding off the needled point. He desperately tried to bring some life back to his injured right arm, but it was still feeling painful, his reactions sluggish.

Bivar sensed victory the way a feral animal sensed weakness in an opponent, and he smiled.

"Near fuckin' end, amigo."

Sweat ran down Ryan's face, seeping behind the patch, stinging the raw, empty socket. He tried to blink it away, suddenly spotting an extraordinary thing.

A toddler had been hiding in the hut, and he now came waddling out, plump and naked, holding a barbed hunting arrow, taller than him, in both hands, like a spear.

He stood staring in bewilderment at the two strange men as they feinted and lunged, sparks struck from the clashing blades. For a moment his face puckered as if he were about to start to cry, then he seemed to change his mind and padded silently toward the man nearer to him.

Bivar.

Intent on his prey, the chief of the slavers never noticed the child.

Until the youngster drove the arrow into his buttocks.

Bivar yelped in pain, half turning, slashing toward the toddler's face, missing him by at least eighteen inches.

The quarter second of stolen time was all that Ryan needed. He hefted the panga in a round-arm swing, aiming at the exposed side of Bivar's neck. At the last splinter of time the slaver started to turn back, dropping his chin, raising his shoulder in a vain attempt at protection.

The broad blade, whetted to a whisper, hacked into the angle of the jaw, cutting through tendons and muscle.

Bivar tried to open his mouth to yelp his agony, but the force of the blow had almost severed the lower jaw, leaving it dangling loose, blood pouring down the man's neck. His tongue flopped grotesquely forward, like some hapless reptile.

As he tried to turn away and run, the lower jaw swung down, hanging across the front of the neck, held only by the threads of gristle on the right side.

It was a truly macabre sight, and Ryan held off for a moment, fascinated by the triple-bizarre injury, unlike anything he'd seen before.

The little boy chortled and dropped the arrow, waving his chubby fists in the air.

Bivar dropped to his knees, using both hands to try to hold the appalling wound together, his dark eyes turning toward Ryan. His voice was muffled, the words garbled by the choking flood of blood that filled his mouth. But with an effort, Ryan could just make out what the desperate man was trying to say.

"Don't let them burn me. Anything... Not the fires and the black swords. You chill me."

Ryan had no affection for the dark-hearted villain, but the torture and sacrifice that he'd witnessed had made him feel sick to his stomach.

The little boy lost his balance and sat down with a thump in the blood-splattered grass.

Ryan stepped in closer to Bivar, still wary, sheathing the blood-slick panga. He picked up the SIG-Sauer with his right hand, pressed the muzzle of the blaster against the kneeling man's nape and squeezed the trigger.

The shock jolted his bruised arm, making him wince at the sudden pain.

Bivar pitched down in the dirt, feet kicking as though he were trying to swim through thick water. After a few seconds the corpse was still and the fight was over.

And the baby started to cry.

RYAN AND HIS COMPANIONS chose not to go to the ceremonial sacrifice of the seven surviving slavers at sunset, preferring to remain quietly in their huts, checking their weapons and recovering from the adrenaline rush of the battle.

"You glad you chilled Bivar, lover?"

Ryan nodded unhesitatingly. "Sure. I'm the number-one man when it comes to scraping scum off the planet. But I don't go for this ritual murder."

The slaughter of the slavers had left only three dead in the village, one of them Rain Flower, and a handful more with minor injuries. Itzcoatl and his elders had been euphoric about the spectacular victory over their hated enemy and almost came to blows with one another as they traded tales of their own individual deeds of bravery.

The chief had come to the hut of the outlander visitors, insisting on shaking hands with each of them, except for Jak, to whom he bowed.

"The old stories were right on the fucking ball," he said. "Since you have all come here to us we have enjoyed great good fortunes."

"How about dead children?" Jak said.

Itzcoatl shrugged. "The wheel turns, we say. The Jaguar folk are gone, and the threat of the whip people vanished like smoke in a strong wind."

He asked them all to come with him to witness and join in the ceremony with the heaped fires and the razored swords of obsidian.

When they refused, Itzcoatl hadn't pressed the matter, though he insisted on their attendance at the banquet that would follow the butchery—or the "gifts to the gods," as he called it.

AFTER THE KILLINGS, the villagers readied themselves for a night of feasting.

Itzcoatl, the priests and the older warriors all wore their richly embroidered finery and their feathered masks. And they brought out the most sacred relic of the village, which was normally kept hidden in a secret place known only to the elder priest and the chief.

It was a full-size human skull carved from a single huge chunk of veined crystal. Chips of jade were set into the center of the eyes, and threads of pure gold outlined the teeth.

"That's one of the most beautiful things I ever saw," Mildred said.

"It is the skull of the white warrior with no shadow, as we call it. Only at the most special occasions is it shown. In a couple of days it is one of our biggest and best holy days, and it will be shown again, the day when Tlazolteotl became pregnant from swallowing the chip of rare white jade and then bore the sun king of our people."

The table was laid with bowls and platters of fish, duck, vegetables and fresh bread.

Beakers of *octli* rested at every place, along with individual dishes of the fiery honeyed maize, *atolli*.

Ryan and the others had agreed that they would leave the village at dawn the next day. Their help was no longer needed, and they had nothing more to offer to the natives.

But they were also united in not telling Itzcoatl until the last moment.

IT HAD BEEN a great celebratory occasion.

The women servers were dressed in yellow to show their link to the food. Some of the priests wore their suits of flayed skin, dyed black, hair matted with fresh

blood, smelling of wood smoke and roasted flesh from
the sacrifices. Some of the warriors had skulls daubed
on their chests in blue, revealing that they had been
active in the ritual slaying of the wounded slaver prisoners. Itzcoatl himself wore vivid green.

During the magnificent banquet, the village leader
three times raised the suggestion that Jak might stay
behind with them and continue to give them the un-
doubted benefits of his own godhead, offering anything to him by way of food or drink or female
company.

And three times the albino teenager rejected him,
politely but firmly.

The chief had taken the disappointment well, nodding silently. He walked out beyond the fires and returned with an embossed silver tray that held a dozen
shining goblets. He placed it on the table.

Mildred leaned across and read the words engraved
on the rim of the tray. "'From the halls of Montezuma to the shores of Tripoli,'" she read. "Must
have once belonged to a Marine unit, back in the predark."

Each of the goblets held the inscription: The Fighting Fortieth.

"This is the finest *octli* we have," Itzcoatl said.
"Brewed and aged in casks of oak for many years.
There is no drink better, and now we should take it and
all honor dead. And swear to the future. For us all."

He handed the nearest goblet on the tray to Jak,
then passed them to everyone at his table, taking the
last one for himself.

"To Coatlicue, mother of all gods." He raised the drink in front of him, holding the silver cup firmly in both hands, gesturing for everyone to follow his example. "And to the ever-young warrior, Huitziopochtli, who others have sometimes called the Hummingbird Wizard. They reside with all the gods of our people on the Mountain of the Star, Citlaltépetl. All united in the place of the gods, Teotihuacán."

The mouth-filling, sonorous names in the ancient language rolled from his tongue, swelling into the stillness of the smoky heart of the village.

"Now all drink!"

Everyone lifted the goblets and drank. At a warning glance from his father, Dean took only a small sip of the burning liquid, managing to stifle a choking cough. The others drained the *octli*, savoring its fire and its sweetness.

Ryan noticed that Itzcoatl and the jade-eyed masks of the other elders had all turned to watch Jak, as though they were linked by a single cord.

There was an inexplicable tension for those few seconds, which eased the moment the white-haired teenager laid his goblet back on the table, empty.

IT WAS AN HOUR or so shy of midnight.

Ryan had suggested that they should rise before dawn and get ready to leave, telling Itzcoatl and the other natives of their intentions only at the last moment.

"Less argument then. So, we could all do with an early night. Any problems?"

Jak slowly put up his hand. "Don't feel good, Ryan. Gut burns. Sweating. Feel sick. Throat tight. Head aches as bad as I can remember."

Mildred stood to go over to him. "Could be something you ate or drank, Jak."

The voice from the doorway interrupted her, stopping her in midstride. "You are right on the ball, lady," Itzcoatl said. "The god is sick because of something he had drinking."

"How's that?" Ryan said, feeling the beginning of anger, overlaid with something that might have been fear. "What do you mean?"

"I mean that Jak has been given poison. By me. In a half day the god will be dead."

# Chapter Thirty-Three

"Poisoned?"

Itzcoatl nodded. He had discarded the ornamental mask, but still wore the long ceremonial robes that rustled as he moved a couple of steps away, toward the door.

Ryan swallowed hard, finding that the SIG-Sauer was already in his hand, the barrel pointing at the head of the retreating native. "You poisoned Jak? Just him? None of the rest of us?"

"Do any of you feel sick?" The dark eyes moved from face to face around the hut. "No? That's your best fortune. We wish no harm to any of you."

Jak moved a few faltering strides toward the chief, resting his hands on the low bed. "Why chill me? Tell me! I'm your fuckin' god!"

"That is the answer. Gods speak in questions and answers. We have given you a secret poison for that reasoning. You are our god. We can't let you go from us."

"How does it help having a dead god?" Ryan asked, waving the blaster at J.B., who'd been circling behind the native. "What's the point?"

Itzcoatl shook his head. "No, Ryan. You don't understand me and my words."

"So tell me." His control was cracking. "Or I swear I'll put your brains all over the wall."

"Be gentle, Ryan. This is our plan. We can cure Jak. We have the herbs to do it. There is time for this."

Ryan sighed. "Oh, I get it. Yeah, clever, Itzcoatl. You want Jak to stay behind and the rest of us to go. We go and you give Jak the antidote."

The chief beamed broadly. "That is the word! *Antidote.* Nobody of us could remember it. Yes, you are right. You go now. Back to your homes. Jak stays. We cure him."

"What if I run off?" Jak grinned, his white face pale and taut with pain, his hands clutching at his stomach. "You haven't thought about that, Chief?"

"Oh, yes. We guard you. It is not for long because..." He checked himself. "We need your being a god for a short time. Perhaps a hand of days."

Mildred suddenly drew her revolver, stepping in very close to the native, ramming the muzzle under his chin. "Why don't you call out and get your people to bring the antidote, Chief? Before you get to be dead."

"No," said Ryan. "I know what he'll—"

But Itzcoatl himself answered. "If you kill me, then I go to live with the gods. So, let it be. I do not know who holds the antidote, or where he is. One of our priests has left the village with it. He will return when a certain note is played on the drum and trumpet and pipe. Only one person in the village knows that signal. I do not. You can shoot us all, every warrior and woman and child, and it will not save the god's life."

"Think he's telling the truth about the illness, Mildred?" Ryan asked. "Could be bluffing."

The woman glared at Itzcoatl, easing the hammer down on the ZKR 551. She turned to Jak. "Get on the bed," she said. "Let's take a look at you."

The albino stripped off his shirt, showing his wiry frame, the skin like ivory, the whipcord muscles gleaming in the light of the torch on the wall. He was biting his lip, sweating like a rainstorm. He laid his right hand across his solar plexus. "Here," he said quietly.

"Fine. Arms at your sides. Now."

The examination took only a couple of minutes, while everyone, including Itzcoatl, watched her in silence. She looked in Jak's red eyes, then checked pulse and respiration, probed at the glands in his throat, down in his groin, making him wriggle uncomfortably. She concentrated on his abdomen.

"Try to relax, Jak," she whispered. "You're stiff as a board, honey."

"Hurts. Like animal eating guts from inside. Fingers going numb."

She straightened, looking at Itzcoatl. "All right, you bastard! I believe you. He's dying. How do we know you got the antidote?"

"Because I tell you so," the chief replied with an impressive dignity. "I tell you how it is. Now, time passes. Will you go?"

"Got us over a barrel, Jak," Ryan said, ignoring the native chief.

"Sure. I know it."

"He digs wisely," Itzcoatl said. "Now take what you want and go. Take the gun of the god. He will not need it."

Dean glanced at his father, then removed the big Colt Python and stuck it in his belt beside his own Browning Hi-Power. Jak made no move to stop him, his ruby eyes looking around at the solemn faces of his friends.

"So long," he said quietly, his voice tight with pain. "Make it quick."

Ryan nodded. "He's right. So long, friend." He leaned over him, whispering, "This isn't the end."

"Hell, I know that," Jak replied in his ear.

Everyone said their goodbyes, either by a clasp of the hand or with a kiss on the feverish cheek. It took only a half minute to collect their possessions and leave the hut without a backward glance. Half the village, all armed, stood outside, watching their exit.

Itzcoatl stood in the doorway. He looked genuinely sorry. "You have given us so great help," he said. "We have no grudge with any of you."

Ryan looked up at him. "How about if we call back here in a couple of weeks, Chief?"

Itzcoatl didn't answer, staring beyond Ryan and the others at the surrounding wall of jungle.

"Yeah," the one-eyed man said. "I get the picture."

"We going, Dad?"

He patted Dean on the shoulder. "I guess . . . afraid so, son. Now."


"I NEVER HAD ANYONE throw me my guns and tell me to run." J.B. Dix stopped suddenly when they were a mile away from the village, halting in a moonlit clearing.

"Don't talk too loud," Ryan warned. "Natives only left us a couple hundred paces back. Could easily be tracking us from the trees."

Doc hunkered on his haunches. "This is the most beastly hole that we've ever found ourselves in. I confess that I had never looked for such a sorry conclusion to this strange expedition."

"Not over till the fat lady sings, Doc," Mildred said. "We have to trust them."

"Why?" Dean was almost in tears, rubbing at his eyes with his sleeve. "Why trust those fuckheads? We helped them. Saved their pesthole ville from the dangers. We did that, and all they do is try to chill Jak."

"Their religion," Krysty said, running her fingers through her hair. "They think it was really Jak who did it all for them. We were just along for the ride. Long as they keep their white-headed god with them, they'll be fine, with good crops and strong, healthy children. Their religion."

"Why didn't he answer, Dad? When you asked about coming by in two weeks?"

"I don't know, son. Got some guesses, but none of them's good ones."

Everyone started to speak at once until Ryan clapped his hands sharply. "Quiet! I've been thinking since we left the village. Simple."

"Go on, lover," Krysty prompted.

"They aren't stupid. They'll expect us to try a rescue. Be looking for us around dawn. We won't be there. Wait out here for the rest of the night." He dropped his voice. "Scout around and see if they're out there, watching us."

"Jak could be dead by the dawn," Mildred stated, "unless they really have an antidote."

Doc coughed. "Nothing else makes sense, Dr. Wyeth, does it? If they have no antidote to the poison, then the lad is doomed. There is nothing we can do to save him, is there? I believe that they will save him. But for what and how long? Those are more pertinent questions."

Ryan looked around him. "We'll go a little farther away, then start to circle. J.B., you can split off from us and backtrack. See if there's someone watching us. But leave that for an hour or so. Give anyone time to give up and go back to the village."

"When do we go in?" Krysty asked.

Ryan leaned his hand against a smooth-boled tree, looking up at the serenely sailing moon. "I think we have to take a chance on this one."

"What kind of chance, Dad?"

"Way I see it, they'll save Jak's life. But they want him for something. I got an uneasy feeling about why they need him. You feel anything, lover?"

Krysty shook her head. "Not really. Nothing I can lay a finger onto."

"But...?"

"But I don't pick any good vibrations. He's their chosen god. Spoken of in the olden times. Mebbe times that are older than anything we can know."

Doc nodded. "There are mysteries back in time that no man can comprehend. Old cities buried beneath the dark weight of the waters. Monstrous horrors from beyond cold space. Entities so blasphemous that a human mind that confronts them can only lose its hold on sanity and become a gibbering madman. In his house at R'lyeh dead Cthulhu waits dreaming.''

''What was that crap, Doc?'' Mildred snapped. ''Times I think you're a few test tubes short of a laboratory.''

He smiled gently at the woman. ''And there are many times that I would agree with you, my dear friend. My mind wanders off on pathways of its own, and I have scant control over it. My apologies to you.''

She shrugged. ''Well... Now you make me feel bad, you old bastard, Doc. Just forget it. I'm worried sick to my heart about young Jak.''

''We all are, Mildred,'' Ryan said. ''And we'll do what we can for him.''

''When?'' J.B. was busily polishing his glasses. ''They'll have a good watch on him.''

''I know it.''

''What if they decide to do something to Jak tomorrow? We won't be able to do a thing.'' He replaced the spectacles on the bridge of his bony nose.

Ryan straightened. ''We'll be close by. Not going to be any rest for anyone tonight. Going to be a long, hard trudge through the forest. Try and get back somewhere close to the village during the morning. Come in from the north. Hide up near that pyramid place. Everyone ready?''

''Need a pee,'' Dean said, scurrying into the heart of a night-flowering bush, rich with the scent of oranges.

''Do you think we will need the rest of this thermite mixture?'' Doc asked. ''It weighs devilish heavy.''

"Might yet come in handy for us," replied the Armorer, who was also carrying part of the ingredients. "It worked well enough, didn't it?"

"In the end, John." Mildred kissed him on the cheek. "Sorry. Don't know what's the matter with me today. Having trouble in the good-words department."

Ryan began to walk along the path, glancing to make sure the others were following him. "Like I said, some hard walking to come. And everyone step light."

THE MOON DRIFTED LOWER in the sky and the jungle grew darker, the shadows deeper.

It was a warm night, the temperature not falling below seventy degrees.

By the time the first glow of the false dawn was lightening the horizon, Ryan had brought them within a mile of the village.

# Chapter Thirty-Four

"Better than blood."

Jak could hear the voice that kept repeating the three words to him, as though it were some sort of religious mantra. It had been speaking for what seemed to be hours.

"Better than blood."

He wanted to scream at whomever it was to shut up. On and on, around and around.

"Better than blood."

For some time, Jak had been aware that he was dying. The herbal poison that the natives had given him was working its claws deeper and deeper into his system. He had a memory, or it might have been a nightmare, that Ryan and the others had abandoned him.

Then he thought he'd still been standing up, or resting on a bed. There'd been a tingling like pins and needles in his fingers, in his hands and toes.

In his arms and legs.

"Better than blood."

The words seemed to be whispered in his ears, like rats scrabbling behind the walls of an old house.

He couldn't remember how long ago it had been since he'd gone blind.

Time no longer meant anything. It was just a word, an empty word in the hollow blackness that had been Jak's world. He was lying in the dark, vaguely aware of the warmth and wetness at his groin.

"Better than blood."

He wanted to stop the voice. Angered and on the edge of tears, Jak bit at his lip.

And the voice stopped.

RYAN AND THE OTHERS had burrowed deep inside a massive clump of flowering orchids. They had a rich scent that Doc said reminded him of visits to a crematorium, but they provided excellent cover.

Despite protests of tiredness from Doc and Dean, Ryan had insisted on leading the group in a huge circle, covering about fifteen miles during the hours of darkness, finishing to the north of the village, then closing back in again, until they were less than a hundred yards away from the steep-sided, flat-topped pyramid.

It was thirty minutes or so from full dawn.

JAK WAS AWARE of hands holding him, helping to move him to what seemed to be an upright position. But his body was stiff, his limbs resisting any attempt to bend. They were trying to get him to drink something, the edge of a pottery vessel pressing against his numb lips.

He heard words in a harsh, guttural language. Occasionally an odd English word would penetrate into the swirling mists of his dying mind.

"God," had been one of them.

"Hope" and "late" had been others.

DEAN WAS ASLEEP, lying curled up, hands jammed between his thighs, snoring quietly.

Doc had also given himself up to rest, lying in a similar fetal position, hands folded on his chest, eyelids twitching with REM.

Mildred smiled at the old man. "Look at him," she said. "I don't know how he keeps up. Tougher than last year's Thanksgiving turkey. Now he's got rapid eye movement, showing how he's enjoying a good session of dreaming."

Krysty lay back against a large moss-covered boulder, feet crossed. "That was a tough march." She yawned. "Wonder how Jak's feeling?"

Ryan moved to the edge of the cover, peering through the broad leaves, making sure that nobody from the village was yet stirring on the nearby trail.

"Mebbe we'll learn something. Overhear a word on how he is. Possible."

"Only happens in some of the predark vids with all those steroid-inflated heroes," J.B. said mockingly. "Just have to wait here and watch."

"Wish I knew how Jak was," Krysty repeated.

THE TASTE WAS SO BITTER that he gagged on it, but the hands were ruthless, gripping both sides of his head like an engineer's vise. Fingers probed at the angle of his jaws, so painful that Jak was forced to open his mouth. Someone else pinched his nose to make sure that he had to swallow or choke.

The bitterness had sweetness to it, lying back on his palate like an afterthought.

And it was hot.

Jak drank and drank until he thought he'd throw up. Just when he couldn't take any more, the cup passed from him and the powerful hands relaxed.

"Be all right," someone said.

J.B. CRAWLED next to Ryan. "Going up to take a look at the top of that pyramid thing," he said.

"Why?"

"Just a bit of an idea. We've only seen it from the side. I want to know what's around the back. Whether it's possible to reach the top without being seen."

"Make sure nobody spots you."

The Armorer grinned. "Sure thing. Just an idea, Ryan. Be back soon."

JAK OPENED HIS EYES, blinking at the brightness of sunshine dazzling through the curtain of glass beads across the front door to the hut.

A black-clad priest sat on the floor by the side of his bed, a frightening figure with a skull mask dotted with shards of broken mirror and obsidian. As soon as Jak began to awaken, the man stood and walked quickly outside, calling in a loud voice to others.

While he lay alone, waiting, Jak took stock of how he felt. Throat and stomach were sore, as though he'd been very sick. The muscles across his abdomen, chest and shoulders were all tender. But he was alive.

"Better than blood," he said experimentally. It didn't sound so bad.

The curtain of beads whispered and Itzcoatl walked in, his feathered green gown sweeping over the floor. He had taken off his mask, and he smiled at the youth.

"You are well again."

"Better than I was. You poisoned me."

"I am sorry, god. It was the only way to keep you safe and to persuade your companions that they should be leaving."

"They've gone?"

"Yes."

"Unharmed?"

"Of course."

"What happens now?"

"Warriors will keep you safe until it is time for you to offer your greatest gift to the people."

Jak didn't like the sound of that, but he let it pass. "When will it be?"

"At sunset. Be a neat time. Until then, ask for whatever you want."

"I want to go."

Itzcoatl shook his head, still beaming at the albino. "No, lord. But any food or drink or the company of girls. All you do is ask."

J.B. WAS GONE FOR MORE than an hour.

The sun rose higher, and the forest around them came to morning life.

Dean woke up, complaining he was thirsty. Ryan told him to pick his way back through the under-growth for about a quarter mile, where they'd crossed a narrow stream, making sure, at all costs, that no-body spotted him.

Doc had also awakened, and he looked around, blinking owlishly. "Stands the church clock at ten to three and is there...something for tea?" He then promptly fell asleep again.

Mildred and Krysty also dropped off, exhausted by the long sleepless night.

Ryan stayed awake, watching for J.B.'s reappearance from his recce up the pyramid.

The Armorer eventually returned, sweating profusely. He'd left the scattergun behind in the bushes, carrying the Uzi machine pistol slung over his shoulder.

Dean had come back with water, and J.B. took three or four deep gulps, throwing his fedora on the grass.

"What did you find?" Ryan asked.

"You think they plan to sacrifice Jak, don't you?" J.B. looked around to make sure none of the others could hear him.

Ryan nodded. "Nothing else makes sense. Itzcoatl almost let it slip out a few times and only just stopped himself in time. You think the same?"

"Yeah. If they do, then it'll be soon. Tonight or tomorrow night is my guess."

"I'll go with that," Ryan said.

"So, what I found up there could be real useful."

THE DAY SLIPPED BY for Jak.

In their eagerness to make sure the poison took effect, the natives had underestimated the dosage. Jak, who was less than five foot five and weighed only a little over one-ten, didn't have the body mass of many of the natives, and the drugs carried on working well past noon.

Itzcoatl had arranged for three of the prettiest young maidens from the village to wait outside the hut in case the god became hungry for tender flesh.

But Jak dozed through the whole day, only waking when the sun was already well down on the western horizon.

He was given a feast, but he could only manage some slices of duck and a goblet of water. Unknown to him, all of the dishes on offer had been liberally dusted with the powerful analgesic drug, *yauhtli*, as a way of keeping him quieted through the ceremony to come—and as a way of relieving him of the worst of the ghastly pain that he was to endure at the height of the great ritual of sacrifice.

Itzcoatl had sat with him, but he left after a few minutes, checking that the fires had been readied on the pyramid and the obsidian swords had been specially honed.

"It must be right," he said to the assembled priests. "It is not given to us to sacrifice a god every day of the week. There must be no mistakes."

THE VILLAGERS had gathered around the base of the pyramid, oblivious to the proximity of the group of outlanders in the center of the huge mutie orchid plant.

Ryan made sure that everyone was fully awake and knew exactly what the plan was. He and J.B. had worked on it for most of the afternoon, trying to find any loopholes, trying to see how they might be blocked, looking at everything that might happen, for better or worse.

Trader used to say that an hour of planning was worth a minute of action.

Dean was restless, kneeling with his big Browning ready in his right hand. He still had Jak's blaster tucked in his belt. Mildred was at his side, keeping up a whispered conversation with the boy, helping to keep his nerves calm, helping to keep her own nerves calm.

Ryan had the Steyr placed in the leaf mold, close to his right hand. A round of 7.62 mm ammo lay under the firing pin.

Krysty was the last of the four. She sat in the lotus position, her hands laid flat on her thighs, her eyes closed, calming herself with the meditation techniques that she'd learned at her mother's knee.

All four were ready.

"IN THIS LAND it will not be said, I slew a sleeping man." Jak sang quietly to himself as he walked through the evening stillness of the forest, surrounded by the colorful masked elders of the village. One of his father's friends, back in the bayous, had possessed a vast repertoire of old predark songs and had taught some of them to the skinny albino teenager.

He felt very good, relaxed, calm, ready for whatever was going to happen.

Itzcoatl walked in front of him, holding a beautiful crystal skull aloft, chanting in his own tongue. Then came a pair of priests, one holding a blazing torch and the other an unsheathed sword of black stone. They wore strange cloaks that seemed to have dangling arms and legs. When one of the priests tripped and nearly fell, Jak couldn't stop from giggling.

Ahead of him he saw a great pyramid of carved stone that seemed to reach toward the orange sky. The whole village stood around its base, and all of them bowed low as he appeared, which made him giggle again.

The steps were steep and Jak had to be helped toward the top of the pyramid.

His legs felt wobbly, his head swimming. The pounding of the drums and the high squealing of the trumpets drove through his skull like white-hot chisels, making him whimper with the pain. But the odd thing was, the pain didn't seem to hurt him. It was all happening, yet once removed.

Below him, the natives were chanting. Far, far below, and far, far away.

"DRUGGED OUT OF HIS DOME," Mildred whispered. "Danger he could fall clear from top to bottom."

"We got that covered," Ryan said.

"Can't I go around the back, as well?" Dean asked urgently. "Please?"

Ryan shook his head. "No. Stay here. Once the shit hits the fan, then it's going to be triple action. Need all our blasters here."

Krysty turned from the small gap in the bushes that had enabled her to watch the unfolding drama. "Nearly at the top," she reported. "Another ten steps."

Ryan brought the Steyr to chin level, settling the walnut stock into his shoulder, finger reaching for the trigger. He pressed his eye to the Starlite night scope, using the laser image enhancer to give him a clearer view of his target.

Jak's shock of white hair filled the sight, and he adjusted upward a little to the figures on the flat apex of the pyramid, standing grouped together, all looking down at their young god. Ryan noticed that one of the black-clad priests, standing at the back, was a great deal taller than any of the others, looking to be close to six-three.

The same height as Doc Tanner.

ITZCOATL HAD TAKEN the center of the ceremony, as befitted his position as chief of the tribe. He stood between the two heaped fires, which waited only the application of a torch. Out of the corner of his eye he noted all the priests of the village, in a row.

He had come up the back of the monument, passing through the small hidden room where the high priests sometimes waited in their main rituals. It contained spare sets of robes in case too much blood was spilled.

After the prolonged giving of the outlander to the older gods, he and the priests would make their way to the back of the flat top, hidden by the pall of smoke from the fires. They would return to the ground down the rear steps of the pyramid, keeping elements of the mystery from the crowd of onlookers from the village.

JAK FINALLY STOOD ALONE, swaying slightly, with the priests circling him, none of them actually laying hands on his serene person.

The drug that they'd administered to him was beginning to wear off, but he still felt kitten weak, sick and dizzy.

One by one in the gathering darkness, the priests came to him and touched him on the heart with their fingers, each whispering an incantation to him.

None of it made any sense, as it was spoken in their guttural tongue.

Yet, oddly, two of the incantations did make sense to him, both coming near the end.

"Hang on, kid, we'll have you out of here."

It sounded like J.B., and Jak automatically started to respond. "Don't call me..." he began, when he realized that this was a part of the illness.

Until the last priest in line, an enormously tall man, also whispered to him in English.

"Avert your eyes from the fire, dear boy, lest you be blinded by it. And hold yourself ready."

On top of the pyramid it was almost dark, and Jak strained to see why Doc's voice was coming from a skull mask of jade and obsidian that topped a cloak of sable feathers.

"Let the fires be lit!" Itzcoatl's voice rang out through the gloom.

The priest with the torch stooped and applied it to the two piles of dry branches, which instantly flared into crackling life, smoke curling into the evening sky.

Itzcoatl stood at the front of the platform, the other characters in the drama ranged around him. Out of the corner of his eye, Jak noticed that one of the priests had moved silently to both fires and pushed something into their hearts, something that looked like a couple of metallic tubes.

"HERE WE GO," said Ryan.

There was no longer any need to whisper. The watching throng of natives was roaring out a rhythmic chant, hands raised, feet stamping, faces lifted toward the crowded top of the pyramid. Jak's slight figure stood alone, the rising flames making his hair glow like living fire.

Ryan's finger tightened on the trigger. He held his breath, waiting for the precise moment, muttering a silent prayer that the thermite would work properly this time.

DESPITE THE EFFECTS of the powerful drug, Jak was recovering his senses. Despite feeling as strong as a drowning mouse, he tensed himself, ready for action. He remembered to avert his eyes from the bright red-and-orange flames, which suddenly turned to a torrent of bright silver fire, flaring out like a supernova, blinding everyone on top of the pyramid.

Everyone except Jak, who'd actually closed his eyes, and J.B. and Doc, who were also ready for the inferno of dazzling light.

Down below, Ryan squeezed the trigger of the Steyr rifle.

# Chapter Thirty-Five

The bullet hit Itzcoatl in the center of the chest, sending him staggering backward, blinded by the ignition of the thermite, to fall into the heart of the nearer fire. The chief screamed once before the intense white heat began to consume him, skin, flesh and bones, swiftly completing the lethal work of the round from the Steyr rifle.

Ryan fired twice more, picking his targets with the greatest care, not taking any risk of hitting either J.B. or Doc.

Krysty, Mildred and Dean had opened fire above the heads of the watching natives, each of them first putting a couple of rounds low, hitting legs, knocking men down, compounding the hysterical terror that had gripped the crowd at the supernatural appearance of the dazzling silver fire and the sudden death of their chief.

On top of the pyramid, Jak stood quite still, his eyes clamped shut, knowing that the light from the thermite might be powerful enough to destroy his fragile night vision. He swayed from side to side, focusing on not falling, arms rigid, swallowing hard as he was aware of the swirling chaos about him.

Jak had heard the cold snap of Ryan's Steyr, then the sound of someone screaming as he went down.

Then there were hands holding him, keeping him steady, familiar voices.

The Armorer fired the Uzi one-handed, clearing away most of the blood-smeared priests in their cloaks of flayed human skin. And then there was good old Doc on the other side, the deafening boom of his gold-engraved Le Mat, the scattergun charge taking out three more of the natives.

"Going down the back," J.B. said, gripping the teenager around the upper arm, steering him between the fires. "Keep your eyes tight shut."

Jak obeyed the voice. Part of his brain was still subdued by the *yauhtli,* so that his feet stumbled and he felt like throwing up. He heard the crack of the Steyr from somewhere way below him and the crackle of shooting from Dean, Mildred and Krysty. His nostrils were flooded with the stench of roasting human flesh, and he wondered who had been sacrificed.

The thermite was a perfect mix, and it was flowing in a molten stream over the top of the pyramid, sliding down the steep steps like a living serpent of fire. It was a terrifying sight to the panicked natives at the bottom, who broke and ran.

IT WAS A MAD RUSH for safety through the jungle.

Despite their collective experience and skill at tracking through a wilderness, there were occasions when none of them was sure which of several winding trails was the one to lead them back to the redoubt.

The soaring moon was hidden behind thick bands of dark cloud, and the night had turned colder. Twice they felt a few heavy spots of rain, pattering down between the thick leaves of the overhanging branches.

Jak was recovering fast.

Once they'd gotten a mile away from the screaming mob of villagers, they stopped while Mildred checked the teenager. She found that pulse and respiration were both a little slow, but he was surprisingly strong and well.

The others took the opportunity to reload their weapons.

Doc was exultant, punching his right fist into his left palm, whooping his delight. "That was *so* good," he said, smiling and showing his perfect teeth. "Teach them to try and turn one of our friends into a human sacrifice."

"Nice shot to take out Itzcoatl," J.B. said. "Difficult at that angle in that poor light."

Ryan grinned. "Helped having that thermite blazing behind him. Best silhouette I ever saw."

"Think they'll come after us, Dad? Still quite a lot of them unchilled."

"Who knows?" He shrugged. "We took out most of their leaders. Put the fear of their gods in the rest of them."

Doc sneezed. "Those pestilential feathers from the mask have brought on my hay fever," he moaned.

"It was the smell of ancient blood that I found so sickening," protested J.B.

"Who burned?" Jak was sitting down, relaxing, following Mildred's orders. He took long slow breaths, resting as the drug abandoned his body.

"Burned?" Ryan said.

"Smelled it."

Doc had holstered the Le Mat. "It was poor Itzcoatl, Jak. I couldn't bring myself to dislike the old rogue. He was only following the traditions of his ancestors. Rather a case of a man having to do what a man had to do. And finding that it's all fallen apart in his hand like wet rot in a buggy wheel. After Ryan shot him, the poor fellow fell smack into the heart of the thermite blaze."

The Armorer clicked the Uzi's safety on and off, head on one side, listening to the action, finally satisfied. "Yeah, not a pretty sight, friends. That thermite burned to the bone, right away. By the time we got young Jak off the top of the pyramid and down through the secret room, the old chief wasn't much more than scorched ashes, top to toe."

Krysty swung around, staring behind them into the blackness, as though she'd heard a twig snap.

"What?" Ryan said, blaster straight into his hand. "What is it, lover?"

"Felt someone out there in the jungle. Coming this way and getting closer."

"The natives?"

She shook her head, the sentient hair seeming to spark like a myriad of tiny fires in the dark. "Can't tell. But definitely coming nearer."

"How far to the redoubt?"

Ryan looked at Mildred. "My guess puts it about another two hours."

"Be close to dawn then." J.B. glanced at the sky as though he were searching for the embryonic sun.

"Right." Ryan checked his wrist chron, angling the face to catch the watery moonlight. "If it's Itzcoatl's brothers after revenge—or after Jak—then they'll know these trails a sight better than us. Let's move it."

KRYSTY AND DEAN had stolen a pile of tortillas from the kitchens before the ritual began, and the friends now shared them, washing them down with cool liquid from a nearby stream.

"Half an hour and we should be there," Ryan said, wiping his mouth on his sleeve. "Beat the dawn."

"Beat the pursuit." For the last half mile Krysty had been looking over her shoulder, prompting a sarcastic comment from Doc, who asked whether she thought that she had a frightful friend walking behind her.

"They close, lover?"

She had been sitting, snatching a few moments' rest. Now she straightened. "Feel them all the time. Feel them on both sides now, sort of closing us in."

"Try an ambush?" Jak suggested.

"No. Not in terrain like this, in this sort of bad light. They'd hold too many cards." Ryan looked around again. "Just keep moving, is all."

"THERE."

To everyone's great relief, the small gateway building finally appeared in front of them, set in the heart of the towering trees. The sec door was closed, and there was no sign of any life around it.

The dark clouds had moved on south, leaving watery moonlight dribbling over the forest.

The narrow path seemed to have closed on itself in the few days since they'd last walked that way.

"There was once a road through the woods," Doc said quietly. "Now the heat and the rain have undone it again and now you would never know..."

"Shut it, Doc," Krysty snapped. "I can feel them closer."

"Open the door, Dean, fast."

"Sure, Dad."

"Rest of us all keep a triple-red watch."

The control lever shifted easily, and the massive vanadium-steel door began to move silently upward. The boy called out once it was high enough for them to get in.

"Ready, Dad."

"Fine."

Was there movement in the deep lake of shadows underneath the flowering shrubs?

"One at a time. J.B., stay and keep them covered."

Cold neon light spilled from the open door, out across the clearing, throwing everyone's shadows toward the edge of the darkness. Despite the cool air, Ryan realized that he was sweating.

He heard the rustling of feet as Krysty, Mildred, Doc and Jak made their way inside the building.

"You next, Ryan," J.B. whispered.

"No, me last. Go."

Combat boots scuffed on the dew-wet turf, then Ryan stood for a moment alone.

He heard a faint whistle, then a response far off to the left, almost behind him. It could have been a night bird.

But Ryan knew that it wasn't.

He backed toward the door and into the gateway, glancing around, shocked to see that the whole place was now covered in layers of vivid green moss.

It was far worse than when they'd made the jump, and his only guess was that in opening the door, they'd let in all manner of spores, damp and heat. Most of the console screens were invisible under the lichen, their panels of lights flickering under the murky blanket.

"I have grave doubts that the actual gateway unit is still functioning, Ryan. I have never seen such advanced botanical sabotage."

"Get into the chamber, quick," Ryan ordered. "Best try it straightaway."

He glanced behind him, but the spillage of light from the control room made it impossible to make out anything beyond the open sec door.

"Should I close that, Dad?"

It was a great temptation. Once it was down, they'd be completely safe from any sort of attack that the natives could manage.

"You can . . . No. Leave it be."

"But if we closed it, we'd be—"

Ryan almost lifted a hand against his son. The presentiment of danger was so pressing that he couldn't bear to tolerate any argument.

"Leave it!"

The boy jumped back as though Ryan had slapped him across the face.

"Sorry, Dad."

"They're close outside. Everyone in the chamber."

Ryan was aware that tiredness was catching up on him. The last days and nights had been filled with too much stress and action, and far too little rest.

Now there was the certainty that the pursuing natives were on top of them, wanting vengeance, wanting outlander bodies to carry to the fires, to remove the living hearts with their gleaming black swords and fill the open cavities with glowing coals. To offer gifts to their gods.

He and J.B. automatically took up the rearguard positions, without a word being spoken between them, backing across the control room.

It was a poor defensive position, even against men armed mainly with bows and blowpipes. Poor cover and too little of it, offering better opportunities to attackers.

"Come on, lover." Krysty's voice was loud and harsh with tension. "Come on!"

An arrow hissed through the door, missing Ryan by a couple of feet, clattering off the back wall and lying near his boots. He glanced down and saw that the barbed tip was smeared with a dark, sticky liquid.

He dropped to his knees behind the last row of desks, J.B. doing the same. Ryan glanced behind to see that everyone else was already in the chamber, standing, holding their blasters.

Trader often said that life generally came down to two choices: a bad one and the other one.

If he and J.B. turned and ran for it, jumping into the chamber and slamming the pale green armaglass door, it would give the natives precious seconds to come after them and trap them before the jump mechanism operated.

So, there was the other choice.

"Get on the floor," he yelled.

Two more arrows and a handful of tiny poisoned darts rattled into the control room through the open sec door. Ryan cursed himself under his breath for not closing it behind them.

But that was spilled milk.

"Ready," Krysty called.

"We stay," he said quietly to J.B.

"Sure, Ryan." There was no need for anything else to be said.

He rose and powered himself forward to slam the armaglass door shut, triggering the jump mechanism.

"Wait for us!" he yelled. "Be along when we can."

He heard shouting from inside, Krysty's voice rising over all of them.

"Don't, lover.... Don't...."

A long arrow struck the door, so close it nicked Ryan's sleeve. He dropped to the floor, crawling back to rejoin the Armorer.

Behind him he knew that the metal disks in the floor and ceiling of the chamber would be glowing, and fine tendrils of mist would be gathering near the top of the six-sided room as the jump began.

In less than a minute, Krysty, Dean, Mildred, Doc and Jak would be somewhere else.

The shouting had already faded into silence.

He and J.B., oldest and best of friends, hunkered in their limited shelter, blasters ready for the inevitable attack.

And waited.

By squinting around the corner, Ryan could see through the open doorway, see the first glow of dawn in the eastern sky.

And see the bright emerald green of the eternal forest.

Waiting.

**Back to the beginning...**

## PILGRIMAGE TO HELL   $4.99
Out of the ruins of worldwide nuclear devastation emerged Deathlands, a world that conspired against survival. Ryan Cawdor and his roving band of post-holocaust survivors begin their quest for survival in a world gone mad.

## RED HOLOCAUST   $4.99
Ryan and his warriors must battle against roaming bands of survivors from Russia who are using Alaska as a staging ground for an impending invasion of America.

## NEUTRON SOLSTICE   $4.99
Deep in the heart of Dixie, Ryan and his companions come upon a small group of survivors who are striving to recreate life as it was once known.

## CRATER LAKE   $4.99
Near what was once the Pacific Northwest, Ryan's band discovers a beautiful valley untouched by the nuclear blast that changed the world forever.

## HOMEWARD BOUND   $4.99
Emerging from a gateway in the ruins of New York City, Ryan decides it is time to face his power-mad brother—and avenge the deaths of his father and older brother.

Here's your chance to find out how it all began!

---

**Don't miss out on the action in these titles featuring
THE EXECUTIONER®, ABLE TEAM® and PHOENIX FORCE®!**

SuperBolan

| | | | |
|---|---|---|---|
| #61438 | AMBUSH | $4.99 U.S.<br>$5.50 CAN. | ☐<br>☐ |
| #61439 | BLOOD STRIKE | $4.99 U.S.<br>$5.50 CAN. | ☐<br>☐ |
| #61440 | KILLPOINT | $4.99 U.S.<br>$5.50 CAN. | ☐<br>☐ |
| #61441 | VENDETTA | $4.99 U.S.<br>$5.50 CAN. | ☐<br>☐ |

Stony Man™

| | | | |
|---|---|---|---|
| #61896 | BLIND EAGLE | $4.99 U.S.<br>$5.50 CAN. | ☐<br>☐ |
| #61897 | WARHEAD | $4.99 U.S.<br>$5.50 CAN. | ☐<br>☐ |
| #61898 | DEADLY AGENT | $4.99 U.S.<br>$5.50 CAN. | ☐<br>☐ |
| #61899 | BLOOD DEBT | $4.99 U.S.<br>$5.50 CAN. | ☐<br>☐ |

(limited quantities available on certain titles)

| | |
|---|---|
| **TOTAL AMOUNT** | $ |
| **POSTAGE & HANDLING** | $ |
| ($1.00 for one book, 50¢ for each additional) | |
| **APPLICABLE TAXES\*** | $_____ |
| **TOTAL PAYABLE** | $_____ |
| (check or money order—please do not send cash) | |

To order, complete this form and send it, along with a check or money order for the total above, payable to Gold Eagle Books, to: **In the U.S.:** 3010 Walden Avenue, P.O. Box 9077, Buffalo, NY 14269-9077; **In Canada:** P.O. Box 636, Fort Erie, Ontario, L2A 5X3.

Name:_____

Address:_____ City:_____

State/Prov.:_____ Zip/Postal Code: _____

\*New York residents remit applicable sales taxes.
 Canadian residents remit applicable GST and provincial taxes.